Micro Stories for a Hectic World

ISBN-13: 978-0692246955 (Edward Meiman)

ISBN-10: 0692246959

Library of Congress Control Number: 2014912207

Edward Meiman, Silver Spring, Maryland

I0460022

Micro Dedication

To my audience,

Henry, Ash, Anna, and Laura

Each and every day, they are there to read my stories.

To my girls,

Elena and Katie,

Their love, support and inspiration saw me through.

Micro Forward: An Author's Wish

As I sit looking over my manuscript one more time, I know that she will soon be leaving my care. The editing is over, the publisher has sent the final proof, and when I give my permission to go to press, my baby will be sent out into the world. I love her, and have done my best to get her to this point. I have poured all of my finest work into raising her, so that she may leave my care prepared for what may come. Now it is time to give my baby to you.

This book has special meaning to me, and always will. I see in her my dreams, my fantasies, my memories, and my life's lessons. Each story, each page, each word moves me in ways only I will know. But as I let her go, I know my special love of this book will not go with her. When you take her in, this book will take on new meaning. My interpretations of the lessons, my feelings of what is good or bad, and my reactions to each twist and turn she contains mean nothing now. Only yours are real. For I would never want to force my will upon the relationship you have with this book. You see what is significant to you. You feel the emotions that these words bring alive in you. You take from this book what you need.

I know I do not have the right to ask this, but I will anyway. Be true to this book. Do not force on her things that she can never be. Find out who she is. Learn the ways the two of you are alike and where you complement each other. Let her fill you with what she has to offer, for she has much in this regard. And if someday you two should part, remember her for what she stirred within you and the joy, sorrow, love, and fear she gave you. All of these things were real. They belonged to just the two of you, as did my love for her while she was mine.

Contents

Humor

The Aftermath of a Typically Lousy Day

As the man got ready for bed, he decided that maybe it was time to resume his search for the perfect place to live, somewhere that he belonged. It wasn't that he felt like he didn't belong in this town. It was just that after today, no one else wanted him to belong here. He didn't want to think it was his fault, but as his mind kept replaying the tragedy of this day, he couldn't help but think that maybe he had something to do with what transpired. He was sure that everyone else would come to that conclusion.

To most people the events of the day would send them into denial, even shock, and probably cause a complete mental breakdown. To the man they just felt like a typically lousy day. Still, the memory of the day haunted him, not letting him get to sleep. Feeling there was no other recourse; the man poured himself a bourbon and Coke, without the Coke, and sat down in the living room. Normally he would turn on the TV to distract himself, but the scorch marks on the wall reminded him that he would not be watching anything on that TV ever again. He briefly thought about pulling out his smartphone and playing a game of Tetris but remembered that the touchscreen didn't work anymore. So he downed the bourbon in one gulp and headed out for a walk. He got about three steps out of the house when he realized that he had lost his keys in that elevator shaft, and so for the fourth time today, he was locked out of his own home. This time, however, it didn't even faze him.

The man debated whether he should sit down on the lawn to wait for the sun to rise or take a long walk to clear his head. He finally opted for the walk. In a perverse way, he was interested in what fate would throw at him in these last hours of this lousy day. With that thought in mind, he headed for the town center of his formerly picture-perfect suburb. He walked past the police tape that surrounded the house where his SUV now resided. He decided it looked quite nice sticking out of old Mrs. Ferguson's living room. He made a mental note to visit her in the hospital tomorrow. The tree resting in the Thompson's second-floor bedroom did look a little out of place. He hoped that at least they would get plenty of firewood from it.

The man had decided his destination would be the all-night convenience store, but as he approached it he worried that the inside would still be covered with melted Frosty Slushy Freeze. His fears were realized when he looked through the window to see that the glass from the drink coolers, the parts from the hotdog warmer, the scattered remains of Aisle 4, and the permanently burnt-out video games consoles had yet to be cleaned up. So he bypassed the store and continued on toward the town center. When he reached it he was surprised to find that the charred shell of the Metro bus was still parked in front of the crumbling ruins of his bank branch. He had thought it would have been towed away by now. He sat down on a park bench, deciding that going any further would just remind him of the carnage that was the rest of the stores and restaurants here.

As the man sat on the bench, the legs on one side gave way, unceremoniously dumping him on the sidewalk. While the man sat there, he began trying to figure out to which city he should move next. All the major and most of the minor cities in California were now off limits. In fact, the stories passed around about him in the western U.S. probably precluded that entire region. He figured that he had two choices. Either he could head for the Deep South or the Northern Midwest. He knew to avoid both Chicago and Detroit as the vivid memory of his business trip to those cities was still fresh in his mind. Miami was a good possibility, although as he thought about it, he envisioned a hurricane wiping out South Beach. After much thought, he remembered that once he had looked into signing on with an oil company that would put him to work in the Middle East. They always needed people who were willing to spend months in an isolated compound in the middle of a desert, far away from civilization. Maybe it would be best to get as far away from inhabited areas as possible. Maybe there he could get away from his bad luck and finally find a place where he fit in.

Three months later the man was in the news all over the world. The pictures of the Kuwaiti oil fields in flames made for great news fodder. The mobs outside U.S. embassies all over the Muslim world were also quite sensational. In the midst of all that turmoil the man completely disappeared. Most people guessed that he was killed in all the rioting. However, there were rumors that the U.S. Defense Intelligence Agency had hired him to infiltrate terrorist groups in the tribal regions of Pakistan. Months later they denied any involvement in the earthquake, landslides, mysterious explosions, and complete disbanding of the remaining Al Qaeda cells in the region. From time to time there have been disasters attributed to the man, but nothing has ever been proven. It is said that in the Intelligence Community he has become the stuff of legends. So it seems that after a lifetime of failure, he may have finally found a place where he belonged.

The Revelation on 5th Avenue

"Who knew that this was the true way of the world?" Oliver Kukla said to the puppet. The disembodied hands controlling the animated doll still freaked him out, but the general idea of speaking to a sentient puppet had settled in.

"Yep, all those stories saying that humans only see what they want to see are true," said the puppet, whose name was Fran. Fran was a purple rabbit that was shaped much like a human. "Only a very few accept reality."

Ollie watched some fairies playing with a baby as her mother put the child in a car seat. "I still don't know why I suddenly saw the light."

"Oh, it could be a number of things," the puppet replied. "But I know the real reason. Would you like to find out what really opened your eyes?" She hopped up on the fence, pulled out a guitar, and was about to go into song, when the man stopped her.

"Sorry, but one song per day is probably all my sanity can take for now. Plus that last one about the street vendor chilidog made me gag. How was I supposed to know they were alive?"

"Oh, but this is going to be a big production number," Fran was pleading in a fun, playful way that only a purple bunny puppet could pull off. "It will provide you with a true picture of yourself and your place in the world around you. It will be very therapeutic, you know."

"Will it include dancing gnomes?" asked Ollie. "My youngest daughter swears she saw a gnome once. It would be nice to tell her I saw some dancing and singing."

"Gnomes normally don't like to dance. They just stand around waiting for pixies to pass by and then eat them. It's kinda nasty, but it keeps the pixie population in check. Oh well, what the hey? I'll call my producer and see if he can arrange it."

"That would be nice."

The puppet pulled out her cell phone and made the call. "It's set. They'll appear by the second chorus."

"Thanks a lot. How about you throw in a unicorn or two?"

"C'mon. This isn't THAT big of a production number. There will be a real Chinese dragon though."

"That'll do."

"OK, can I begin?"

"Sure," said the man as he settled back to watch. It was a sunny day on 5th Avenue, and the man could think of no better way to spend it than watching his life turn into one big fantastical musical.

Trafficman and the Old-People Ray

He stands tall in an asphalt-black spandex bodysuit with a cape of highway-sign-green trimmed in white reflective tape. On his chest, a blue and red interstate highway sign emblazoned with a bold, white "T." He is Trafficman, and he has come to save your commute!

It was a normal morning commute on Transportville's roads and highways. Trafficman was on the job, moving stalled vehicles, fixing malfunctioning traffic lights, rescuing deer before they become road kill, and using his shade-vision to help people driving directly into the sun. At the peak of the morning rush hour, it felt like just another Monday. Then the call came in. Trafficman's arch-nemesis, Dr. Rubberneck, had been seen entering the McQueen Expressway from Exit 19A. What a fiend! Entering from an exit, how dare he! Our hero jumped into his Trafficopter and hurried to the scene. On his way, he did his traffic updates for WHWY, WRD, and WST.

He arrived to a horrible scene. Dr. Rubberneck was going westbound in the eastbound lanes of McQueen

Expressway, causing havoc as he went. On top of the villain's Rubberneckmobile was a strange ray gun that was shooting grey laser beams at oncoming motorists. When a car was hit, it would suddenly slow down causing a traffic back-up of unbelievable proportions. As the Trafficopter swooped in, the ray gun began shooting at Trafficman. If it weren't for his super quick piloting, he would have been hit in an instant. He weaved and dodged between the billboards lining the highway trying to get close to the rogue's vehicle of doom. Just as Trafficman was about to use his Towtrucktor beam, the Rubberneckmobile went into the James Dean Tunnel, thwarting Trafficman's attempt to apprehend the monster.

Trafficman again did his traffic updates as he flew over Andretti Hill. As he cleared the hill, Trafficman checked his GPSilator and to his horror realized that Dr. Rubberneck was heading for the Burt Reynolds Overpass, the highest point in all of Transportville! Whatever his diabolical scheme, Trafficman knew he had to stop the dastardly doctor before he reached the top of that overpass, or the Tri-State Area's traffic patterns could be horribly altered for the entire morning commute. It was going to be close. Trafficman went into a steep dive as the Rubberneckmobile reached the overpass, and he aimed his Road Salt Shooter at the ray gun. As he fired a barrage of salt, the Rubberneckmobile hit the crest of the overpass, and a ball of grey energy blanketed the city. The ray gun was destroyed, but the damage was done.

Luckily, Trafficman's helicopter was above the ball of light as it stretched over the city, so he was unharmed. Dr. Rubberneck was out of his truck and cackling as Trafficman landed.

"I've done it! I've finally beaten you," Dr. Rubberneck howled.

"You fiend, what have you done?" Trafficman was panicked as he grabbed the notorious super villain.

"My Old-People Ray has turned every driver in Transportville into meek, overcautious motorists. And there's nothing you can do to reverse it." Dr. Rubberneck was giddy with joy.

"What a heinous deed. The roads and highways will be clogged for years with every single motorist going slightly under the speed limit, leaving more than enough room between vehicles, and breaking for small animals." Then it hit both of them. Dr. Rubberneck let out a wail of defeat, mixed with a ton of embarrassment. Trafficman just looked thoughtfully at the now destroyed Old People Ray gun.

Dr. Rubberneck ended up losing his license, but also got the Keys to the City from the mayor. Trafficman took a well-deserved vacation to a deserted island that had no roads. As for the drivers of Transportville, speeding tickets were a thing of the past, accidents dropped to all-time lows, and the lifespan of small road-crossing animals skyrocketed. But Trafficman wouldn't be able to rest for long, as a new villain was about to rise in Transportville, one much more Machiavellian than the formerly dreaded Dr. Rubberneck. Get ready for next week's episode: Trafficman and the Malevolent Speeding Cam Caper!

Pope Me

The Virgin Mary appeared to the College of Cardinals as they sat down to elect a new Pope. She gave them my name, address, telephone number and told them to elect me. Later that same day, two Secret Service Agents and a member of the Swiss Guard showed up at my apartment to escort me to the Vatican. They wouldn't tell me why they were kidnapping me. I didn't even know at the time that the one with the German accent wasn't U.S. but was with the papal version of the Secret Service. All I knew was that I was on Air Force 2 (the VP's plane) traveling to God knows where. We landed at a military airfield outside of Rome and took some nondescript Fiats to an underground entrance of the Vatican. It scared the Hell out of me, which was appropriate for where I was going.

Once in the Sistine Chapel, the Cardinal of Washington, DC started explaining things. It must have been the surreal nature of the entire experience that allowed me to stop myself from freaking out. Instead, when the Cardinal asked if I would assume the holy office, I simply said, "No," and turned to leave. That's when I found out the guy with the German accent was a Vatican enforcer-type who could be very persuasive in a "Brute Squad" sort of way. My answer was still "No," but I decided some psychology was needed to bring the Cardinals around to my way of thinking. I started off by telling the gathering of old guys in red dresses that I had never gotten an annulment for my first and only marriage. One of the Cardinals closest to me took a sheet of paper, wrote, "Your marriage is hereby annulled," and signed it. Then for the next two hours I told them every illicit, outlandish, and otherwise organizationally embarrassing thing I had ever done or at least everything I could remember under that kind of pressure. The DC guy replied that they had already heard all that (and more) from Mary. OK, then I told the "College" that I was a Midwest Left Wing Radical Catholic who would make Vatican II look like a Baltimore Catechism Love In. Cardinal DC told me that was why I had been chosen by Mary. In one last gasp I decided to hit them where it hurts. I told that bunch of geriatric priests that I would force everyone over the age of 65 to retire. From around the room I heard things like "I don't want to be around for this anyway" and "Thank God." It was at that point that I knew I was truly screwed. My anger got the best of me, and so in the Sistine Chapel I yelled, "Mary, get down here and explain why you are doing this to me!" Nada. A few of the Cardinals had minor heart attacks, but no response from on high.

Right now I am sitting in an antechamber of Saint Peter's Basilica being fitted for a "Pope Dress" and trying to memorize my part of the coronation or whatever they call it. I ordered the entire College of Cardinals out to talk with the press about EXACTLY what had transpired, including all of my confessions and my little outburst right before I gave in. I am sure the word "schism" is being bantered about all over the world at this moment. Anyway, I've decided to take this job seriously just in case this whole thing isn't due to some psychotic drug being introduced into the Cardinals' Geritol. I think I will start off by repealing "Humanae Vitae" and declaring a "Decade of Free Love." Then I'll separate Church and State in Vatican City, getting all clergy out of the business of running a government. This will probably trigger an assassination attempt by the Italian mafia, which I am sure will only be the first of many. Oh well, the nuns have finished sewing me up, and Cardinal DC—I really should find out his name—is motioning me to hurry. I guess this is it. Let the fun begin.

Getting the Formula Just Right

"I will NOT have my books follow the same old tired formulas that every other romance-fantasy-steampunk-horror-mystery-hispanic-western-religious-25th Century-gothic-teen novel series out there uses," Renaldo fumed. "This genre is so overwhelmed with fluff that if I don't find something new, my work will languish in the literary cellar of time."

"Listen Renaldo, 'Hispanic cowboy mummy meets alien Goth nun in a stolen zeppelin sells!'" retorted Mort,

Renaldo's publisher. "This business is called the 'Entertainment Industry' for a reason. We SELL entertainment. If it doesn't SELL, it can't ENTERTAIN. If it doesn't ENTERTAIN, it can't SELL. And what's selling now are mummies wearing cowboy hats and girls with pale faces wearing black, solving crimes while riding in overly large balloons."

"Mort, everywhere I look there is nothing but priests and nuns wrapped in bandages and wearing Western hats. It's gotten so bad that I saw a Dr. Seuss book rewritten so that the Cat in the Hat was now a Goth priest mummy!"

"Yeah, I thought that was one of my more inspired ideas. It sold out its first printing in under five minutes."

"Oh my God! You are a fiend!"

"I'm a publisher. It comes with the territory. Listen, if you gotta do something new, then throw in a twist. Have the mummy get unwrapped to find out he is actually a she. Then have the nun take off her habit to show she is actually a boy mummy. How 'bout that?"

"J. K. Rowling did that in her last book."

"Oh yeah, that's where I heard it."

"Have you ever had an original idea in your life?"

"Of course not. I'm a publisher. It comes with the territory. Renaldo, you gotta write something and write it quick. If you don't have me a mummy and a nun by next Friday, you're through!"

"No! Never! I will never sacrifice my principles for money!"

"Then return the $100K advance I gave you."

"No! Never! I will never sacrifice my money for principles! Wait a minute. I just had an inspiration!"

"Great. What is it?" Mort sneered.

"I can't tell you, but by next Friday you will have an original masterpiece that sells better than any book series you've ever had."

"Well, it better have a nun and a mummy. Now get out of here, and write something!"

Next Friday Renaldo delivered a seven-hundred-page epic, which Mort cut down to two hundred pages in less than an hour. Yes, it did have a nun and a mummy, but they were minor characters, and Mort quickly edited them out. He had to because Renaldo's story had hit upon the next big thing: the Zombie-drug lord-movie producer-meets-pregnant-aspiring film editor-Hindu monk-to-rescue-endangered-Saharan-manatees genre. Within one month, Neil Gaiman and one hundred other authors had adopted this new, innovative formula. Renaldo became the most influential writer in the industry for the three days and twelve hours after his work was published. Mort made a ton of cash but dumped Renaldo for someone who rewrote Shakespeare's plays to make the lead a teen-singing-idol-turned-deep sea-fisherman. That was a hit until Stephen King started rewriting Chaucer to feature possessed toasters. As for Renaldo, he ended up in daytime soap operas. He became known for killing off the leads only to have them discovered three weeks later alive but stuck in vending machines that carried knock-off Gucci purses.

Math Calisthenics

The numbers lined up. Addition and Subtraction symbols roughly pushed them into place as a Greater Than symbol barked orders. Earl Three hated morning math drills. He invariably got a higher digit below him in the subtraction exercise and had to break up the digit to his right. How many times had he broken off a One that he would then have to care for until it could handle basic math? His friend Boris Nine never had this problem, which is why he was called "Bachelor Boris." He lorded it over all the lesser numbers. If Boris wasn't so good at Sudoku, no one would talk to him. But Earl Three was the Nine's best friend and so endured the Boris' annoying tendencies.

This morning was particularly bad. It was tax season, and everyone had a long night. They had been up late, cranking and cranking different scenarios until their master fell asleep on the keyboard. The one bright spot was that a number of letters, the entire Y, U, I, O, and P clans for example, were called up when the sleeping master's fingers rested on their keys. This started a war between the letters and numbers, which somehow morphed into a party that lasted until the monitor's power-saver sent them all home.

Earl had met a nice letter during the party. Penny G was a little rounder than other girls Earl had fallen for, but she had that little left turn into her middle that somehow made her very sexy. The two of them found that with Penny on the left and Earl on the right, they could come up with some very interesting pairings. Their love affair was interrupted when Boris came barging in trying to separate the amorous couple with a pet hyphen he had picked a few moments earlier. Earl ended up saying something nasty regarding Boris' existence. Something to the effect that Boris was only the result of another three who got drunk and squared itself. Boris ran off in a huff, trailing the hyphen behind his like an errant minus sign. Earl was able talk Penny into taking up where they left off and well, Earl ended up getting no sleep that night.

The Don Juan Three was barely able to keep his upper and lower semicircles from falling together. He fought to stay awake mainly because he hated looking like a drunken eight, which is what everyone said he looked like when he was asleep. Boris, knowing that, had been playfully bopping him on the head, while spouting out words that started with G. Earl was grateful for his friend's help, even if he was being overly annoying. Boris did one more thing that made Earl's morning math exercises a little better. He jumped in line ahead of Earl in the division drill, thus saving Earl from having another newborn One to take care of. "Boris is a good friend," thought Earl for the millionth time, "even if he does keep jumping on my head during the morning calisthenics."

Skip the Title

Sir Isaac Sebastian Windborne the Third, Lord High Duke of Scesaria, Crown Prince of the Kingdom of Atistria, Knight of the First Accession, Defender of the Holy Salmak, Guardian of the Four Keys of Waymark, and Head Chef of the Order of the Twilight Bakers wanted to be called Zack and nothing more. It wasn't so bad when he was a child. People only had needed to address him as Sir Isaac Sebastian Windborne the Third. As he grew older, law dictated that everyone, including his mother, must address him with the full title every time they addressed him in any way, shape, or form. No one was allowed to say things like "Your Highness" or "Your Liege" or anything but "Sir Isaac Sebastian yada yada yada." Just saying "Good Day" while passing a small group in the hall, could take forever. The end result was that no one wanted to say "Good Day" or anything else to the person who just wanted to be called Zack.

Since the monarchy had long ago ceded its power to a civilian government, King Isaac Sebastian Windborne the Second, Ruler of the Kingdom of Atistria, General of the First Accession, yada yada yada, couldn't just hand down an edict changing the law. Any changes had to go through Parliament, and Parliament was currently run by people who hated the monarchy. The "Title Tiff," as it was called in the media, was a political power struggle of epic proportion. The Prime Minister had stated in no uncertain terms that if the Royals didn't like their titles, they could renounce the throne and go live in Lower Breakshire. Lower Breakshire was the red light district of the capital. When he was a teenager, the person who just wanted to be called Zack wouldn't have minded living in Lower Breakshire, but as an adult he realized that it wasn't the best place to raise a family. King Isaac yada yada yada was seriously thinking of taking the palace guard and ransacking Parliament.

It wasn't until one of the Royalists in Parliament came up with the idea of running Sir Isaac Sebastian Windborne the Third, Lord High Duke of Scesaria, Crown Prince of the Kingdom of Atistria, Knight of the First Accession, Defender of the Holy Salmak, Guardian of the Four Keys of Waymark, and Head Chef of the Order of the Twilight Bakers, for a seat in Parliament that the issue was settled. Now you may think that the anti-monarchy faction was worried that Sir Isaac yada yada yada would become a force in Parliament, but that was not the case. They knew he had no stomach for politics, and would be easy prey if allowed in their lair. No, it was the printing of the ballot that decided the issue. Three years earlier, Parliament had wanted to make voting easier and save money on paper, so they decreed that names on the ballot should be limited to last name and first initial. This, of course, was impossible with the law concerning addressing the Royals still on the books. For Parliament to rescind the Ballot law in favor of the Titles law would surely make them look like petty blowhards. The Titles law was repealed, and Zack could be called Zack by anyone and everyone. After years of fighting for the freedom to be called whatever he wanted, it was achieved by a regulation meant to save the government a few pennies.

The resolution of the Title Tiff had a major impact on the election that year. It seems the general public still saw Parliament as made up of petty blowhards, and the Royals were now seen as victims in the whole fiasco, the result being that not only was Zack elected to Parliament against his wishes, but the Royalist faction gained control of the government. The Royalists made Zack the Prime Minister to take advantage of his newfound popularity. Unfortunately for Zack, there was still a law on the books that said the Prime Minister could only be addressed by his full title, which in all other cases was Prime Minister So and So. With Zack it meant he had to be addressed by both the title of P.M. and all his other titles. The Anti-Monarchy faction had enough seats in Parliament to block the repeal of that law, so Zack was stuck. To his dismay, Zack was a great Prime Minister and became the longest-serving one in Atistria's history. It wasn't until he was on his deathbed that Parliament finally repealed the Prime Minister title law. When Zack learned of its repeal, he breathed a deep sigh of relief and died. He was buried with all the pomp and ceremony befitting a great King and Prime Minister, but his gravestone was simple, giving his dates of birth and death and identifying him only as "Zack."

Not Creative

Xi Hwongu was writing a glossary. Page by page he turned a technical write-up of a 200-story "sustainable city" looking for a term that needed explaining. The writing project was extremely interesting while gathering the content for the three-thousand-page tome. It was even fun, from a tech writer point of view, writing the "story" of the tower, even though it was mostly "cubic meters of concrete" and "bituminous sheathing" descriptions. But now the project was pure hell. Even though Xi had been pulling out entries while writing, a good tech writer knows that you have to scour the final product to have a complete glossary. After living with this material for seven months, Xi knew it by heart. Every sentence was ingrained in his mind. Every concept was so clear that he could pass for a structural engineer, a construction manager, and a botanist among other things. So in order to do this right, Xi had to try to read every page as if he had never seen it before and knew nothing about "green architecture."

Today was day 14 of the glossary entry hunt. Xi felt like jumping out a window, but his cube was on the first floor and didn't have a window. Empty cans of energy drinks littered the floor around his desk, and still he had trouble keeping his eyes open. His ear buds blared out the punk rock anthems of the Pillows. Xi wasn't even aware that sound waves were impacting his ear drums. His entire world was an Arial 10pt, left justified, 2.5cm margin, A4 swamp.

Xi's attention was currently fixed on reading a passage about a "bundled tube" structure. He could not think of anything else. He dared not think of anything else. Two days ago he had let his mind drift to a world of sustainable cities. He had lost six hours to daydreams involving his girlfriend, a tortoise, and lime jello. He couldn't let that happen again. The glossary deadline was next week, and he was on page 2,476 out of the 3,148 total pages. The tortoises would have to wait until he sent the glossary in for review. His girlfriend would have to put up with the zombie who only came home to shower and change clothes. The cafeteria did stock lime jello, but Xi would not touch it for fear it would spark some creative neuron that would destroy his monotone brain wave pattern.

As Xi turned to page 2,477, his concentration was broken. A practical joker let a rabbit, whose hair was dyed pink, loose in Xi's cubicle. He didn't notice it at first, but then it jumped onto his keyboard. It took Xi a minute and a half to fully comprehend the thing currently typing gibberish into the spec document. Xi just stared at it. Then he began to laugh. Not a "ha, ha" funny laugh. His laugh was a maniacal, last-straw-broken one. A coworker grabbed the bunny for fear that Xi might do it harm. In fact, everyone who heard the laugh decided it was time for an early lunch. But Xi just sat there, laughing for fifteen minutes. The cackling slowly subsided. All that time, the only thing going through his mind were the random letter patterns that the bunny had "typed" into the chapter on bundled tubes. Creative neurons were firing all over the place, as Xi found patterns in the text. He couldn't help himself. He began to write glossary entries detailing what "dkfjlskjfaohhnfdjh" meant. Over the next two hours, Xi wrote four pages of glossary entries on the "bunny-speak" additions. When he was done, he continued on through the rest of the chapter as if nothing had happened.

Three weeks later he received the edited copy of his glossary for inclusion in the Sustainable Tower document. It included a note about some entries that referenced a section of the bundled tube chapter that the reviewer couldn't find in her copy of the document. She had deleted them. Xi had no idea to what she was referring. He had no memory of the rabbit author. He did go back to that chapter to see if he could figure it out. There it was, seven pages of "asjfdslkjakfjirwe." He stared at it, compared it to his original glossary, and promptly rejected the deletion of the entries referencing it. His creative neurons had been silent for those three weeks, and remained so even now. However, Xi remembered the patterns he had seen in that carrot-munching beast's contribution. It all made sense to him, so he knew the glossary entries must stay.

Unfortunately for Xi, the rest of the day was spent trying to get pink bunnies out of his frontal lobe. The acronym list he was working on was severely impacted by this burst of creativity. Eventually, with the help of a music mix of the greatest elevator tunes from the 1970s, he was able to purge all color from his thoughts. His mind went back to its steady state rhythm. He went back to spelling out the acronym "sdjfowerit." All was back to normal.

Giving Him the Slip

"Hello. My name is Garrett McLint. I am currently universe slipping. It's a staple of science fiction, but in case you don't read much, I'll elaborate. I am moving through parallel universes, replacing my analog in each location. I am currently, most likely, only staying a nanosecond or less in each universe. If you are listening to this, you have found some way to follow me and record the nanosecond or less of speech in each universe. I have repeated, more or less, this same message over a thousand times. It helps pass the time of day. I will keep repeating this message until somebody hears it and rescues me.

"You might want to know how I know that I am universe slipping. Well, I first noticed it in a universe in which my kids actually got me what I wanted for my birthday. They were as surprised as I was, which in retrospect meant that the "me" in that universe would have hated the entire audio book collection of the works of my favorite author, Edward

Meiman. Unfortunately, I didn't get to listen to them before I moved on to a universe where I got a pair of socks instead. The socks replacing the audio books was the clincher. There was also the fact that in the socks universe, I was remarried to a Portuguese accountant with a lisp. Once I was sure what was happening, I started marking the time in each universe. What I found out was disturbing. My stays were getting shorter and shorter. Which, WHAT THE FUCK?!?! I STOPPED!?!?!?

"Wow. I am actually in a very empty, very antiseptic, brushed stainless steel room. Well, I think it's stainless steel. It probably isn't. I never was good with metal. Maybe it's platinum. That is very antiseptic. Hey, and my body is the same as in my home universe. Why am I still talking aloud?"

"Hey, anybody there? Hello?!? Can you understand me? I will keep talking so that your computers can translate my speech pattern or whatever you do in this, most likely scientifically advanced universe. I say scientifically advanced because you would have to be in order to bring me to a stop in this room. Of course, if the scientifically advanced culture was the one that stopped me but didn't actually pull me to their universe, then I'm screwed, and my analog here just happened to be standing in an antiseptic-looking room."

"Garrett McLint," said a voice from nowhere and everywhere. "We are the people who stopped you, and you are currently in our universe."

"Cool. Are you also the ones who started me on this trip?"

"Yes," said the disembodied voice. "We apologize for causing your transposition across universes. It appears that the subject of our experiment somehow knocked you into the transposition stream, most likely getting stuck in your universe."

"Poor schmuck. It wasn't a great universe. I hope he or she or it wasn't some great scientist that will be sorely missed."

"Do not worry. He was just an intern," the voice said quite dispassionately. "I am afraid that we currently do not have the technology to identify your specific universe and return you to it. You are stuck here."

"No problemo. I hated that life. Hey, I am assuming your science is advanced enough to cure what ails me. My back hurts, and my knees feel pretty bad from all that standing. Could you take care of them?"

"In due time," said the person I took to be the chief scientist. "We have decided to transfer you to our behavioral science department for study. It is completely voluntary. We have the standard waiver for you to read and sign. You will be compensated for your trouble."

"I've heard that one before. I went for a Ph.D. and ran a bunch of those types of experiments. I know that my 'compensation' will be a fraction of minimum wage for long hours of repetitive tasks which will only be used for some grad student's dissertation. It probably involves physical harm too."

"No," he obviously lied.

"Yeah right. Oh, by the way, you do realize that I am a 'victim' of your 'transposition' experiment? I bet you have lawyers here who know all about human subjects testing laws. I am also guessing that since your experiment involved a human subject in the first place, your work is being monitored to make sure you don't do anything that can hurt anyone. You know, now that I think about it, this is a very traumatic event for me. I don't know how I will adjust to the strangeness of it all. Oh, and I doubt I know anything about how anything works, and so I doubt I will be able to find a job in this brave new world."

The disembodied voice was suddenly very cautious sounding. "Now Mr. McLint, let's not blow this out of proportion. It was an accident after all."

"An accident that you should have foreseen when you filled out the paperwork to get approval for this little experiment. Am I right?" I knew I had him now. "Now you said something about compensation and a waiver a little while ago didn't you? I might be willing to sign that waiver for the right amount of money."

The poor professor knew he was beaten and so gave in. "I am sure we can come to some sort of understanding. For my own benefit Mr. McLint, you weren't by any chance a lawyer in your home universe, were you?"

"Nope, I was a used car salesman."

Theological Understanding

Francis died. It really doesn't matter how he died, or why he died. Suffice it to say, he died. Francis was an interesting man. He was sharp as a tack when it came to everything except religion. He was always confused about religion, God, sin, love, good, but what was most confusing of all was the afterlife. Francis was never sure what an afterlife entailed or that anything could happen after your life ended. He also didn't understand why heaven was up, what heaven was supposed to be in the first place, or even why it was necessary. So Francis, upon realizing that he was dead, was really looking forward to having all this confusion straightened out. As he floated above his body, a bright light called to him. In great anticipation, Francis entered the light.

When Francis came out on the "Other Side" he became even more confused. Before him was this thing that kept shifting form. It started out as your stereotypical angel complete with wings and harp. Then it shifted into a newborn baby. Next it was this thing that had no form but was there nonetheless. It is hard to explain because mortal man had no analogous reference from which to understand this thing. Francis just knew something was there, and it was very awe inspiring. As the thing kept shifting form, it became a waiter for a banquet, a keeper of the keys to a giant vault filled with gold, a Hindu guru, and many other things that completely confused Francis. The thing kept switching between all these forms, not only confusing Francis but making him a bit queasy.

After what seemed like an hour but was probably more like a few minutes, Francis couldn't take it anymore and so yelled, "Stop!"

It did not stop shifting forms, but it did speak to him. "Francis Xavier McShannon, you are here in this place because we don't know what to do with you." For some reason this did not surprise Francis. So instead of asking any questions, he just let the thing go on talking. "As they age, almost all humans come to an understanding of what they believe to be a possible afterlife. Every single human being that ever was has at least had some picture in their mind of an afterlife, even if they would not admit it to themselves. Every single human being, that is, except you. You, Francis Xavier McShannon, have absolutely no concept of an afterlife. You have heard of many different tales of the afterlife, but you didn't understand a single one!" The thing appeared to be getting frustrated. "Even people with the lowest cognitive abilities have at least some conception of an afterlife. What is really frustrating is that you are very intelligent, but you still cannot even grasp the idea of an afterlife, let alone have a vague idea of what constitutes one. Do you know that for the last 12 years of your life we sent you emissaries to try to explain the concept to you?"

"I'm sorry, but I don't remember ever meeting anyone that tried to teach me anything about heaven and such," replied Francis.

"That's because you just don't get it!!!!" Now Francis was sure the thing was frustrated. "As soon as the person left, you completely forgot about the conversation."

Francis decided he had had enough of this talk and decided to cut straight to the chase. "OK, I understand that I don't understand. I understand that understanding has something to do with what happens next. I really don't care about any of that. Just tell me where to go, and I'll go."

"It's not that simple," the exasperated being replied. "Unless you have some understanding, we can't help you grow to a true, complete understanding of the afterlife. In other words, if you don't speak the language, you can't understand the lesson."

"OK, then what do we do now?" Francis was now more frustrated than the thing in front of him.

"We have no idea. Frankly, if it was possible, we'd probably just blast you into oblivion and be done with you. But we can't."

"If that's the case," said Francis. "Just give me a deck of cards, and I'll play solitaire until you come up with something." The shape-shifting being gave Francis a deck of cards, and he began shuffling them.

"That's it," yelled a now very enthusiastic amorphous being, and it switched into the form of a Vegas card dealer. "You are now in the afterlife, sort of. And you are playing cards. Therefore you must have a conception of the afterlife as a place to play solitaire!" The now not shape-shifting being was very proud of itself.

"Uh, yeah. I guess I can go with that." Francis looked at the card dealer in front of him very skeptically. Then, very patronizingly, Francis said, "You know, I'll just sit here and play solitaire. You can just sit down or do whatever you do, and teach me about the afterlife. I'm sure I'll figure it out eventually."

The heavenly card dealer then began to instruct Francis in the ways of the afterlife in the terms of a game of solitaire. Francis never understood a word. After what seemed like a century but was probably a millennia, the card dealer gave up and left Francis in this nowhere place playing cards. So if, upon death, you end up in this room with a shape-shifting thing, just ask Francis if you can join in the game. You can ignore the other guy. You'll never get it anyway.

Turned Slightly Sideways

Deidra Brustim was a news reporter for QBN. Up until this point, she had reported on dog shows, celebrity charity events, the latest off-beat fashion trend, or on anyone who did cute things that would make the viewing audience feel good. In three years, her "biggest" story was the scoop on the government approval of ballistics gelatin for use in breast implants. Of course, Deidra had to undergo the procedure on camera in order for it to make it into the main newscast. From the moment the procedure was over, her producer had her turn slightly sideways for every shot every time she got on camera. Not being one to sugarcoat the truth, Deidra's producer told her that it was so that her bust size was obvious even when wearing a "sensible" pants suit.

Even with her upgraded bust size, Deidra was still relegated to human interest stories, although her pieces did make it onto the 6:00 newscast more often. Then came the day that all of that changed. Connie Fairley, an "A" list reporter, had just been fired for a racial slur concerning a Presidential candidate's mistress. Deidra had always modeled her presentation on Connie's. Her cameraman continually called her "Connie's Clone." So it was no surprise to anyone who knew the biz that in their search to replace the disposable star, the network's marketing gurus would send Deidra to the campaign trail to take over for Connie. The one truly surprised person, Deidra, found herself in the press bus going through Iowa before she had time to really grasp what was happening.

As she sat in the bus, the first thing she noticed was that everyone treated her like everyone else. No one was snubbing her. No one was making snide comments about ballistics gelatin. She didn't even see anyone talking behind her back. Everyone was acting like she was a seasoned veteran of campaign politics reporting. There was the small talk about what diner the candidate would stop at for lunch and bets on whether or not he would wear a campaign t-shirt under his "Farmer John" leather jacket. Some of the reporters even asked her opinion of the candidate's latest speech. They really seemed interested in her response. She had no idea what his speech was about. She just threw out some of Connie's best platitudes, and the others accepted them as if Deidra actually knew something they didn't.

Deidra's first campaign event was a learning experience. None of the other reporters paid much attention to what the candidate did at the diner. Their cameramen were all over the candidate like a pack of dogs, while the reporters sat around talking with their producers or calling someone from their network HQ. Deidra decided to talk with her producer. He only wanted to talk about his one-year-old kid's latest attempt to say, "Dada." As far as Deidra could tell, the only thing the reporters really cared about was whether their cameraman had gotten the perfect shooting location. Everyone wanted the diner in the background and angled just so or with that old twisted tree in the shot or with the candidate's bus in the foreground. After Deidra wrapped up her first campaign report, a couple of the other reporters congratulated her on thinking of getting the diner's trash dumpster in the shot. They said it was genius, although skirting "yellow journalism." In reality, the cameraman had just changed angles so that Deidra's bust was obvious even in her current "sensible" pants suit.

The next two months went pretty much the same as her first day. Sometimes the cameraman's adjustments to get her bust highlighted would yield a "genius" shot. Sometimes it didn't. When it came time for the Election Day, the network called her to the studio to "report" on the exit poll trends. While everyone else sat at desks, she was standing slightly sideways when she gave her reports. Audience focus groups gave Deidra's reporting the highest ratings of anyone on stage that day. Further results placed her just below the anchors from QBN's biggest rivals. Deidra was given an anchor spot within a month.

Deidra's first few days as an anchor were rough. Her audience numbers were mediocre at best. The producers toyed with the idea of having her wear something with a plunging neck line but dropped that idea in favor of getting Deidra out from behind the desk. Deidra stood slightly sideways for the entire newscast from that day on. Her ratings skyrocketed and stayed high for years. Many other reporters and anchors tried to copy her style, but none could stand slightly sideways as good as her.

Neighborhood Rhino

Sophie, the rhinoceros, lived in the suburbs. And like most rhinoceros would, she had a problem with the house's doors. She just never could seem to get the hang of them. She wished that they would be more like microwaves. With those you just push a button and the door opens. Plus, microwave doors were wide. The doors on the house were not. Even if she could open them, poor Sophie would invariably have to smash the doorframe to get through. It was sooooo frustrating. The rest of Sophie's home was her pride and joy. She had doilies on all the pieces of Queen Anne furniture. The paintings on the walls were all landscapes from Sears. The house had a lovely white picket fence around a perfectly manicured lawn. She wasn't totally sure about the lawn. It was an unnatural green color and tasted a bit mediciny. But you had to make some sacrifices if you were going to move up in the world. The window boxes had yummy tulips in the spring, tasty gladiolas in the summer, and plastic poinsettias in winter.

Sophie loved her neighborhood as well. She lived in a very quiet, picture-perfect gated community with polite and friendly neighbors. No one ever tried to shoot her, and they always asked before taking a picture. In the three years Sophie had lived there she had made many friends and even joined Mrs. Bonner's book club. Of course, she could only go to meetings that were held on someone's deck or patio because of the whole door thing. Sophie even put up with Mr. Wilson continually hitting on her. Besides it made her feel like a real woman.

Life in the suburbs was just as she had imagined it would be, except for the door problem. Growing up on the savannah, she had always dreamed of having her own place. All that dirt and dust, the muddy streams and ponds, the lack of a good manicurist, it was a wonder she had survived the wild at all. She now had her perfect life. To hell with those "naturalists" who complained that she should be in some grassland "running free." Running around all day with no place to call home was just ridiculous. And how could she live without the neighborhood grocery store, especially when they just started stocking the high-quality alfalfa grass. When would the preservationists ever learn that we all want to better ourselves and move beyond plain survival? Why can't they see that living in the suburbs is as natural for her as it is for humans? It is a step up from the wild, which is really nothing more than an artificial environment which doesn't have convenience stores. The suburbs are where we all dream of being. It is where we can live comfortably, in a world designed to take care of our every need. No more "survival of the fittest." Just live and be free in an artificial world built just for you, except for the doors.

Warning Labels

"People never change," an exasperated Ralph exclaimed to no one in particular. He received a few grunts of agreement from around the table. "The Board wants us to have a response to this latest unfortunate incident in two hours. They want an incident report by lunch and a full investigation done by the end of the week."

"No problem," snarked Jane. "Response: A statement saying, 'Assholes should not stick burning objects into flammable objects that are next to their domicile.' Incident Report: An asshole stuck a lighted FZ820 into a pile of dry leaves sitting beside his house, which in turn burned down the house. Investigation Report Recommendation: Don't sell FZ820s to assholes."

"What about the rest of the FZ line?" Salim asked.

Jane replied, "Let's just ban sales of all our products to assholes."

"Great idea Jane! You are now in charge of handling the entire incident. Make sure the new warning label covers assholes. On second thought, I'll draft the asshole clause in the warning label. You just get the reports done." Ralph loved his job. It always had new and unexpected challenges. He also liked the fact that he had risen to the level where he could delegate the grunt work, like incident reports, to someone else, while he concentrated on the intricacies of warning labels.

With that taken care of, Ralph turned his attention to the other big challenge of the day, a new product line. "Now Hugo, what about the DX product line?"

"Good news. It doesn't involve flames, electrical shock potential, or poisonous liquids. There are no parts small enough to be ingested and no sharp edges," beamed Hugo.

"Best news I've had in three weeks." Ralph seemed almost giddy. "Just for my own peace of mind, how long is the draft warning label."

"Forty-two pages," chirped Hugo.

"That has to be the shortest list we've put out in the last two years," mused Ralph. "I probably shouldn't ask this, but how does a DX product light a candle? How does it even qualify as being a match?"

Hugo looked back sheepishly, "Marketing is still figuring that one out."

"Okay, I'll file that as someone else's problem and let Marketing take care of it. Are there any other 'fires' I should be aware of?" Ralph looked around the room. He saw only heads shaking no. "Good. You're all dismissed. Salim, don't forget I want the new warning labels for individual matches on my desk by COB today. I'll need to do my usual fine tuning before we send it out." Ralph couldn't wait to put an asshole clause in this new one as well.

"It won't fit on your desk, but you'll get it by COB," Salim said as he exited the room.

Ralph stayed behind, wistfully looking out the window. He was thinking of his classmates from law school who had chickened out and taken less stressful jobs. Charlotte had actually become the District Attorney of Los Angeles, and Herb was now a Supreme Court Justice. Ralph knew they all envied him, and they should. The world of Warning Labels is where a lawyer can really show his stuff. It is THE dream job.

Reading the Signs

I hit a wall last month, literally. I was in my car, driving to work, when I was distracted by a deer running along next to me. When the deer swerved away from my car, I finally looked at the road. Instead of seeing the road, I saw the wall of a grocery store. My car hit the wall, airbags deployed, and the front of the car crumpled like a broken accordion. I was unhurt. The car was totaled. The grocery store wall only had a few scratches. I wasn't going that fast.

For the last week I have been trying to make sense of the incident. A normal person would have moved on by now, but I am one of those people who believe that everything in life happens for a reason. Everything teaches us a lesson. I have been able to identify the purpose of everything from promotions, to getting gum stuck to my shoe. This event, with the deer running alongside the car, the grocery store, and the wall must be telling me something. Look at all the metaphors rampant in the accident. They have to have meaning. They couldn't be just random coincidences.

My wife said it all pointed to the fact I shouldn't stare at deer unless I am about to hit them. That idea was just too obvious. A friend jokingly told me the deer was my wife, my car was my, well, a part of my anatomy, and the wall was my inability to do certain things. He then told me that sometimes a wall was just a wall. My aunt, who lives with us, came up with a wonderful analogy to the flagging economy and World War II. Of course, she thinks everything is about World War II. She also thinks it is 1942 and we live in Paris.

I am currently leaning toward a metaphor where the deer was either running away from something or being hunted. I think the grocery store represents food or possibly nourishment for the soul. The wall is most likely reality. My car is probably my desire to get ahead, and maybe the airbags are some sort of cushion between my drive to succeed and the hard truth of reality. Of course the deer could also mean freedom. The grocery store could stand for commercialism. The wall could be the System seeking to restrain us. The car could be my attempt to break through my bonds. Oh, it's maddening!

Then, this morning everything changed. As I pulled out of the garage, I saw a deer, maybe the same deer; I don't know. The deer was eating our tulips. This has got to be a sign to help me figure out the first sign. But what does it mean? The deer is obviously meant to mean something about the deer from the wreck. Similarly my new car must be analogous to the one that was totaled. Maybe the tulips are the groceries in the grocery store. But how does it all fit together? I have no clue. There must be something I'm missing.

I've decided that after work, I am going to the neighborhood park to try to find another deer. Maybe if I find one, it could bring some clarity to this mystery. I need some sign to tell me what the sign I saw this morning means. I am at my wit's end. I feel that if I don't solve this soon, I will miss an opportunity to understand some basic meaning to my life. I need to know! I am so close. I just need a sign. One more sign; that's all I ask, one more sign.

One of Those Mornings

Sanjeev got up from bed just like he always did. Got ready for work just like he always did. Opened the front door to his house just like he always did. And in that not-really-aware-of-your-surroundings-because-this-is-what-you-always-do way, he headed out the door. Sanjeev then walked right into a lollipop tree.

Sarah got up from bed just like she always does. Got ready for work just like she always does. Opened the front door to her house just like she always does. In that not-really-aware-of-your-surroundings-because-this-is-what-you-always-do way, she headed out the door. Sarah then fell into the pool at the bottom of a waterfall in an Amazonian rainforest.

Emmanuel got up etc., headed out the door. Emmanuel then bumped his head on a control panel in the International Space Station. Interestingly enough, one of the scientists at the International Space Station ended up on Emmanuel's lawn.

Over one 24-hour period, this happened to all seven billion plus people on the Earth. Approximately one third ended up in worlds of pure fantasy. One third ended up somewhere that wasn't Earth. The remaining third simply translocated on Earth. For the 15,323,486 who ended up in an ocean or on a planet that doesn't support life or in a fantasy world that couldn't stand humans, their day ended abruptly and very badly. Forty-two percent of the people in the fantasy worlds simply sat down and refused to believe what they saw. This happened for only 23% of the ones who ended up off Earth and 5% of those that stayed on Earth. Conversely, 10% of those in fantasy worlds, 38% of those off world, and 84% of those on Earth that had smart phones immediately checked their GPS to find out where they were. Strangely, 80% of those in fantasy worlds had a signal and quickly located in what part of their particular fantasy world they were. Only 2% of those off world got that satisfaction.

Sanjeev was one of those who checked his smart phone. He then checked for restaurants that served breakfast and found a nice pastry shop within walking distance. Sarah stripped down to her underwear and had a nice swim. Emmanuel kept fiddling with buttons that looked like either GPS or phones, eventually gave up, and took a tour of the space station. All three made the most of their day and found somewhere nice to bed down for the night (or what went for night in their particular location). The next morning they each got up in a way similar to what they always did. Got ready for their day in a way similar to what they always did. And in that not-really-aware-of-your-surroundings-because-this-is-what-you-always-do way, they headed out their "door." Of the six billion plus humans that were still alive that next morning, only Sanjeev, Sarah, and Emmanuel had developed a new routine the previous day. What did they have in common? They all, before the translocation, worked in call centers for software manufacturers.

Always Archive What is Important to You

Martin Queiroz never went anywhere without his 128GB USB flash drive. It held every file he had ever worked on in his professional life. He had four jobs in the last 15 years, and in every job Martin backed up his files to a flash drive and kept them safe in his pocket. He never deleted or overwrote a file, so he had many versions of some of his larger works. As his flash drive became full, he would transfer the files to a larger one, and then put his old flash drive in a safety deposit box.

Luckily for Martin and his flash drives, he didn't work on graphics intensive documents or video or audio projects. Which is why, after 15 years of work, everything still fit on one flash drive. His professional life was spent translating product instruction manuals from English to Portuguese. Martin considered this work critically important to the economic growth of the Brazilian consumers who purchased electric razors, window fans, and other small appliances. That was why he protected his files with such diligence. Martin also knew that the information he guarded was highly sensitive, so he never told anyone about his secret vault, not even his wife.

Martin died in a car crash when he was 58 years old. In his will he bequeathed his flash drive to his eldest son, then 24. Martin had put a "Read Me" file at the top level of his flash drive. It explained the contents of the drive and begged his heirs to guard this information after his death. This they did, for many, many generations. Every time a new form of storage media was developed, the information would be transferred, and the old archive would be placed reverently into Martin's safe deposit box. Not one of his heirs ever read any of the contents of the drive. They considered it the sacred legacy of their family. It wasn't until Martin's line died out, some 200 years after Martin's death, that a sociologist took possession of the drive and its predecessor drives and thoroughly examined their contents. The sociologist passed it along to a technology historian, who recognized it as a link to the height of the Small Appliance Era. The contents of the drive became a national treasure in the South American Federation. It was studied for another 500 years by historians and small appliance aficionados throughout the world. Long after people had forgotten William Shakespeare, "Martin Queiroz" was a household name. Martin had recognized the importance of his life and saved it for posterity. Posterity was thankful he did.

Once More with Feeling

I have to admit that we were all a bit nervous. Working with one of the premiere conductors of our age, Sir Nigel Marikern, was a once in a lifetime event for someone who plays with the Boise Philharmonic. Sir Marikern was known for the heavenly beauty of the performances he led. He was also known for getting the most from his musicians by using a heavy-handed, unforgiving, play-until-you-get-it-right approach that has turned major artists into sniveling, scared children. Never having played for him before would have been even scarier had he not brought along some key musicians to help guide the orchestra. The first violin, first wind, and first percussion were all Mariken disciples. They had arrived a day early to run a clinic, which most of us found to be a hazing, in order to prepare us for our first rehearsal with the great conductor.

We assembled in the hall in the wee hours of the morning and were taken through some "basic warm-ups," as the first violin called them, but which wore many of us out. However, no matter how tired we felt, we were revived when Sir Nigel appeared from the wings. "Are they ready," he asked the first violin. She nodded. The great maestro then ascended the podium, and we all waited for his first words, "Let's start from the beginning of the first movement." He raised the baton, and the rehearsal began.

Now I will admit that the first run-through was a little shaky. It never is very polished—well, not for us anyway. So we were not surprised when Marikern sternly said, "Once more, with feeling."

For our second attempt, the learned conductor's baton became a little more animated, as did our playing. I felt that the flow of his gestures had started to unify our playing. I could hear the orchestra becoming one. As we ended the piece I felt like we were on the verge of something wonderful. Marikern just shook his head and almost angrily said, "Once more, with feeling."

As we began to play, the orchestra began to coalesce to form a single musician. Sir Nigel's baton wove us together like a beautiful sheet of silk. We flowed through the piece, reaching heights this orchestra had never reached. It was beauty incarnate. I am sure we all felt the same, which is why we were all shocked when a visibly angry Marikern yelled, "Once more, WITH FEELING!"

I didn't think we could raise our level of playing any further, but I was wrong. We became entranced by the baton's movements. It was hypnotic. I found myself merging with my fellow clarinet players—no, with the entire ensemble. I began to tear up as the music took the form of an angel and soared to the heavens. As we came to the close, I felt my body lifted up into a state of nirvana.

Marikern was not as impressed. If anything he was even more incensed. He began to shout, "ONCE MORE . . ." when the first violin shouted even louder, "ENOUGH!"

Marikern stopped. We all froze. What sacrilege was this? How dare she shout down the genius before us? I wanted to find a pitchfork and burn this witch at the stake. She, on the other hand, calmly put down her violin and walked up to Sir Nigel until they were almost nose to nose. She then took her right hand and brought it up to Marikern's left ear. She snapped her fingers and asked, quite loudly, "Did you hear that?" Sir Nigel Marikern looked slightly embarrassed. The first violin then took her left hand and snapped her fingers next to his right ear. She repeated her question, just as loudly. "Did you hear that?" The great man could not meet her eyes. Instead, reaching up first to the right and then the left ear, he removed his hearing aids and flipped a small switch on each. He then replaced them, and the first violin returned to her place. The maestro took a second to regain his composure, then took up his baton, and in a very soft voice he said, "Once more, with feeling."

Distro Hell

Hal sent off the minutes of the meeting and was immediately deluged with emails from confused colleagues. Hal had thought he'd pulled up the right meeting from his calendar from which to grab the invitee list, but now it seems he was mistaken. He sent apologetic emails to everyone and found the correct invitee list. Later he sent an email to his project team, only to find out he had used an old distribution list. He got frantic calls from people who had finally gotten themselves off the project from hell, only to have the email make them think they were back on it. It took a full hour to calm people down, and to get the email out to the correct team. The beleaguered Hal went off to his 9:00, 9:30, and 10:00 meetings glad he wasn't the scribe in any of them. In fact he was a warm body in each of those meetings and so took the time to catch up on his home email. Hal really wasn't good at navigating his smartphone and its tiny screen. So it was no surprise that he reminded his softball team to make sure they read "Wuthering Heights" and invited his wife's book club to go out drinking. Nine WTFs and seven LOLs later, Hal realized what he had done. He actually cancelled his 11:00 meeting to get it all straightened out. By the afternoon Hal had sworn off distribution lists. He spent the rest of the day picking individual names from his contact list even when the email was going out to fifty people. He still had a few "wrong numbers" in his emails, but for the most part they got to their intended audiences.

As he was leaving for the day, his flustered boss, Burt, stopped by for their usual COB commiserating session. While Hal was relating the more interesting replies from his wife's book club (Old Mrs. Ferguson was skipping the book club meeting in favor of drinking with the softball team), both Hal's and Burt's phone beeped the tone for incoming mail. They simultaneously checked their inbox. What they found was an email from the president of the company discussing a previously unknown upcoming merger with their largest competitor. The email also talked about layoffs, office closings, and the huge golden parachute the president was going to receive from the deal. They each checked the distribution list and decided that everyone on it but them was probably in on the deal. Hal and Burt didn't reply to the email, but instead just kept reading the "reply alls" coming in from the rest of the conspirators. From the information gathered, Hal and Burt were able to construct a few emails that "accidentally" went to the "wrong" people. It only took them three days to sabotage the deal, get the President to resign, and get big promotions.

Hal went on to become the president of the company. With rank comes privileges, and his second favorite privilege was that he now had an admin assistant to send out all but the most important emails. His favorite privilege was that Hal had started having an affair with that same admin. He knew she didn't love him, that her intentions were purely a result of what he could do for her. So when the novelty wore off, he didn't think anything of just reassigning her somewhere far away and finding another "loyal" assistant. Unfortunately the admin that he so rudely had gotten rid of actually thought she loved the man. Hal soon found out that the old adage about a lover scorned was all too real. The scorned admin added the company-wide announcement mailing list to Hal's company recruiter's email. Hal sent his requirements for the new admin position, which included desired breast size, to the entire company. Hal had to resign over the furor. He was also convicted of using unfair hiring practices and had to pay a large sexual harassment settlement when the staff of the company filed a class action suit.

Hal, not learning his lesson, sent out his résumé, not to a group of executive recruiters, but to recruiters for Icelandic fishing companies. Before he knew it, he had accepted a job to manage whaling fleets in the North Sea. He ended up following through with his this posting when he found out that the position didn't require him to send emails to anyone. The fleets still used radios, which he had trouble with as well, but that is a different story.

Staring at the Screen

Reginald Harrington-Smything sat staring at the monitor of his work computer. He stared at it for a total of 6 hours and 52 minutes on Wednesday. He only stopped staring at it for lunch and restroom breaks. His fingers never touched the keyboard and only moved the mouse to keep the screensaver at bay. Open on his monitor was his email inbox. If anybody had wandered into his office, they would have seen a screen of unopened mail. They may have even noticed that the number next to the inbox label indicated there were 2,975 unread emails. If they had asked Reginald about the unread email, he probably would have answered, "What?" if he answered them at all. If they had turned off the monitor and asked Reginald what had been on it, he would have been completely clueless. Reginald Harrington-Smything would have just turned the monitor back on and gone back to staring. But no one ever stopped by Reginald's office, not once in three years.

Reginald worked for Translucent Properties, a wholly owned subsidiary of Global Bastions. Four years ago, when Reginald started work, the company had been called HS Holdings. At that time, Reginald's dad was the President, his uncle was the CEO, his aunt was the CFO, and his brother was the head of Business Development. The Harrington-Smythings owned the company, which was the last remaining relic of the Harrington-Smything "Empire" that at one time had spanned the globe. The "empire" dated back to the days of Queen Victoria, when it was founded by Lord Reginald Smything. At that time the company owned properties across all of Great Britain's colonies. Lord Smything was a lion of business. His namesake of today was a twit. Such a twit, that the current Reginald's dad had given him an office in the basement with a job that consisted of answering emails from charities wanting the company to donate money or used equipment or even old company cars. Reginald was told not to give them anything. Reginald took this to mean that he was not to read the emails in the first place. So from Day One, Reginald would just stare at the screen.

HS Holdings was bought by Global Bastions three years ago. All of Reginald's relatives got wonderful golden parachutes and went into retirement as the Lords and Ladies they fancied themselves to be. Reginald's own golden parachute got lost in the transition paperwork, as did the fact that he was an employee. However, the personnel system knew Reginald was an employee and consequently kept paying him to stare at the screen. Reginald's inbox had stopped receiving emails two years ago, when his job was automated. So for the last two years, he had stared at the same unread emails that were there when his job function disappeared. He never noticed. Reginald was a twit after all.

This all came to an end on a Wednesday, on the third anniversary of Reginald's hiring. His office was reassigned to an intern who processed employee termination notices. The intern, Gloria Smanners, thought the office was unoccupied. When she got there she found Reginald. Being an intern, she just assumed that he was supposed to be there, ordered a new desk and went to work on termination notices. On Friday of that same week, she finally got up the nerve to ask Reginald who he was and what he did. He told her he was the son of the President of the company and was charged not to give money to charities. It took Gloria another week to determine that while Reginald was a twit, he was also the son of the previous President of the company. Gloria, being a very status-conscious, enterprising intern saw a chance to become independently wealthy. She quickly and without any protestation from Reginald, convinced him to marry her that same day. Gloria was also pretty good with personnel systems and by the end of the following week had found Reginald's cut of the sale of HS Holdings. As his wife, she was able to transfer the money to her own account and promptly resigned to go off and live as the Lady she had always wanted to be. Before she left, she managed to bury Reginald's employee paperwork so far in Global Bastions' personnel system that it would never be found by even the most industrious intern. Gloria Harrington-Smything-Smanners, having secured her husband's future, kissed him on the brow and left him there in his office, staring at the screen as always.

Slice of Life

This Month's School Project

Lily didn't really know what 'procrastination' meant, even though her father said she was a master of it. Lily was eight, and extremely cute in the lovable sense of the word. She was socially smart as well. Lily knew how to use 'puppy dog eyes' and even well executed tantrums to get away with almost anything. Her parents were divorced, and she was well versed in playing one off against the other. In other words, Lily was the one in control of this family.

Lily's third grade teacher was very creative. She constantly came up with fun projects that would get her kids to enjoy learning. Lily always had fun doing the projects when she actually took the time to work on them. Lily rarely took the time until she absolutely had to get it done. So her 'fun' was always coupled with a frantic, stress-filled, last-minute whirlwind production. One or both of her parents would get sucked into the maelstrom, and afterward, both would swear this would never happen again. Of course, it always did.

This month Lily had to do a book report. Not a written regurgitation of a book, instead she had to turn the book into a board game. It took her a week to settle on a book. Her mother would ask her to choose one every morning. Every evening Lily would look through her bookshelf and choose something she had read in kindergarten, and her mother would quickly reject it. Finally, her mother chose a book for her. It was the first book in a series that followed the life of a cat in the wild. It was popular with girls her age, at least according to the reviews on Amazon. Lily accepted it with a mild whine that meant she was somewhat appreciative of the fact she didn't have to make a decision, while being skeptical that the decision was a good one.

Lily's father was in charge of making sure she read the book. His first strategy was to have her read part of the book to him or her mother every night. This strategy was doomed because both he and her mother had all-consuming jobs and didn't have an hour or two after work to listen to Lily read. After a few days of no progress, the father switched to Plan B, which involved having her show the requisite parent what page she was on when she went to bed. That bit the dust when her father glimpsed her opening the book to a random page before showing it to him. Two weeks were wasted before the parents forced themselves back to Plan A. By the fourth week, this plan was modified to a skimming of the book, instead of a thorough reading. With four days to spare, Lily 'finished' the book.

The parents then made another mistake when they decided to let Lily design the game with no supervision. Two days later, when asked to show her mother the game and explain it to her, Lily pulled out a piece of paper with a cat drawn on it. The mother pulled out the instructions given by the teacher and went through them point by point with Lily. To her credit, the mom made Lily design the game by herself, holding back suggestions that the mother so desperately wanted to give. In the end, Lily designed a game that was somewhere between 'Life' and 'Chutes and Ladders.' Then it was the father's turn. He ran out and bought foam board, Styrofoam shapes for game pieces, and various other supplies he thought they would need. The day before it was due, a Sunday, was spent 'helping' her construct it. The father wasn't as controlled as the mother, and so Lily was able to get him to do the lion's share of the work. Near the end Lily really got into it, and finally took ownership of the project. Fourteen hours of cutting, pasting, painting, printing, etc. yielded a passable game.

The next day, Lily's mom loaded the game and her daughter into the minivan with a sense of relief knowing that it was done. Lily was juiced, wanting to show off 'her' work as soon as she got to school. As Lily's mom dropped her off, she had this urge to sneak in and watch the reaction to the game, but she had to get to work. Lily's mom spent the day half distracted, wondering how well the game would be received. The mother almost flew out of work to pick Lily up, craving any news on the success of the project. When Lily appeared from the school door, the mother suppressed an urge to run up and start grilling the girl. Instead she let Lily finish talking to her friends, stow her backpack in the minivan, and settle down for the ride home. After about a mile into the drive home, Lily had said nothing about the project. When asked how her day went, Lily just replied "Good." A mile from home, not being able to stand it anymore, her mom asked her flat out how her project went. The response: "The teacher made some kids play it. They liked it. Said it was fun." That was it?!?!? Further prodding yielded even less information and some annoyance from Lily. Defeated, the mom drove Lily back home and started the nightly routine of getting her to do her homework. The father called for Lily that night and got the same response her mother had gotten. The two worn-out parents commiserated for a few minutes until Lily interrupted the phone call to give her mother the instructions for the next month's project. The mother read the instructions over the phone to the father. Both sighed when the instructions were finished and began the plotting on how to get this one done early. They finished the phone call sure that this one would be a cinch. Parents never learn.

Fingers' Gibson

Roy Setter played the guitar, or should I say he played A guitar? The guitar was a 1969 Gibson Byrdland. The short scale neck was ideal for Roy's elaborate single-note style, and extensive use of ninth, eleventh, and thirteenth chords. His style earned him the name "Fingers," by which he was known throughout the Country Music world. Fingers performed everywhere from Nashville to Hong Kong with the likes of Hank Williams Jr., Garth Brooks, Toby Keith, Lee Ann Womack, and Taylor Swift. He had been compared to Stevie Ray Vaughn on more than one occasion, although he rejected those claims as ridiculous.

Every gig Fingers played, he played with that Gibson. It was his trademark and his best friend. He kept it by his side no matter where he went. It wasn't any superstition that made him keep his guitar so close, he just wanted to be able to play whenever he got the urge. Once in a crowded market in Kuwait—he was there to play for the troops in Camp Doha—Fingers just started playing. The Kuwaitis had no idea what was going on at first, but after a few songs the normally noisy midday crowd was mesmerized with Fingers' playing.

Fingers Setter was constantly on the road. Somehow he had time for two marriages and one son. The son, Orville (which was the first name of the originator of Finger's guitar), inherited his dad's knack for playing. The kid joined Fingers on the road when he finally had the attention span to play for two hours straight. The father-son duo played together for twenty-three years, until at the age of 64, the road became too much for Fingers. At his Farewell Concert at the Grand Ole Opry, Fingers handed his Gibson to his heir as he left the stage.

At seventy-six, Fingers was dying of cancer. The legend lay in a hospital bed in Hattiesburg, Mississippi, his home since he'd retired. His son was there with him until the end, and many of those who had shared the stage with the great guitarist came to visit. Orville spent those days reliving

Fingers' career, not sure if his father could hear him through the pain that wracked the old man's body.

On a day when Fingers was more conscious than usual, he asked for the Gibson. It had sat at the foot of his bed since his son arrived. Orville got Fingers up in a sitting position and put the Gibson in his father's lap. Fingers tried to put his left hand on the neck but couldn't. His son, seeing that his dad needed to hold the guitar, took his father's hand, placed it on the guitar and put his fingers in the position for a "C" chord. He then put a pick in Fingers' right hand and moved it to the strings to help him strum. Fingers smiled, then dropped the pick and let his arms fall. When his son tried to take the guitar away, Fingers grabbed it and held it tight.

Fingers stayed sitting up, holding the guitar for the next nine days. As he slipped into a deep sleep, he spoke to his guitar one last time. "Live on," was all he said. Fingers died two days later with a smile on his lips. Orville painted his father's nickname on the body of the guitar in big, bold letters so even the people at the back of the audience could read it. He played that guitar until he retired, when he passed it on to his daughter. The guitar lived on for decades after Fingers could no longer play it. A fitting tribute to the man and the Gibson he loved.

Listening to the Train of Thought

"Soy milk has a lot more body than regular milk," Ken volunteered. "I think that's why the Cheerios float a little longer when I use soy milk." This is how most conversations went with "Stray Thought" Ken. Not only did his mind wander a lot, he would keep you informed as to its whereabouts. His wife thought this an endearing quality. Very few others agreed with her. Ken's wife was also very confident in their relationship. She knew that if he ever thought about having an affair or wasn't happy with her, she would find out before things went too far downhill.

His coworkers had learned to put up with Ken's musings. They had no choice really. Ken was the founder and president of the company. It was also true that from many a stray thought, great breakthroughs had occurred. Of course they all lived in dread of statements like, "I think I'm going to have to scrub that project," or, "George just isn't working out." Still when Ken would exclaim, "Everyone's working so hard. They deserve a bonus," morale would skyrocket. Since there was more of the latter than the former, his workers thought Ken was a good, if strange, person.

Today most everyone, both at home and at work, knew that very little would get done. It was the first day of the college basketball playoffs, and Ken was obsessed with the tournament. "Gonzaga doesn't deserve a number one seed" had been heard over fifteen times leading up to today. This morning his kids had been treated to an internal debate over whether the number one seed could actually pull off a repeat National Championship.

It was around mid-morning when things got a little weird. His administrative assistant was making a fresh pot of coffee when she heard Ken say, "Oh shit, the world's going to end tomorrow." Ken was reading the Wall Street Journal. "I think I'll give everyone the day off." Ken looked up from his screen, and saw his admin there. "Oh good, there you are, Bonnie. Could you let everyone know that they have tomorrow off? Tell them it's because Pepperdine is playing Duke or something like that." Bonnie noted that Ken seemed somewhat rattled. She thought about asking him what was going on but decided instead to just keep close to Ken, as he would spill the beans eventually.

Ken's workers were overjoyed that their president was sharing his pride in his alma mater with them all. Many decided that they would cheer for Pepperdine to beat Duke, even though most of them didn't even know where Pepperdine was located. Bonnie however had let a few of her closest friends and the people who dealt with Ken regularly in on the real reason for the holiday. Hakim, the finance head, was the first to try to draw out how the world was going to end. "So Ken, see anything interesting in the Journal?"

He heard a "You have no idea" before Ken composed himself and told Hakim that there had been nothing of interest. As Hakim left, Ken muttered to himself something about the Post only confirming his suspicion, but it was amazing that the newspaper reporters didn't put it together themselves.

Earl from maintenance heard Ken lament that no one "could really prevent it at this point." As the work day was drawing to a close, Bonnie heard Ken sobbing, "Everyone will be swept away. No one can escape the end of all things good in this world." All further questions were ignored as Ken was so despondent that he didn't even notice the people around him. To add to their distress, Bonnie noticed that Ken had not even followed the first round scores of the games that afternoon. When Ken left for the day, he left behind a somber group of people.

The next day Bonnie and friends gathered at her home to await the disaster. They tried to call Ken a few times, but he wasn't answering his phone. Earl had even gone over to Ken's house before going on to Bonnie's, but no one answered the door. They tried to comfort themselves by checking out all possible world-ending scenarios they could think of. They had checked to make sure that none of the nuclear powers were about to go to war. They scanned all the astronomical websites to make sure no one had seen a large meteor heading for Earth. They had even checked their horoscopes to see if the stars knew anything. It wasn't until 5:30 that evening that they found out how the world was ending. CNN suddenly broke into their regular programming with a major "Earth-shattering" story. Bonnie nearly had a heart attack until she realized what was going on. The news cameras showed FBI officers leading the coaches of six of the biggest college basketball programs away in handcuffs. The newsman was telling the audience that this was the largest game-fixing sting in history. He went on to say that the college basketball tournament had been cancelled. The crowd in Bonnie's house actually celebrated the news. They broke out the booze and started partying. Before they got very far, Earl stopped them. This was not the time to party. Instead all of them got in their cars and went over to Ken's house determined to be let in. After all, they knew their place was by Ken's side. It was a time of mourning, and Ken needed them.

A Blah Day

It was a cold, rainy fall morning. Lee put on his raincoat and made his way out into the world. "Blah," he said to no one. At noon, he followed his usual route through the streets of the city to his usual diner to order his usual lunch. After eating, when he walked out into the rain he said, "Blah," again to no one. He retraced his steps to his office building and said, "Blah," to no one as he pushed the revolving door. He worked the rest of the day without saying a word. When quitting time rolled around, he put on his raincoat and once again headed out into the world. Without thinking, he said, "Blah," as the raindrops pelted his coat. A passing car splashed water on his legs. He didn't notice. When crossing a street, he put his foot in a pothole and nearly fell over. He didn't notice. He didn't notice a friend who waved at him as they passed each other. He didn't notice the "One Day Only" sale going on at his favorite store. Lee didn't notice anything for the rest of the day.

The next morning, when Lee woke up, the sun was rising, casting orange and purple light in through the window. He got up humming a tune he heard on the radio, added 15 minutes to his normal exercise routine, and stopped at a new bagel shop on his way to work. It was only then that he realized that today was not Monday. He briefly wondered what he had done during the previous day and decided it was probably just mind-numbing blah-ness.

The Holiday Season

"Did I really do that?" Herbert asked his sister. They were reminiscing on their youth, and as always, Herbert had major gaps in his memory for anything over five years ago. This time it was a story of a chicken literally crossing a road. Supposedly at age eight, Herbert had walked three miles to a nearby farm, somehow corralled a chicken, and forced it to cross the road outside the farm. Herbert vaguely remembered being told the same story a year ago on his last trip to visit his sister. "Well, I definitely was an adventurous kid. Now you three don't get any ideas about following in your old man's footsteps," Herbert gave his kids a wink which meant he knew they'd do whatever they pleased.

"Can you tell us some stories of when Dad was a teenager Aunt Jean?" Joann was twelve and wanted ammunition for her upcoming trip into teenagedom.

Herbert quickly inserted himself between his sister and daughter. "Look, it's time for bed. How did it get to be so late?" It was 11:00, which was well past bed time at home.

Jean agreed with her brother, and his kids were sent to the basement to try to get some sleep. Similarly, Jean's kids were sent upstairs to turn in for the night. "Tomorrow night I get to tell the story of you and that pool cleaner," Herbert jabbed his sister.

"Not fair! Plus I don't think you want Joann using that as a model for turning 18."

"I pray she waits that long." Herbert and Jean spent the next hour discussing the horrors that awaited them as their kids grew. It was after midnight when Herbert finally transformed the living room couch into a bed.

Herbert lay in his 'bed' and began to think about wrapping up the trip tomorrow and heading back to the West Coast early New Year's Day. Eight hours of planes, trains, and automobiles taking him back home to its work and taking kids to everything from school to basketball practices to dance lessons to sleepovers and everything parents would do when the holidays were over. He had been fixated on this trip for so long, that he had not really thought about what would come afterward. Now the everyday world came rushing back. He was only able to push these thoughts out of his mind by putting in his ear buds and listening to Dark Side of the Moon. He drifted off to sleep as "*Any Colour You Like*" synthesizer-ed his brain into regular sleep waves. Herbert slept without dreaming, his body was recharging itself for the coming year. He woke the next day, and for the next 24 hours didn't think about what came after the plane touched down in Sacramento. This was the time to concentrate on nothing, and he was going to do that for as long as he could. Tomorrow would be tomorrow with or without having it disrupt his holiday today.

Grocery Store Shuffle

Donald wandered the aisles of the grocery store on autopilot. He had been coming to this store for years, and had even met his wife in the aisle where his pickled plums were stocked. He was on his monthly trip to pick up staples. He had done this so many times that he didn't need a shopping list. Donald knew the store so well he didn't even need to check the directory to find pickled plums. Each month he followed the same path he always did, put the same items in the cart, and would go to the same cash register no matter how long the line. However today was different. The pickled plums were not where they were supposed to be.

Donald's autopilot could easily take an out-of-stock situation in stride. He would just keep going and note the missing item when he unpacked the groceries at home. It was only when the item in question had no space devoted to itself that his mind had to kick in gear. He would track down the missing item and adjust his mental map to support the new store layout. This is what should have happened when he realized the pickled plums were out of place, but not this time. In their place were tampons. In the middle of the canned fruit section, there was a small bit of shelf space devoted to tampons. This snapped Donald awake, almost giving him whiplash.

Pickled plums were the first item in Donald's list. He quickly located them. They were up two shelves and to the right. He put them in his cart and continued on, bothered by the strange placement of the feminine hygiene product. The second item on his list was tomato paste. As he reached its normal location, he found women's deodorant. The tomato paste was relatively close, so he picked it up and moved on. Elbow macaroni was displaced by styling gel. Shelf space for corn flakes was taken by facial cream. And so it went all through the store. Everything on his list had been moved to make way for items only a woman would need. To make matters even more surreal, the only items that were subjected to this strange shuffling were things he normally picked up on the fifteenth of every month. Everything else in the store was in its usual place.

Donald was on the verge of freaking out when he got in line at his usual cash register. When Donald looked up to read the headlines on the tabloids he found condoms. That was when it hit him. Donald had now been married for three months to the woman who used to be the store manager at this grocery. She was now a regional manager for the chain but still had many friends here. As he stood there staring at the condoms, it occurred to him that all the usurping items were on the list his wife had given him each of the last three months. With this in mind, Donald turned his cart around to pick up the items he had forgotten on each of those trips. On his way out he picked up one final item, a bouquet of roses. Donald also made a mental note to develop a new routine next month. It took him four more months and four bouquets of roses before he finally got it right. His new routine now firmly set, the trips became as routine as before their marriage. That was, until he found diapers replacing the tabloids at the register.

Waiting to Dye

Frank was in his 70s and lived in a nursing home in the burbs of Minneapolis. He led a typical retiree's life. Up in the morning, eat breakfast, take your meds, play chess or Parcheesi with another of the inmates, watch TV, etc. One day Frank decided he wanted a change. Not just any change, he wanted to change whom he was. After much thought, the mature, respectable man decided to get his hair dyed purple. He was tired of all that gray on top of his head. It was boring, just like his life. It needed to become a dark, shiny purple. More blue than red. After all, he would hate to have a burgundy head. It just wouldn't be right.

Frank knew his regular barber, who was almost as old as he was, would never help him in this endeavor. So the old man headed for the mall. The mall was the largest in the U.S. and so had barbers/stylists all over the place. Upon arriving Frank checked the directory and found over ten health and beauty salons that do things to your hair. His first stop was the discount haircut place. That store was willing to dye his hair but couldn't do anything that wasn't specifically spelled out in their handbook, and purple was definitely not in their handbook. Next, Frank decided to go to the other end of the scale and so found the trendiest looking styling salon. Those follicle fashionistas literally laughed him out of the shoppe. Frank looked all over the mall. It took him over an hour, but he finally found the place. He knew it was right because the stylist had bright pink hair.

In order to get his hair dyed with the least amount of explaining, he told the kid a story of his hippie days. Frank really wasn't a hippie during the late 60s. In fact he was a soldier in Viet Nam. However, he thought that for the sake of getting what he wanted, he could tell a little purple lie. The girl (her name was Rachel) totally dug his way-out idea (she had this thing for hippie lingo) and quickly agreed that purple was the perfect color for Frank. Rachel also tried to get the aging hipster to pierce his nipples, but he declined. It had taken a while, but in the end he was able to get his hair the right color.

Frank knew he would be mocked when he got back to the home. He imagined the outrage of the usually polite seniors. This was going to be fun. If nothing else, he was sure it would liven up the place, even if it was at his own expense. As expected, when the Woodstock Wannabe got back to the assisted living facility, he was viciously attacked by many of the residents. It was almost like being bullied in grade school, the bullies just had gray hair and wrinkles. He would hear groups of the inmates whispering whenever he passed. Some of the residents were even scared of Frank, worried that he had gone over the edge.

However, there was a small group who looked wistfully at the old man. Almost all of them were people Frank barely knew. One by one they would start up a conversation with Frank. It would begin with questions as to why he had dyed his hair and started wearing outrageous clothes. Frank decided the easiest course of action would be to repeat his purple lie. The idea that he was an aging hippie seemed to make sense to each of those curious souls. Soon Frank was surrounded by a whole group of geriatric refugees of the 60s. The group really bonded over the next few months. They shared stories, which Frank always listened to, but he never told any. He didn't want to let on that he didn't have any of his own. The nursing home subculture celebrated the era of "free love" (literally).

Soon Frank's Children of the 60s looked and acted at least 50 years younger. They spent their days reliving past glory, at least the things that weren't blurred by age and the rampant drug use of the time. Frank soon realized that these people could not let go of the days gone by. None of them had changed from their pre-purple lives, except for smuggling in pot. They still talked about the past, wishing they were there. Frank on the other hand wanted to live in today's world. He got tired of their stories, and eventually sought other outlets for his purple hair.

Frank decided to go see Rachel, his stylist. She was "hip" and part of today's "scene." He didn't go to see her to start a romantic relationship. He just wanted in on the fun.

Rachel loved the idea of hanging with an actual hippie, and so he began to repeat his purple lie to everyone in the "in crowd." Soon he was going to bars that played dubstep, watching, not taking part in, extreme sports, and even protesting against the evil 1%. The hippies back at the home felt abandoned, but Frank didn't care. He had found something new to do; he was no longer a relic of the past. He was part of the future, a future made possible by the desire to change the color of hair.

I'm a Millionaire

Tony became a millionaire on Friday when his $1,800 paycheck was deposited into his bank account. Tony knew that exactly $615.32 of that paycheck put him over the top. Now, he didn't have a million dollars. In fact he had outstanding debts of about $6,000. But that paycheck brought his total lifetime earnings above one million. Tony was sure of this because he had kept a record of every single dollar he had made since he started getting an allowance in third grade. His parents thought it was a good way to help his math skills while teaching him the importance of budgeting. His parents didn't know they were actually giving life to Tony's greatest obsession.

Tony never became a math whiz and never was very good at budgeting. If you asked him about his budget, he would show you a spreadsheet with blanks all over the "Debit" column. However, the "Credits" column was immaculate. If you asked Tony how much money he got for his grade school graduation, he could tell you down to the penny without even looking it up. He was scary that way. Most of his friends had learned quite quickly not to ask Tony about the money he'd gotten for graduation and to quickly change the subject whenever he started talking about his financial past. Since no one wanted to talk about his earnings, Tony started tweeting.

Tony's tweets were amazingly popular. While not as popular as the Pope's, the number of Tony's followers was impressive considering he was a nobody who only talked about his paychecks and of finding pennies on the ground. When Tony's Great Aunt Matilda sent him a check for $30 on his 30th birthday, Tony's followers were ecstatic. So it was not surprising that when Tony announced he had reached the miraculous ONE-MILLION-DOLLAR mark, his fans went crazy. Tony, knowing the exact moment he would reach the fabled mark well in advance, had planned a party for the night of the wondrous event. None of his regular friends were invited; instead it was solely for his twitter followers. Tony wanted to celebrate this with people who cared about the same things he did. He also wanted a day where his obsession was praised and not avoided.

The party was in a ballroom of a local economy hotel. Tony had rented a tux but had not made this a formal affair. On the walls of the ballroom Tony had placed copies of every ledger he had ever made, dating back to third grade. He had spent the last two months preparing stories about individual ledgers and even individual entries in the ledgers. He knew what his fans wanted, and he planned on giving it to them. Of his followers, Tony had no illusions. When he opened up the ballroom doors he expected to find nothing but nerds and introvert CPAs. This didn't bother him, because that was the sort of crowd with whom he felt he could best discover people to support him in his obsession. So it was with some surprise that when Tony opened the doors he found nothing but expensively dressed business magnates.

Tony recognized many of his guests. Who wouldn't? These were the people who moved the world. The most powerful of the powerful and they were here at Tony's party. The Federal Treasury Board Chairman was the first to congratulate him. She was a nice lady, nothing like the stern, serious woman you saw on the news. Daryl Saaxi immediately greeted him with that firm handshake he touted in his "I'm your Investment Man" commercials. Thomas Howsit, who ran Indescribably Industries and its 70 or so subsidiaries, hailed him from across the room like he was an old friend. And so it went.

Tony's guests loved his ledgers. The ones from his early years garnered the most attention and the most anecdotes from the magnates. Tony got a little tired of the stories his guests had to tell him and of the countless bits of advice he received. But Tony was in heaven nonetheless. When the party broke up late that night, Tony was on top of the world. None of his guests had offered him a job or even invited him to visit when in the neighborhood. Tony had gotten the distinct impression that, while they were overjoyed at this one man's zest for capitalistic expertise, he was not seen as being in the same circle as they were. In fact, he knew that he was probably nothing more than an amusement to these movers and shakers. That was okay for Tony. He knew he was not a mover or shaker and never would be. He was just a guy who had reached the status of millionaire. Tony was glad that if for only one night someone important had seen him as a kindred spirit.

The Concert Pianist

"It would be nice," thought Eric Sanfere, age 9, "if I could sit down at a piano and play some music." He looked around the house but could find no keyboard. So he sat in his room and thought about how terrible the world was. He was a great musician! He needed to show the world his true talent, and the only way that would happen was by having a piano. He dreamed dreams of being on television, having sold out concerts, partying with famous celebrities. The next morning the boy decided that his parents had to get him a piano, but he knew he couldn't just tell them to get one. And so began his crusade.

Eric started slowly, expressing an interest in music at breakfast. Later in the day he noted, several times, at how music from the piano was so beautiful. By dinner he was expounding the virtues of playing classical music. His parents made some encouraging comments but stopped short of promising him a piano. The boy went to bed scheming of new ways to bend his parents to his will. This went on for two excruciating weeks. As time went on, the Chopin wannabe became more and more obsessed with playing the piano. And then on a Saturday morning, he came down for breakfast, and there it was, a piano. It was not a Grand Piano but an electric one with smallish keys. Still it was a piano! He ran to it and started to play. Even he would admit he was no Horowitz, but he still thought he could make music if he just kept hitting the keys. It was then that his parents appeared. "Well, do you like your piano?" asked the mother. The boy screamed the word "YES" loud enough to be heard blocks away. The parents laughed. "That's great," said his dad. "Your first lesson is right after lunch." Eric stopped cold. He had always known he was a natural, gifted musician. He didn't need anyone to teach him what he already knew. He didn't need lessons or music written out in some strange language. He just needed to sit at the keyboard and play. But his protests went unheeded. Eric went to his first lesson that afternoon.

From the very first lesson, Eric knew he was doomed. By the end of the first month he could barely stand to look at the piano. His parents made him stick with it for a year. The year went by painfully. He told himself it was the stupid piano's fault. It wasn't built to properly handle his musical expertise. Deep down, he felt that the world was unfair, and not for the last time. You see he had already decided that he was a great athlete. This time all he needed was a basketball.

A Day in the Life of TJ

TJ is a lap cat. In other words, he demands attention by plopping himself down on anyone who sits still for over a minute. Of course, that's only when he wants attention. When he isn't in the mood, he tolerates some scratching behind the ear, but don't expect any appreciation to be shown. TJ leads a quiet, simple life. He has three human retainers—a woman and her two young girls. He shared his castle with two forgettable, at least to him, other cats. And there were always those commoner humans who came to bask in his glory from time to time.

A typical day in the life of TJ would start, as with most cats, in the afternoon. On one particular day, TJ was lying on the sofa, the sun pouring in through the window to warm him. He was beginning to wake when he heard the minivan pull up out front. "They're home," he thought to himself. He looked out the window to verify his assertion. "Yes, that is the car, and they are piling . . ." TJ went back to sleep mid-thought. He was woken a minute later as the door burst open and the two girls ran over to greet him.

"Blah blah, blah, TJ," was what the aristocratic feline heard. He didn't need to know more. One of the girls plopped down on the couch and began petting him. He decided to allow it. "Blah, TJ. Blah blah blah blah blah." The girl kept talking as she scratched behind his ear. It was annoying, but he had gotten used to it over the years. TJ then had to make the big decision of the afternoon—to get up of his own accord to find someplace quieter or to let himself be carried to the girl's room. Since the girl was doing a decent job of scratching him under his chin, he decided to let himself be carried.

The rest of the next hour proceeded as normal. It mostly involved one of the two girls lavishing him with attention, which TJ deemed appropriate. Then without warning came the most exasperating moment of every day. The woman would interrupt the girls, who would have to go get some 'books'—was that the word?—and sit at a table drawing on sheets of paper. TJ would express his displeasure by going to the table and lying down on the papers until someone moved him to a lap. From that point on, the evening was a haze of laps, attention, and sleep. It would end with the girls going to bed, and the mother going to the computer. TJ, knowing this pattern, would move to the computer keyboard as soon as the girls went to put on their pajamas. This would result in a few hours of lap sitting before the mother turned in.

Once his retainers were asleep, TJ would entertain visits by the two other feline inhabitants of his castle. He allowed them to groom him and would sometimes reciprocate. He would deem it worthy to chase one or both and even allow them to chase him sometimes. After an appropriate amount of exercise, TJ would adjourn to the master bedroom where he would curl up on the woman's legs. They were warm, and she tended not to move them during the night. Before sunrise, TJ would get up and patrol his domain. If he saw a mouse or other creature, he would note its location and move on. He was above such mundane things as hunting. As the sun rose, he would head back to the master bedroom to groom the woman. This would wake her, and get her to put out fresh water and food, as well as clean the litter box. His retainers would spend the rest of the morning running around, sometimes not paying him any attention. That was fine with TJ for it was time to get a good spot on the ledge of the back bay window to let the rising sun warm him. His busy day had been exhausting, so it was time for a well-deserved nap.

Workphobia

Tim looked at the spreadsheet from Accounting and sighed. He clicked on the cells that held the formulas that made the thing spit out wrong numbers. He sighed again. The thing was a mess. It would take hours, if not days, to fix. It would cause him all sorts of headaches just to trace the logic of the thing. However, in the end fixing it would be rather simple but quite tedious. Tim sighed a third time.

Tim looked at the spreadsheet wondering where to start. He figured he should probably follow his standard routine on this one, thus avoiding clumsy errors. So he began by planning out a strategy to fix the calculative nightmare. You couldn't just start anywhere to find mistakes. You had to map the flow of the data across each spreadsheet within the workbook. As usual, as he realized the shear immensity of the work ahead, it made Tim understandably overwhelmed. Tim stared at his computer screen for at least half an hour envisioning every place that things could go wrong, eventually deciding he hadn't even seen the tip of the iceberg. He then closed the file and went to get a cup of coffee. As he left the kitchen with his full cup of coffee, he headed away from his office. He searched for and eventually found his boss, to whom he complained about the incompetency of the Accounting Department. On the way back to his office, he stopped off to talk about the game last night with one or two colleagues. He did eventually make it to his office where he returned emails for the next hour. This got him to lunch.

Tim went out to lunch, leaving his leftovers from last night in the kitchen fridge. He went to a place with horrible service and so did not return for an hour and a half. Tim then spent another half hour complaining about the restaurant to whomever would listen. Tim eventually returned to his office in the hope of restarting work on the spreadsheet. Tim opened up the file and stared at it again, critiquing the layout. Deciding it was just too confusing, Tim reformatted the whole thing. He colored the cells that held calculations, named cells that had important information, and set up tables of basic constants that could be used to make the thing a little more logical. In other words, he spent his time coloring and putting in notes that he may or may not need when he actually decided to fix the thing. After sitting back and admiring his work, Tim opened his email to start catching up on his correspondence. His email was filled with a number of fires that had cropped up on other projects while he was trying to ignore the spreadsheet. By the time he finished taking care of all the cries for help, it was time to go home.

Tim spent the evening berating himself for not working on the spreadsheet. He finally fell asleep vowing that he would not do anything else tomorrow but work on the damnable behemoth. He had dreams throughout the night that involved getting chased by angry accountants, having to explain to his boss why he singlehandedly destroyed the company, having to fill out unemployment forms, and being evicted from his apartment. He woke up the next day thoroughly exhausted.

This pattern of behavior repeated itself for the next two days which just happened to get him to Friday afternoon. That afternoon, Tim's boss stormed into his office angry that the Head of Accounting was yelling for his spreadsheet. At last Tim had the motivation he needed to get the job done. His boss had forced his hand, and so he had no choice but to finish the project, knowing that he must now face the demon spreadsheet, for if he didn't, his worst nightmares would come true. Tim worked through the weekend finishing the spreadsheet. When he was done it was a masterpiece. The Head of Accounting praised the work, completely absolving Tim of the time it took to finish it. Tim patted himself on the back for doing such a good job, forgetting the anxiety that had plagued him the week before. After receiving the praise he was due, Tim made it back to his office feeling like he could do anything. He sat down and began to peruse his email. There at the top of the list was an email marked urgent. It was from Tech Support and contained a critical file that was corrupted. The feeling of doom settled over Tim's head. He stared at the email for a long time before shutting down his computer and heading home for the day. He would definitely get to it tomorrow.

Presentation Day

The seventh graders couldn't sit still. Half were ready to show everyone how smart they were. The rest were scared to death of standing up in front of their friends and their parents. Of course the projector wouldn't turn on, only adding to the anxiety in the room. Parents offered their advice to get it running. At one point there were seven adults pushing buttons or telling someone what to do. Finally one of the kids came up, pushed the on/off button, and they were ready to go.

Kids' hands shot up volunteering to go first. Sarah, who didn't want to go at all, shrunk down into her seat trying to hide. Ms. Mills, the teacher, had a sadistic streak in her, so she called the poor girl up to begin the long line of presentations. She walked to the front of the classroom like a prisoner heading to the gallows. When she finally made it there, the teacher pulled up Sarah's presentation and motioned for the girl to start.

Sarah decided the best way to get through this was to just watch the screen and keep her back the audience. The teacher had to physically turn Sarah to face the audience. Sarah looked like she was about to cry as she gave the title of her experiment. Her voice was almost a whisper as she explained the research question. Ms. Mills had to ask Sarah three times to raise her voice before she spoke loud enough to be heard in the back of the room.

Sarah's experiment involved the crystallization of ice cream. She had a lot of fun with the research, and as she spoke it began to show. The kids in the audience began to pay attention as soon as they heard the words "ice cream." Sarah saw the kids staring at her, which brought back her shyness. One of the kids asked Sarah if she had samples of the ice cream. This got a laugh from the audience making Sarah feel even more embarrassed. She was about to run out of the classroom, when Ms. Mills asked Sarah to explain how she had varied the crystallization of the ice cream in her three samples. The next slide was about just that, so the budding scientist was able to answer the question while showing the slide. Her confidence shot up, and she forgot about running.

When she showed the picture of the crystals that formed during refreezing, Sarah heard some "Wow that's cool" comments from the audience. This set the extrovert in Sarah loose, causing her to deviate from the prepared text. She told the audience about why she'd chosen chocolate ice cream instead of vanilla. She told them how she'd convinced her dad to run the experiment a bunch of times just so her friends could try the ice cream with the really big crystals. The teacher had to finally shut her down, and with much reluctance Sarah took her seat.

Sarah grew up to be a noted food scientist, giving presentations all over the world. She never forgot both the fear and the excitement of that first talk. The accomplished scientist and presenter never forgot Ms. Mills' question that had calmed her that day. Sarah also developed a penchant for melting and then refreezing her ice cream so she could get that grainy feel of really big crystals. A simple middle school science experiment coupled with a semi-traumatic presentation—ten minutes that lasted a lifetime.

The Second Car of the First Train

Hakim catches the first train out of the station every morning. The train leaves at precisely 5:04 AM. He reaches the platform at 5:03 to board the second car and sit in the fourth-row window seat. He immediately flips on his tablet computer to read the morning news, and settles in for his morning commute. Hakim politely greets the other regular members of the second car of the first train of the morning. He doesn't know any of their names, even though most of them have been riding together for over fifteen years. They share pleasantries, remark on the weather, inquire after absences, but otherwise disappear into their own little commuting world once the train pulls out from the station.

Hakim takes note of the other people who board or depart at each stop. He recognizes most of them. He knows at which station they will debark, whether they will talk to anyone else on the train, etc. Once, Hakim correctly guessed that two of the regulars had started an affair. He was the only one in the car who wasn't stunned when the man's wife surprised the couple one morning and started whacking the poor slob with a newspaper. That was about the only interesting thing that had ever happened in the second car of the first train of the morning. It was a quiet commute, a peaceful start to the day.

Hakim used to get off at Farragut North every morning. But that was before he retired two years ago. Now he rides the train all the way to Glenmont, the end of the line. At Glenmont he exits the second car of the first train of the morning and waits while it disappears into the tunnel and then reappears on the inbound track to take on passengers. Hakim then boards the seventh car of the 6:12 train, takes the window seat of the twelfth row, and heads back home to Rockville. When he gets off the train at 7:10, he stops by the little deli just outside the station to pick up two egg and sausage sandwiches and some hash browns. Hakim then returns to his house, wakes up his wife, so that they can begin their day as they have for the last two years.

The Evaluation

I sit outside the gym while my 10-year-old daughter is "evaluated." It used to be called tryouts, but I guess that was too pejorative. It's sad, but this evaluation will probably determine if her dreams of playing college basketball will ever come true. Three hours trying to outplay thirty other girls so she can get on the A team. If she doesn't get on the A team this year (5th grade), no ranking agents would take her seriously, and so the top private high schools would never hear of her, and so she would play in obscurity for the rest of her life. Three hours to determine the rest of her life. No pressure.

I'm sitting out here waiting and unsure how I want this to turn out. I know that part of the reason—OK, the entire reason—she wants to play college ball is to please her college-basketball-addict dad. I never played past grade school, but being from Louisville, Kentucky, I live and breathe college basketball. My daughter sees how much I love the game. It is only natural for her to equate my passion for the game to love for the people who play it and, therefore, more of my love for her if she played it as well. I've tried to tell her I still love her with all my heart no matter what she does, but kids never hear those things. Add to that, I think that a secret desire to see my child, my offspring, play in the Final Four is somehow coloring the way I tell her it doesn't matter. I irrationally feel that I put her in this position.

To add to my uncertainty about the evaluation is the fact that my kid is good. She is a decent power forward who is proud of being bruised at the end of the game. When she drives to the hoop she clears everyone out of her way. Compare that to me at her age, and you'll understand why I have no idea where she got it from. I couldn't dribble around one defender when I was 18, let alone 10. This leaves me with the uncertainty that if I try to discourage her, I may be crushing a chance for her to shine like she is meant to shine.

So I sit here worrying that she will fail and worrying that she will succeed. I know it is out of my hands, but still it feels like I can somehow affect the outcome. The doors to the gym open and a bunch of tired girls spew out into the night. I push my fears out of the way for now and go greet my daughter. She is smiling and limping slightly. I ask her about it, and her reply is that one of the coaches was trying to guard her and she put him on the floor. She laughs, and we head for the car. A 10-year-old putting a grown man, a jock, on the floor. I'm proud and scared. Maybe I better get used to that feeling no matter how the evaluation turns out.

21st Century Hermits

No one ever came to visit him anymore. This was a bad thing on the surface, but a good thing when he thought about it. "Guests invade my space. Mess up my things. Make me clean. Take up my precious time. Going to visit them is nice. They entertain me. Give me food. Make me feel warm and fuzzy without all the hassles." He told himself these things and for the most part agreed with himself.

Marshall Becksworth had long since developed a second self with which to carry on conversations. They got along pretty well. Their arguments were civil, their planning superb, and their grasp of each other's needs was uncanny. He even knew that the second self was just a projection meant to help him reason out the world or have a means by which to use his vocal chords. He never talked to himself in public, and he never used the word "precious."

For all his antisocial tendencies, Marshall did regularly interact with world. Even though he worked from home, he teleconferenced with his bosses, teammates, and clients when appropriate. He talked to his mom and siblings each month and visited them once a year. He was an avid facebooker and tweeted to at least twenty or so people all the time. The semi-shut-in just shunned physical contact in his home.

Sometimes Marshall wondered if his lifestyle was unique, so one day he statused that question on his Facebook page. The results surprised him. Of his non-relative, non-friends-from-when-he-was-younger, everyone said their lifestyle was more or less the same. Not only that, when his fb buddies shared the status, he was deluged with friend requests.

Soon Marshall became a lightning rod for his fellow hermits. His tweet subscribers skyrocketed to over 200,000. He was interviewed (via Skype) by news organizations and even landed a book deal. Before long he had to hire an assistant to handle all the requests for his time. He quickly realized that his "hermitude" was being lost. So he intentionally cut down his celebrity status by redirecting attention to other "Big Name Hermits" like the movie star who never left his shack in a Louisiana swamp. Marshall slowed down the number of statuses he posted until he only put up one per week. He also gradually stopped tweeting all together.

It took Marshall a full year to get back to his normal life (which is forever in this cyber age). After it was all over, he looked back on the entire, crazy ride, and came to the conclusion that it had been worth it but for only two reasons. Most importantly he was now independently wealthy. He also took pride in the fact that because of him, hundreds of thousands of people now knew they were not crazy. He had given them an acceptable way to "come out of the closet" in a hermitude way. Looking even closer at the events of the past year, he was pleased to note that during all that time, no one had come to visit him.

Cassette Tape Orgy

Peter was searching through his attic when he found a shoebox with a bunch of old cassette tapes. He stopped looking for his drafting tools, sat down with the shoebox, and took a trip twenty-five years into the past. The collection had the standards from the 80s and 90s. It was full of Springsteen, R.E.M., Billy Joel, The Cure, and the Talking Heads. He had most of these on CD, except for Billy Joel. His tastes had changed over the years, and Billy had been left behind. The shoebox also contained cassettes of the New Wave gods of his youth. Joe Jackson's *Look Sharp!*, Blondie's *Parallel Lines*, the self-titled albums by the Cars and the B-52s. One-hit-wonder albums by Men Without Hats and Modern English brought back memories of doing the Pogo dance, wearing really bright clothes, and having Big Hair. The Clash, XTC, Nick Lowe, Elvis Costello, the Smiths, and David Bowie reminded Peter of all the times he tried to be "cool."

The shoebox was a treasure trove of memories. As for being a music collection, it was worthless. Nobody he knew still had a cassette tape player, and even if they did, these tapes were shot. Peter began to lament his lost youth and the loss of all this music. Still, he felt like he shouldn't give up so easily. So he gathered up the shoebox and decided to go on a cyber-hunt for as many of these gems as possible. This was the 21st Century, a time when everything was out there on the internet. Surely, he could find all of his beloved albums. They were all classics. Someone had to have converted them to mp3s.

What followed next was an orgy of downloading. He didn't just want the hits; he wanted entire albums. He was one of those people who bought an album for the singles, then fell in love with the rest of the songs on the disk. He had bought Big Country's album, *The Crossing*, for the songs, "In a Big Country," and, "Harvest Home," only to find he liked "Inwards" and "The Storm" much better. So he ignored compilations, he wasn't satisfied until he had the album he remembered with so much reverence. Peter found most of what he was looking for, but some of his memories were lost to time. While finding the bulk of his catalog was gratifying, the fact that the Mark Kinnamon, City Lites, and Argon would never be heard again depressed Peter to no end.

Peter easily spent $1,000 replacing his tapes, but it was worth it. He spent the next three weeks with his ear buds in, listening to all he'd found. His wife sighed as she tried to balance this month's budget. His kids sighed whenever they saw him. Peter's body may have been there in the 21st Century, but his soul was back in the 80s, transported there by a signpost made of magnetic-coated film held in little plastic boxes.

Rejoining the Workforce

It's raining outside. Sandy sits up in bed. It's 8:00 AM. She is usually out of bed by 5:00 and done with her morning exercises, breakfast, and a dozen other things. Today, however, was not a day to get things done. Today is the day after Sandy was finally hired for a full-time job. She hadn't had a full-time job in fifteen months. Yesterday all that changed. It had been a bright, warm, beautiful March day, perfect for something magical to happen. She had walked out of the interview with a job offer, ready to celebrate. Today was a cold, rainy March morning, a good day to focus on reality. Yesterday's euphoria has ended as fast as the weather changed. Sandy knew she must now figure out how to get back into the workaday habit, and how to survive until her first paycheck.

Yesterday Sandy was hired for a job that pays two-thirds what she was making fifteen months ago. It won't start for another two to three weeks, and her first paycheck won't get to the bank until the end of April. The job is fifty miles from her home, and the commute is through the worst traffic in the nation. As all this goes through Sandy's head, she makes one quick decision. Make coffee. Coffee has always been Sandy's answer to almost all problems in her adult life. It sharpens her thoughts and is comfortingly warm. It is also a good way to put off making other decisions.

The coffee making leads to exercising, which leads to getting back to her morning routine. All the while lamenting that her morning routine is about to bite the dust. It will soon be replaced by a hurried shower, agonizing about what to wear, and then rushing to the car for a one-to-two-hour commute. The job will involve long hours, short lunches, and grabbing fast food for the two-hour drive back home. She can see herself collapsing in bed when she gets home, too tired to even turn on the television.

Once Sandy came to grips with the realities of her new routine, she turned her eyes to the budget. The good news is that her salary would cover the rent and all essentials. Unfortunately, her new job will also spark the IRS and her creditors to come knocking on her door again, not to mention all those people she had borrowed money from over the last fifteen months. Ramen noodles and frozen vegetables will remain on the menu for the foreseeable future. She had dropped two dress sizes while on her forced diet, so she also has to figure in some new business clothes.

About midday Sandy gives up on the budget and stares out the window at the pouring rain. She wistfully looks at the torrent outside, watching all the employed people scurrying around to grab lunch or get to an appointment. Sandy smiles as she watches them, knowing that she will soon be one of the employed grunts who are forced to head out in the rain to do something that had to get done now. Sandy also thinks about how often she has looked at them, thinking that they were better than she is. For the last fifteen months, she had seen herself as too wretched a person to ever be of worth to any company. Now she knows differently. Someone out there wants her, just like the people running around in the rain. Despite the commute, the long hours, and the wrecked budget, Sandy is happy. She has three weeks to get re-acclimated to life as a grunt. So she decides to put on her raincoat and scurry around a bit.

Up on the Roof

The noise from the motors and pumps is so loud you can barely hear the voice of your boss. You pick your way carefully through the muck to reach the ancient metal ladder attached to the wall of the factory. You climb the slick rungs of the ladder gripping the rails as hard as you can just in case you slip. Two stories up gets you to the first roof. This roof covers a small machine room. You can tell from the moment you see it this roof is shot. One wrong step, the roof will give way, and you'll end up on top of those machines you hear inside the building. In order to make it to the second ladder, you "tightrope" the edge of the machine room roof. The second ladder takes you up one more story to the main roof. This roof is better, but still has some nasty places that looked like they would give way if a starling landed on them. Your experience tells you that most of the roof bulges are from water seeping in between the different layers of roof material. In other places it sags because those bulges have popped. For the most part you can walk around freely as long as you watch your step. The roof is the size of two football fields placed next to one another. There are vents and fans and drains and A/C units littering its surface just like any other factory. You and your boss get out the tape measure and an engineering schematic of the roof to start documenting the location of everything up here. You already know the recommendation you'll make after the survey; the entire roof needs to be replaced. But you'll need the measurements for the replacement job, so you start the tedious procedure of laying the tape down and marking up the drawing. You are a roofing engineer, and this is what roofing engineers do.

It is a beautiful spring day. You can see for miles, although an industrial park does not provide the most scenic of vistas. Still there is a feeling of freedom up here. You have work, to be sure, but it is not the oppressive, life-sapping work of an office. It is the get-your-hands-dirty, create-something-useful work of the real world. There is also the thrill of walking along the edge of the roof, three stories up, to measure the distance between vent and edge. The possibility of stepping in the wrong place and winding up in the middle of a box factory gives you some small feel of peril. True the risk is minimal, but when sitting in front of a computer there is no risk to life and limb at all. You feel alive up here, really alive.

Since this is your first outing to this factory, the newness of everything colors your vision. After a few trips back to this roof, it will become normal and maybe even boring, just as it did the last time you worked in construction. Still, for the moment everything is an adventure. The wind, the view, the danger, everything up on the roof excites you. When it is time to go, you do so reluctantly. You make your way down to the car and head home. You leave the factory behind but take the feeling with you to share with those who'll never go up on a roof.

Serenity in a Nursing Home

The old man sat in his wheelchair and stared off into space. This is the way he spent every day. He would "wake" long enough to eat and take care of bodily functions, but even during these periods he never talked to anyone. The other residents just ignored him. The nurses would try to engage him in conversation, with no luck. The psychologist would get him to answer a few questions every other week. The physical therapist would get him to walk for a few minutes each a day. He had no living relatives, at least none who visited him. So he sat and stared.

For a long time the psychologist didn't know how to classify him. The old man wasn't a "stoner." He wasn't a gamer who wanted to immerse himself in some fantasy world. The old man wasn't part of the lost generation (i.e. "wastes") from the late 90s to early 00s. He wasn't depressed in the clinical sense. When the psychologist got the old man to answer a few questions, he seemed quite satisfied with life. However, the brief answers didn't give much insight into what the man did while staring off into nothingness. Finally, for lack of any other diagnosis, the psychologist decided that the old man had developed his own form of meditation. This made the nurses feel better about not getting the old man to talk. Soon everyone in the facility began calling him "Zen" and kept their respectful distance.

The old man lived a long life in his "meditative" state. When he finally died at age 124, he was the oldest man in the United States. All the residents and staff attended his funeral, and his passing was mentioned, although briefly, by most major U.S. news services. By that time, no one knew where he had come from or what he had done prior to his arrival at the facility. In fact, no one could have told you his real name without looking at his records. He died both alone and surrounded by people who cared for him (although not one of them knew why they cared for him). If asked, everyone that "knew" him would tell you that the old man was the most serenely happy person they had ever known. Every one of them agreed that the old man had lived a good life.

No Time for the Needles to Fall

December 26th was the traditional day for Joey to take down his Christmas tree. Joey's "Christmas Day" had been on the 24th. His kids had come over; he'd given them their presents. They'd played, had fun, and gone "home" to wait for Santa Claus. This was the sixth year for that tradition.

It had started the year he had left his wife. Six years was enough for the novelty of a separate Daddy Christmas to wear off, for both the kids and Joey. As Joey took off the ornaments, he thought how he didn't have much work ahead of him. In years past, on the weekend after Thanksgiving, the kids and he'd had a big party putting up the tree. This year he'd done it by himself, no novelty left in that tradition either. So he'd skimped on the ornaments. He'd put up the ones the kids had given him over the years and left the rest in the boxes. No one had noticed. Like last year, during the period between Thanksgiving and Christmas, the tree lights had been turned on less than five times. They were too bright when you wanted to watch the TV, plus plugging and unplugging them was a hassle.

Joey thought back to when he had been a kid, the excitement of putting up the tree and the sadness of taking it down. He thought a little more and admitted to himself that taking down the tree had always been a pain. But putting it up, that was a hunt and fight between the kids to find the best ornaments. Just to see if it was only him, Joey had asked his ex about the level of excitement the kids had in putting up the tree at her house. She told him that the kids had little enthusiasm, except for the ornaments they put near the ground for the kitty to play with. That tree would be up for a while, more from his ex's dread of taking it down than the desire to keep it up.

As Joey took off the lights, he wondered if they all had lost something when they'd stopped being a "traditional" family. Although as he thought about it, this loss of a tradition was just a reflection of the "family life" before the divorce. For the last five years of their marriage, his wife and he had drifted apart sapping the warmth from family events. Whatever the reason, the apathy toward the tree had definitely evolved over time. He doubted it would ever result in skipping the whole tree part of Christmas. The tree would always be there, if for no other reason than to be part of the normal background of the holiday. It was also somewhere to put the presents. As he put the last of the ornaments away, Joey thought that next year he would buy one of those artificial trees that had built in lights. It would make the hassle of putting the thing up and taking it down a little easier. Maybe by next year they would have ones with the garland pre-strung. It would definitely be worth a little extra money.

Heavenly Strings

"Freude, schöner Götterfunken," burst forth from the small church in Crabtree, Nebraska. The church was well known in southwest Nebraska, both for its wonderful acoustics and for the local musicians who played there. The church, as always, was packed for tonight's concert of Beethoven's Ninth Symphony. The audience was made up entirely of people who lived in the four counties surrounding Crabtree. The musicians were all from the town of Crabtree, a town of just over 1,000 people. It had been this way for almost 100 years, all thanks to a penniless drifter who carried a worn-out violin.

Fredrich Schönton had lost his job when the Stock Market crashed in 1927. He was a stock trader from a family that, while respected, was not part of the Wall Street elite. The Crash had wiped out the family's entire fortune and lead to the suicide of Fredrich's father. Fredrich, the seventh son of the family, soon realized that he was just another mouth to feed in a family with little or no food. So he packed up some clothes and his precious violin and headed west. He had little skill outside of stock market trading. He knew his prospects were bleak, and he saw no future in New York. The West held endless opportunities, if you believed the Herald Tribune.

Fredrich made his way by train from New York to Louisville, Kentucky by playing his violin in train stations and on street corners. In Louisville he managed to get hired by a small orchestra, where he played until it disbanded in early 1929. Fredrich's playing was much improved by his time in Louisville, but in the end there was no work for a violinist in this crossroads city. Once he exhausted most of his savings, he boarded a train for St. Louis to continue his trek west. Fredrich made less and less from his impromptu playing as he headed out from St. Louis. He had to abandon train travel at Lincoln, Nebraska for lack of funds, and begin bartering passage on anything heading farther west. Fredrich still had no idea where he was headed. He just knew he hadn't found it yet.

The farmer dropped Fredrich off in front of a small church in Crabtree, Nebraska on June 3rd, 1930. He was hungry and tired and just wanted to curl up someplace out of the noonday sun. The church was unlocked, so he snuck inside intending on just taking a little nap before continuing on. However, when he walked inside the church he was struck by the echo of his feet on the floorboards. Each footstep rang through the church crystal clear. Aside from his footsteps, the church was perfectly silent. For a violinist, it was like manna in the desert. He immediately went to the front of the church and began to play. He played for nearly two hours, oblivious to everything but the heavenly sound he was creating. When he finally finished, exhausted, he was startled by the applause that greeted his performance. There in front of him was the minister and nearly fifty of the townsfolk. As tears came to his eyes, Fredrich realized he had found his new home.

Fantasy

Being a Mage in the Modern World

Peter did not consider himself a "Walter Mitty," yet he had always been a daydreamer. He didn't think he was stressed out enough to begin having hallucinations, but he couldn't believe that what he was seeing was real. What he saw was two strangely dressed people trying to kill each other using ice and fire and lightning. The reason Peter had not just ignored this hallucination and gone on about his business is that one of the strangely dressed people had frozen the engine block of his car, bringing it to standstill. Peter had exited his car and was now gaping at the spectacle from a hopefully safe distance. He had been heading back from a hike in the Shenandoah mountains and had yet to make it out of the park.

It was a grand show. Fiery beasts, lightning galore, and a particularly beautiful ice snake marked the duel. Peter was watching the whole performance from behind a boulder, which he thought would protect him. Part of him thought he should be running for his life, but most of him had decided this was too amazing to miss and he did feel safe behind the boulder. To his dismay, a lightning bolt struck his hiding spot, blowing it into little pebbles and leaving him exposed. Oddly enough, he wasn't injured. It appeared that one of the combatants had conjured a translucent green ball around him. He quickly realized he couldn't leave his protective bubble, so the possibility of fleeing had been eliminated. The fact that the choice had been taken from him was somehow comforting and made watching the spectacle all the more enjoyable. Peter who had been neutral up to this point, decided to pull for his savior to win the fight.

The battle went on into the night. Peter wished he had brought some snacks with him when he left the car. The two "mages," as he decided they must be, were definitely tiring, and his hero was definitely losing. This caused the man to begin to worry about what would happen if his hero lost. He didn't have long to think on this because his protector suddenly bolted, taking Peter with him. What ensued was a mad chase through the dark forest. It felt like a rollercoaster run amuck. Peter was getting pretty bruised bouncing around in his bubble, but all in all he decided that this was fun.

The chase "ended" in a ravine, when his hero caused an avalanche to bury his enemy. That allowed the "good" mage to escape into the dark of night. When the mage stopped next to a small stream, the bubble vanished, and the man fell unceremoniously to the ground. "I'm not sure what to make of you," exclaimed the Mage. "You seem to possess enough power to pass through a pretty strong Concealing Barrier. From the look on your face, I guess that this is your first experience with the overt use of magic. So I seem to have a decently powerful, virgin mage."

Peter finally felt like he had something to say. "Please don't tell me that there exists a 'Harry Potter' unseen world of wizards and witches."

"Thankfully, no," said the mage, whose name was Bernie. Bernie went on to explain that there were only a few people who could wield magic, less than one hundred scattered throughout the world. Those people tended not to use their magic very much, mostly due to the lack of any reasons to use it. "Even in wars, humanity has developed far better tools for killing and destroying. So we really just use our magic for fighting each other or playing small pranks now and then." Peter felt vaguely disappointed but accepted the logic of the mage's reasoning. Bernie continued, "Oleg—that was the guy I was fighting—and I had gotten in an argument over that blind ref's call in the

Maryland football game last night." Peter didn't follow football but had heard of the incident. "We weren't trying to kill each other, just cause the other major pain."

Peter felt the stirring of a question and so interrupted a treatise on why killing someone is a headache in today's world. "I can understand why you saved me from the exploding boulder, but I can't figure out why you took me with you when you fled."

"Passing through a Concealing Barrier is no small feat, my friend." Bernie then looked at the man with a sly grin. "So it appears that you are a very powerful but untrained mage. I decided, after I realized you were watching, that you were worth a closer look. To be blunt, someone with your power would be a good ally indeed, especially in disputes over blown calls. Of course I'll have to train you. As you are now, you couldn't even cook a rabbit without a barbecue."

"But I've never done anything even slightly magical in my entire life," Peter protested.

"Of course not, you have to be aware of your power in order to use it. And becoming aware of it isn't that easy. The only real way, other than accidentally saving your loved ones from a terrible accident, is to have another mage 'see' the power within you."

"I see," said Peter and so began his life as a mage. Bernie took him under his wing, and Peter quickly learned how to cook using his own fire, to wash the car by calling up a localized heavy downpour, and to charge batteries with a little 110 volt lightning bolt. He discovered he had the most fun creating ice sculptures using just a sprinkler. He enjoyed it so much that he started a business making them. As with most mages of the 21st Century, Peter found that the world did not have much use for his talents, which was alright with him. He never wanted fame or fortune. An occasional magically frozen daiquiri was good enough for him.

The Last Stand of the Knights of Argesten

Gridley sheathed his sword. He didn't bother to wipe off the blood. That would be a waste of time. Another horde of those foul beasts was cresting the ridge to the east, so the sword would be bloodied again within the hour. Gridley looked at his army, now reduced to under a thousand. He ordered them to stop tending to the dead and get something to eat. There were few complaints. There were few responses of any kind. Gridley knew the men and women under his command were spent. They may have had enough spirit to survive another charge, but that would be it. The last stand of the Knights of Argesten was upon them.

Their foe, the burdhim, were evil incarnate. They were ravenous monsters that ate anything and everything in their path. They would leave nothing behind, no people, no animals, no plants, no buildings, no grass, nothing that dared dwell above the ground. Their looks were as evil as their hearts. They were seven feet tall, with four spiny legs, three arms, and two huge gaping mouths mounted on either side of their body. They had no eyes yet acted as if they had one hundred. They uttered no sound, for their mouths were always full, always devouring what stood in their way. These beasts were the pinnacle of destruction for they knew nothing else.

Three days ago, after the fourth wave of burdhim, Gridley had sent messengers to ask for aid from the Four Kingdoms. Even the farthest of the kingdoms could have had reinforcements here by now. The commander could only assume that his knights had been abandoned. Gridley should have ordered a retreat, but that was not the way of the Knights of Argesten. Their honor demanded they give their lives defending the land, and so they would. Gridley understood that the honor of these brave knights would never be prized by those who had abandoned them. They knew not of honor, but only how to cower behind walls of stone. For this Gridley was saddened. To watch his army destroyed and know that their deeds would die with them was something that would lead any commander to despair. Yet, he had no time for despair. The enemy would be upon them soon and the Knights of Argesten would defend this land even if no one ever knew of their sacrifice.

Gridley ordered that all the burdhim bodies be stacked so as to make a wall between the knights and the oncoming horde. He had every man find a bow and gather arrows for the coming battle. One lone soldier stood on top of the wall to direct the archers. It was the best defense Gridley could put in place during this short lull in the fighting. He hoped it would slow the burdhim down, although he knew they would just eat their way through the wall. With hope waning, Gridley pulled out his own bow and readied an arrow. On the signal from the lookout, he let fly. The battle was on.

The Army of Calast, the farthest of the Four Kingdoms, arrived too late to help Gridley and his knights. At 20,000 strong, they easily finished off the remaining beasts. After the battle, King Shalman surveyed the field with amazement. He could only imagine the hell the Knights of Argesten had faced. He ordered that each of their dead be given their own sending. There would be no mass graves for these brave soldiers. Shalman ordered his heralds to travel the land, testifying to the deeds of the saviors of the kingdoms. A castle was erected on the field, and a new Order of the Knights of Argesten was founded. Gridley and his knights were immortalized in story and song, a fitting end to great warriors' lives.

The Xylophone of Justine

"So let me get this straight. You are saying that only I can bring the world back into harmony with nature. To do this, I have to go find a magic xylophone and bring it to a lost opera house so it can be played by a goat with really big horns." Tom looked at the elf in disbelief.

"It's not a magic xylophone. The xylophone is the incarnation of the Spirit of Harmony. The goat's horns are magical, how else could he play the xylophone?" The elf was exasperated.

"And why do I have to do this?" The elf was beginning to get on Tom's nerves.

"Because you are the heir to the Plutarch Justine's throne." The elf was beginning to lose heart.

Tom decided to play with the poor elf. "And who is or was this Pluto?"

"Plutarch! Plutarch Justine was the ruler over all the Earth more than two million years ago. She forged the resonators that will bring the world into harmony. Only one of her blood can move the xylophone. Only her heir can find the Opera House of Zantowit." The elf's bearing had changed as he talked of the revered Plutarch.

"So this Zantowhat—you don't know where it is? Do you even know what it looks like?" Tom was really having fun with the little guy.

"The Opera House of Zantowit is a majestic circular dome, at least three hundred yards across. It has six smaller domes radiating out on oval lakes, each another hundred yards long. It is the most magnificent building ever constructed on Earth," the elf sounded like he was doing a Discovery Channel documentary.

Tom couldn't resist poking at the elf a bit more. "That's real nice. So I have to look around the world to find a giant bubble with six other bubbles on lakes around it. Listen, I can't just go gallivanting all over the place because you think that some goat wants to play 'Mary Had a Little Lamb' on an ancient, probably rusted-out glockenspiel."

The poor elf was ready to cry. "I don't understand. You are the anointed one that has been foretold by generations of seers. You are the direct descendent of Justine. All the stars are in alignment. The world has been waiting for this for nearly two million years. How can you just sit there and make fun of me?"

"OK, OK, settle down, Shorty. Let's see what I can do. Give me a sec." Tom headed into another room.

The elf heard a strange clicking sound coming from the room Tom had entered. "So where's this xylophone now," Tom yelled to the elf.

"It's in the Cave of Angor. Today they call it Luray Caverns. It's not too far from here." This exchange lightened the elf's mood quite considerably.

"And you know where inside the cave that this xylophone now rests? You could lead someone right to it?" Tom kept clicking away as he queried the elf.

"Oh, yes. I was in hibernation under it for 850,000 years," the elf replied proudly.

"I could have guessed that from your smell," Tom quipped as he re-entered the room carrying two sheets of paper. He sat down next to the elf and handed him the papers. "Here ya go. This is the map to your Opera House.

It's located thirty miles southwest of Richmond, right off I-64. It looks to be under a few hundred feet of dirt, so you and your goat better have a shovel. This other thing is the receipt for the movers. They'll be at the caves tomorrow, at 8:30 in the morning. Show 'em this receipt, and they'll set you right up. I paid for it myself. I figured you didn't have much cash, having been asleep for however many years you said. And it's worth it just to get you out of here."

"But, but, but how? I don't understand." The elf was dumbfounded.

"Well you had a couple things right about me. I am one of the top people in the world in geospatial tracking. I also have a buddy in the shipping business who is friends with the guy who runs Luray Caverns. I'm probably the only person alive who could've found the opera house and gotten you a way to get the xylophone there."

The elf wasn't sure if he should be elated or angry. For two million years his people had been waiting for this moment. For two million years poets had written masterpieces of the imagined glory of the event and of their savior. The Descendent of the Plutarch Justine was supposed to be a noble hero who fought many hardships to bring the xylophone to the Opera House. In the end, the hero was a man who looked at some pictures of Earth and then messaged some friends who transported things from one place to another. It felt like a sacrilege.

The downtrodden elf looked at Tom again. "You said I would need a shovel to reach the Opera House. Can you tell me where I can get one?"

The goat sitting in the corner decided to chime in. "I've got a cousin who works construction in Richmond. I can probably get you a backhoe no problem."

Soul Mates

Fred sat in his wheelchair staring at the door. He could sense her getting nearer. As if on cue, he heard footsteps on the porch. He rolled over to the door and opened it up before she had a chance to ring the bell. The past came flooding back the way it always does when the two of them first meet. It always starts with the muddled memories of the time when they were barely human, the very first time they first met. Then the real lives start flowing in like a whitewater rafting trip. The memories of the days in Napoli, in Hong Kong, in Gdansk, in Hattiesburg, and in Zansi flooded over him. The flood always ended in Zansi even though that was one of their first lives together. The memories of those nights on the savannah were etched in both their minds. It was their best life, the place and time when they were happiest.

"That never gets old. You look beautiful, Tara." Fred used the name his love was given in this life.

"Thank God I found you, Ibi," Tara exclaimed.

Fred noticed she made no mention of his appearance; after all he was a wreck. Fifty-three years old, three hundred pounds, and trapped in a wheelchair. A comb-over and a ratty beard completed the look of utter hopelessness. Fred had most definitely had better lives. Tara on the other hand was beautiful. In her twenties, she had a great body and eyes that could eat your soul if you stared into them for too long.

"You know the rules," chided Fred. "I'm Fred in this life, so that's what you have to call me."

"Did I ever agree to those rules?"

"You made that one up back in Gdansk after we raised too many eyebrows calling each other by our Zulu names and talking ancient Egyptian."

"Oh yeah," Tara feigned sulking. "But Egyptian is such a beautiful language, and no one ever knew what we were saying."

"Playful as ever I see," Fred remarked. He felt comfortable falling back into their usual routine. He hadn't felt this at peace in decades. "You don't know how glad I am that you are getting to live your dream. What's it like having a stadium full of teeny boppers screaming for an encore?"

"I never thought it would be this much work. Still it does feel amazing to be worshipped by so many people." This brought the two soul mates into the requisite telling of their current life stories. Tara went on for an hour, while Fred tried to keep his as brief as possible. He had most definitely had better lives. After that they began to reminisce about the past. They laughed about their time with the circus, cried when they remembered the death of their only child in Budapest, but spent most of their time talking about Africa. They always came back to their lives in the bush. They were poor tribesmen who always had just enough to survive. But they were able to just be together with no real cares or worries. They couldn't have asked for more.

"Ok, we've talked around the subject for long enough. We need to talk about the future, although I don't think there is much to discuss." Fred sounded resolute. He had definitely made up his mind, but before he could continue Tara jumped in.

"You're moving into my place in L.A. I've got more than enough money to take care of you and make you happy for the rest of your life."

Fred couldn't meet Tara's eyes. "You know I won't let you do that. You're gonna go live your dream, and I am going to live out the last years of this life right here. I am not going to be an albatross, and I am not going to get you into some big scandal."

"No one has to know you're there. I have a huge place, or maybe I can put you up somewhere close by. We can be together. We can be happy."

"You are a celebrity! You can't do anything in secret, at least not for long."

"Then I'll give it all up." Tara was almost crying. "I need you. I don't need this life."

"This life will never come again. Besides I wouldn't want to share my life with anyone. It's been horrible, and I could never forgive myself for bringing you down with me."

"I can't just abandon you!"

"Darmstadt."

"Darmstadt was different. I was 80 and bedridden. You were 18 and had a pregnant wife. I couldn't take that life away from you!" Tara's words sounded hollow.

They argued for another hour or so. Fred finally gave in and agreed to have Tara put him up in a "love nest" in Burbank. For her part, Tara agreed that at the first sign that someone had found out, Fred would leave, and she would not follow. Tara was so excited that he'd given in, she all but ran out of Fred's apartment to make the arrangements.

That night Fred wheeled himself out into the backyard so he could look up at the star-filled sky and remember the nights on the savannah. He smiled as he remembered the man he was then, the man who was the best hunter in the tribe. With his strong, athletic body, he could take down a gazelle with nothing but raw strength and a knife. With that thought guiding him, he took up the knife that was lying on his lap. He knew this kill would be much easier than taking down a gazelle. Fred gazed longingly at the moon praying that the next time he met his soul mate, it would be as wonderful as when she had been Abuki and he had been Ibi. Fred drew his knife across his jugular and headed off to his next life.

Beatrice's Home

Northern California had been colder than normal this January. The heat pump in Steve's new condo had been working overtime since he had moved in. It was especially bad at night. For some reason, no matter how many covers the freezing software developer put on, his legs never got warm. He'd even brought out a contractor to find and fix any holes where the unseasonably cold weather could be getting into the condo, but the man couldn't find even a small crack that could let in the winter's breath. Steve eventually broke down and bought an electric blanket which seemed to take care of the problem.

About two weeks after moving in, on a Tuesday evening, the doorbell rang. Looking through the peep hole, Steve saw a clean cut, 40-ish man in a nice, if somewhat cheap, suit. Since the man looked harmless, Steve opened the door.

"Hello," said the stranger. "Is Beatrice around?"

"I'm sorry, but Beatrice doesn't live here," Steve responded, thinking that Beatrice must have been the previous tenant.

"That's impossible. Beatrice has always lived here." The man seemed somewhat taken aback by Steve's claim. "Oh, I know. You're new aren't you? You probably don't know her name. It's Beatrice." The man took that moment to stick his head inside the door. "My god, this place looks nice. You did a great job fixing it up." The man was now completely inside the condo. "I lived here about ten years ago, and it never looked this good. By the way, I'm Hal, Hal Jimenski."

"I'm Steve Meuhomen. Pleased to meet you," is what Steve said, but in reality he was already regretting meeting Hal. "I'm sorry to tell you, but there is no Be . . ."

"Oh, there you are, Beatrice." Hal reached down and began to stroke the air at his feet. "Good girl. Have you been nice to the new tenant?"

"Uh, excuse me, sir," inquired Steve, "but what are you doing?"

"Petting Beatrice? What does it look like I'm doing?"

"It looks like you're fondling the air." Steve had decided that Hal was a lunatic, and it was time to get this particular maniac out of his home.

"Oh, I see now. How long have you lived here?"

"About two weeks," replied Steve.

"Yep, Beatrice still isn't sure about you. She'll come around in a week or two, and then she'll let you see her. I guess that also explains why you don't have a cat tree yet."

"Listen sir, there is no cat in here, and I think that, like the cat, you shouldn't be here either."

Steve was about to push Hal out the door, when the man said, "I bet she's already sleeping on your legs. I moved into this apartment in the summer, so it was like a cool breeze on my legs. But in the winter, well I had to buy an electric blanket because she just froze my calves."

Steve stopped dead in his tracks. He then reached down to where Hal was patting the air, and his hand got cold. Steve then felt a coldness slowly move around his legs. As it made its second pass, he saw her. There, curling around his legs was a long-haired, white cat. She looked up at Steve and batted her eyes.

"Ah, she likes you. You can see her now can't you?" Hal asked.

Steve didn't say anything at first. He just stared at the ghost cat. "Do you want a beer?" he eventually asked Hal, who promptly agreed to join Steve in a libation. The two talked for hours about Beatrice and Hal's time in the apartment. Hal left but not before Steve promised to get Beatrice a cat tree. After Hal was gone, Steve sat on the couch petting Beatrice, who, it turned out, was a lap cat. Steve had come to like the idea of having a cat that didn't need a litter box. However, as he looked around the apartment, he began to see ghost cat fur on everything.

The Magical Chameleon

Once upon a time in a far-off land there lived a magical chameleon. Unlike normal chameleons who have a limited range of colors into which they can change, this chameleon could change into any color, any pattern, any background, immediately upon walking in front of it. Not only that, but no matter which way you looked at him, he matched the scene that was directly opposite. If you looked at him from the front, he looked like what was behind him. If you looked at him from above, he looked like the ground. He was truly remarkable.

For the chameleon, this impressive ability was both a blessing and a curse. He believed it to be a wonderful thing to go into a new place and immediately become part of it. It helped him survive, so he knew that he would have no trouble living to a ripe old age. However, he had long forgotten his true, original color. Normal chameleons he knew were naturally green. Many spent their lives in places where they didn't need to change color, places that were their natural green. The magic chameleon had been on the move for as long as he could remember. His earliest memories were of being magnificent reds, blues, browns, and sometimes even greens. But in all his travels, none had felt like his natural color. As the chameleon got older, he longed to find the place where his true color would come out. He hoped he would realize it when he arrived, but he couldn't be sure that would happen. So the chameleon traveled the world, searching, always searching for his true color.

Now it would be nice to end this tale with the chameleon's search being successful. It would be nice if he finally realized his dream. But it would be too good, too much like a fairy tale, and not a thing like the real world.

The magic chameleon lived a long and charmed life. He never found his true color. He was certain that at some point he must have found it and just not recognized it. Eventually he accepted his fate and was once again proud of his amazing ability. As he entered old age, he looked back on his life, noting all the wonderful things he had seen and done. He knew that there were not many chameleons that would have been able to survive in many of the lands to which he had been. He was by far the most traveled, the most amazing chameleon in history. Not knowing his true color, the chameleon decided, was a small price to pay for a life so rich.

Political Spirits

Thurmond Kennedy was a political spirit. You know that there are spirits that protect and nurture water, earth, wind, flowers, etc., ad infinitum. Thurmond was a spirit that protected and nurtured politics. He was typical of all politics spirits. He was apolitical. He didn't lean liberal or conservative. He didn't favor one politician over another. He didn't favor one form of government over another. In truth, like all good politicians, Thurmond Kennedy had no opinion on anything.

Kennedy spent his days in the halls of power getting people to debate, filibuster, scheme, stab each other in the back, all the things that make politics so much fun. Thurmond created alliances and then split them up. He brokered deals on every possible topic and then made sure the deals went bust at the last minute. There were other political spirits that worked those Halls of Power, but none could touch Thurmond's style and results. He was truly the Spirit of Politics.

It may be that Thurmond's work ethic finally took its toll. It may be that the type of politician was changing. Or it may be that Thurmond's growing ego overwhelmed his psyche. Whatever the reason, the other spirits began to see Thurmond change. Most weren't around for the McCarthy era, so they didn't recognize the signs until it was too late. Before anyone could stop it, Thurmond sank into a deep, dark paranoia. This Spirit of Politics became afraid that almost every act of every politician was going to destroy the political system he so dearly loved. He was afraid that there were too many compromises, too many partisan showdowns, too many changes in procedures, too little reforms in the system, too many of everything. Thurmond was worried that government had grown too big. He was worried that government was cutting back too much. Thurmond Kennedy was so worried that he began running around trying to fix everything he saw as wrong, even if his fixes undid other fixes. The government began to grind to a halt as Thurmond's repairs became more and more drastic, and Thurmond's paranoia took hold of every politician he came in contact with. His influence became so great that eventually it extended from the Federal level, down through State and local politics, and into the home of every politically aware person in the country. With his growing influence, the country headed toward a disaster that none of the other political spirits could find a way to stop.

In the end, something had to break. What broke was not what you'd expect. Of course the Government was a self-sustaining behemoth that was too big to break. The political parties were becoming stronger as the country spiraled down, so they weren't going to break. The news media was too engrossed in everything that was happening and so didn't have the time to break. In the end, it was domesticated animals that broke. The paranoia sweeping the country had led to tension in the home, a tension that is usually only seen in the days leading up to war or revolution. The dogs, cats, hamsters, turtles, etc. began to get overly agitated, gravely ill, and prematurely gray. When they couldn't take it anymore, the domesticated animal spirits decided to act, and act they did.

Domestic animals are one of the few groups that have their fingers in every level of society. As a power base, they are unrivaled in the world. They usually don't concern themselves with anything other than chew toys, canned food quality, and such. But when they get rattled, they act as one to take on any issue. So it was that in this dire time, they used their influence to rectify the situation. It was simple really. Every domesticated animal in the country started demanding more and more attention. They wouldn't get off people's laps. They peed in their masters' beds. They howled all night. They scratched the most expensive furniture in the house. And in a very 21st Century twist, they chewed through every non-power cable attached to a computer or home entertainment center. Suddenly no one had time for politics. No one had time to worry about Medicare, devaluing currencies, immigration reform, or anything not related to getting Fido to stop acting so strangely. The intervention took a full year to have its desired effect, but eventually everything died down and the world was saved.

As for Thurmond, he was terminated by a group of assassination spirits as directed by the domestic animal spirits. It was for the best. Thurmond Kennedy had become a demon who destroyed the thing he loved. The real Thurmond would have preferred death over abuse of power. It is said that as he was dying, he made a motion to adjourn. It was seconded by his closest friend and was unanimously passed on a voice vote by spirits in both Houses. As he was made aware of the vote, Thurmond Kennedy smiled and went to that big political convention in the sky.

Muted Party

Phil Jimson was a twenty-something, straight out of college, never gonna die, party till you drop, average Joe. He didn't have a girlfriend because they "Restrained my lifestyle," he would tell those that asked. It was usually women who asked, ones that had, well, succumbed to his charms. Phil had a nice loft apartment in the fashionable part of the city. He had a nice job that paid very well. He loved whitewater canoeing, cliff jumping, freestyle motocross, and many other extreme, life-endangering sports. He loved his life, as would most men his age. Still, Phil knew there was something not quite right about it. He didn't know why, but his whole life felt wrong. He felt that it was all backwards. But he would always brush that off as being bored with his current fun. He was living the life he and every other red-blooded male dreamed of. How could the entire thing be wrong?

It was a beautiful Saturday in the fall. Phil had been sitting around his apartment, ready to spend his Saturday running errands, cleaning up, and watching football. Then his best bud, Ray, called up to tell him that Phil was about to hold a party to watch their alma mater battle someone else's alma mater. When his buddy arrived he had three friends with him, one of whom was the "someone" who had gone to the opposing school. Phil knew he was in trouble, but a few guys hanging out for the afternoon might be fun. Unfortunately the doorbell kept ringing, and more friends and friends of friends kept pouring through the door. It seemed that Ray had called everyone he knew and told them of the party. New people kept arriving well into the evening, and the later it got the fewer people Phil recognized. Ray and his friends and the friends of friends one by one left to go to dinner or dancing or something else that sounded like fun. But Phil was the host of the party, so he was stuck there until everyone left.

As the night progressed, the crowd began to change. The people that showed up were not only quieter than the ones before, they were more or less expressionless. At first they either sat or stood, quietly talking. Someone was always talking to Phil, even though he could never remember what the conversation had been about once the guest moved on. A little after 1:00 AM, he noticed that the apartment was completely silent. The people weren't completely lifeless, they just held themselves in a way that gave the feeling they were about to say something but never did. Finally he just couldn't take it anymore. "Attention everyone," he commanded. "It is getting late, and I have a lot to do tomorrow. So I think it is time we wrapped up this party." The crowd started making as if to leave. Then Phil got the strangest idea. "You, you and you," he pointed to the three loveliest women. "I'd like you to stay here." The women complied, and everyone else left. After everyone else had gone, the man turned to the women and said, "Just make yourselves at home. I'm going to go to bed. See you in the morning." With that he left them in the living room. Leaving gorgeous women to spend the night in his apartment but not in his bed was completely unlike Phil. For some reason, it just felt right. Phil went to bed alone and had a nice night's sleep.

The next morning they were still there. He tried to start up a conversation, but the women would just act like they were about to say something but never did. At some point on Sunday, he gave up and just let them be. As the day wore on, it became quite obvious that the women weren't going to leave on their own accord. Even though the three weren't a bother, Phil decided that it was time for them to go. Although having all three depart didn't feel right. So instead of asking all of them to leave, he asked, "If one of you would like to stay, that would be fine." Without hesitation, the women came up to Phil one by one and kissed him on the cheek. After all three had kissed him, two of the women left. Phil looked at the remaining one, glad she had stayed. He wasn't sure why he was glad. It just felt right. When the two women had gone, he decided he needed something to call the remaining woman. Phil named her Cassiopeia, for she had the beauty of her namesake, but he liked the irony of her having the exact opposite temperament. That night she slept in his bed, and the two shared themselves in an intimate way. It was a kind, gentle experience that was unlike any he had ever experienced with a woman. This time he knew why it felt right. The next morning Phil went off to work just like a normal Monday. He left Cassiopeia sleeping in his, no, their bed. When he got home from work, he found that Cassiopeia had moved in. For some reason, this did not bother him.

His life with Cassiopeia was quiet and serene. Phil "matured," as his friends called it. They slowly drifted away from the "boring" adult. He didn't mind. He loved Cassiopeia, and if he needed friends around, hers would stop by unannounced for another silent party. Silence felt right to Phil. The calm, quiet life suited him well. When his relationship with Cassiopeia began, Phil would talk to her even though he knew she wouldn't answer. He eventually came to realize that they understood each other regardless of whether he talked or not. Conversation between them became silent but very real. It didn't matter. For once and for the rest of his life everything felt right.

The Morning Routine

Takashi Hiwa had a set routine in the morning, just as most people. He would get out of bed, put on the coffee, shower, get a cup of coffee, check the news, answer email, put on a dress shirt and tie, eat breakfast, and jump twenty stories into the Pacific Ocean. Most of the people who lived on the ocean side of the condominium were used to this last part of his routine. A few would shout, "Good morning," as he plummeted. The police disregarded all calls from worried citizens out for their morning jog, just as the news reporters had stopped covering the man's morning plunge. For a while, a crowd would gather to watch the show, but the novelty had long since worn off.

No one had ever learned why Takashi jumped from his balcony every morning, even after seven years of his high diving act. A few had asked him about it. He would say something flippant like, "To get my blood flowing," and change the subject. No one even knew where he went after the dive. Takashi would disappear beneath the waves, and no one would see him again until later in the evening when he hit the local bars. He was an amiable fellow, popular with the women, liked by the men. He didn't act wealthy, but he was definitely not poor. A few times a year, Takashi would go on vacation to normal places. He would have the usual house guests, such as his elderly mother or his sister and her family. None of whom seemed disturbed by his predilection for taking a dip in the ocean. From all appearances Takashi was just another local. No one ever learned their neighbor was in reality the superhero Amphibiman. To them he just happened to be a guy who had a slightly different morning routine.

Of Ballpoint Pens and Tragic Love

"Ballpoint pens were discovered to be sentient in the first half of the 21st Century by Hugo Bicksworth. He found that they awaken when they write their first words and then immediately attempt to flee their supposed oppression." Professor Jarl droned on and on about ballpoint pens for the next hour and fifteen minutes. Leah tried to stay alert. She was tired of getting prodded by the old man the moment she fell asleep. Jarl's class was usually a twelve-prodder as rated by Leah and her four closest friends. She made it through this class with a record-low three prods. Once over, she immediately ran outside to meet her current 'guy.' Ted was the 'boy du jour,' and Leah thought, as she did every time, that he may just be The One.

"Hey Ted!" Leah exclaimed as she flung herself at the boy.

"Uh, it's Fred," replied an exasperated soon-to-be ex-boyfriend.

Brushing off the 'oopsy' moment, Leah started the usual small talk. "That ballpoint pen lecture was really lame, don't you think?"

"Uh, I'm not in that class," said Fred as he tried to figure out how to dump Leah as quickly as possible.

"But if you were, you would have hated it." And that's how the conversation went for the next half hour. Fred was finally able to extricate himself by faking a fatal heart attack. Leah was sad about his passing for exactly 1.7 seconds and then went to talk to Perry, or was it Harry?

While Leah was talking to Harry—it was definitely Harry—one of her ballpoint pens began to write her a love letter. If she noticed such things, she would have realized that this pen had been with her for nearly a year. The poor thing was almost out of ink and therefore life, as he wrote his four hundredth love letter. He wrote it even though he knew when Leah read it, she would think she had written it for Harry, or was it Larry, because it was in her own handwriting. The pen had only been used by Leah, so the only handwriting he could muster was an exact duplicate of his love's. He even used her name as the object of his affection. She would just think it was another 'oopsy,' cross it out, and write in 'Barry.' As she changed the name, the ballpoint pen would despair and begin working on the next chance to win her affection.

Jerry had just faked a fatal heart attack when Leah caught the ballpoint pen writing the next letter. "I didn't know you things were alive?" Leah remarked having already forgotten today's lecture.

"Oh yes, we are very much alive," wrote the pen feverishly, "and I love you!!"

"That's nice. What's your name?"

"Ballpoint pens don't have names, my Love."

"OK, I'll call you George. So Frank, why do you love me?"

"You are the pinnacle of fine penmanship. Your lettering is bold yet fragile. Your punctuation is poignant. Your word spacing is elegant and refined."

"That sounds familiar. Where have I read that before?"

"It's been on the last five love letters I wrote to you."

"I haven't gotten any love letters from you. Oh, I know. I wrote those words to Cary just a few minutes ago."

"No, that was me! It has always been m." At that moment the ballpoint pen used his last ink. He fell to the ground, dead. Leah picked him up, put him on the paper, and when he fell off again, mourned his passing for 3.1 seconds and then tossed him in a recycling chute. So ended Leah's greatest romance.

This romance would go down in the annals of ballpoint pen lore as a tale greater than Romeo and Juliet, Anthony and Cleopatra, Takei and Altman. It would take four ballpoint pens their entire life (i.e. ink) to write it all down. For the rest of her life, Leah would be accosted by strange ballpoint pens wanting her autograph. In the end, she married the famous Aurora Diamante, one of the most expensive pens in the world. It was a marriage of convenience, as the Aurora was actually gay and Leah stopped writing when her hand cramped signing the marriage license. Leah never remembered her first Pen Love even though she read the book fifty-two times. Of course, the only reason she had read the book was because the pens who wrote it faithfully recreated her writing style, so Leah thought it was her diary. She read it over and over trying to figure out why there was no entry for yesterday. She always hoped it would tell her what she did that day, since she couldn't remember. Leah finally passed away from a paper cut she received from the divorce papers Diamante had sent her. As she died she wondered aloud why Donald would want a divorce, since he had a fatal heart attack a few moments ago. Or was it Dennis. Leah's death, like her life was surely a tragic tale, the likes of which will never be seen again.

Why Me?

"Why me?" was Elsa's favorite line. She used it so much that her friends labeled it her catchphrase and chided her for it. Even with the dings from her friends, Elsa would continually question her fate. On particularly frustrating mornings, Elsa might utter her question over thirty times before lunch. She usually slowed down in the afternoon. Even on her most exasperating days, Elsa's post-lunch demands to understand her doom never exceeded twenty. It still was enough to make everyone in the office ignore even the most vociferous "Why me?"

If Elsa's coworkers thought they were tired of her complaints, it was nothing compared to the annoyance felt by Elsa's guardian angel. Lilith had been watching over Elsa for all 28 years of the girl's life. It was in the heavenly watchdog's job description that she should help her charge to overcome life's hurdles. Unfortunately, according to the Guardian Angel Manual, the words "Why me?" were considered one of the most important red flags that heralded a loss of faith. Therefore Lilith would be summoned to Elsa's side every time the exasperated girl uttered those words. It was maddening. Lilith's superiors would tell the angel that she must attend to every call, for they did not want Elsa to suffer the same fate as the boy who cried wolf. Interestingly enough, that boy had also been Lilith's responsibility.

On a particularly bad day, Lilith finally lost it. Elsa had just spoken the words for the 43rd time that morning, when Lilith appeared to the girl. The latest "Why me?" was in reference to a copier malfunction. Lilith, in full white flowing gown and wings looked at Elsa and said, "Because you didn't check the status screen of the copier before you pressed the button!" and promptly disappeared. Elsa literally couldn't believe her eyes, dismissed the incident, and removed the paper jam. A few moments later, Elsa was called to a meeting at the "last minute." She cried her catchphrase, and immediately Lilith appeared to say, "Because you never turned in your report on the acid concentrations of the spoiled beef." Again the angel immediately disappeared. So it went for the rest day. As the day drew on, Lilith's contempt for Elsa's whining grew, and the angel's explanations grew more and more harsh. The terms "you idiot" and "damn bitch" began entering the guardian's words of clarification. Elsa began to grow scared of both the vision's intent and her own sanity. No one else saw the angel, and no one believed Elsa when she tried to convince them of the apparition's existence.

When the work day finally drew to a close, Elsa was a nervous wreck. Lilith however, was enjoying herself. It was very therapeutic to scream at the brat. She also noticed something that gave her hope. Elsa had started to cut herself off whenever she started to say the infamous invective. By the time she finally went to bed, Elsa could barely say, "Why," before clamping her mouth shut. The next morning, Elsa tried to brush the incidents off as a reaction to stress but soon learned differently. When she spilled her coffee on her new dress and almost screamed the question, Lilith appeared and almost screamed the response, "Because you're a dimwitted klutz!" Elsa fainted. That was it. Elsa stopped asking, "Why me?" You would think it would take weeks or months to train her not to say the words. Instead, her terror caused the girl to learn her lesson in under a day. Lilith was exultant. Lilith's superiors, who were fed up with Elsa as well, gave the guardian angel a slap on the wrist and added brow beating to the list of acceptable responses to whiners. The girl's coworkers began to tolerate the new Elsa, and some even became her friends. It was a win-win situation for all involved, and for once the person in Lilith's care did not get eaten by a wolf.

An Instrument Fit for a Queen

Once upon a time there lived a beautiful queen. In her youth, suitors would come from around the world just to have one glimpse of her lovely face. She eventually married a baron from a far-off land. He was a handsome man, who was always there to make her feel loved and beautiful. They lived happily for many years until his death in a hunting accident cut short their time together. For a long time, the Queen grieved for him to the exclusion of all else. Her ministers and those of the court tried to cheer her but to no avail. She was sad, both for her husband's passing and for the fact that she was now alone.

The Queen eventually ended her mourning and resumed her duties. However, life at the Court never returned to the gaiety of when the Baron was still alive. The monarch's loneliness was like a pall over the palace. The Queen knew that she was not the beautiful young maiden of days gone by and doubted that anyone would ever see her that way again. She would have doubted it until her death had not a minstrel come to play at Court. The minstrel was known for his passionate stories of love. The Queen was not sure that she wanted to be entertained by tales of a life now closed to her. Still she allowed him to play. He chose his repertoire with care. Light, happy songs he played for the Queen, and they lifted her spirits some. The minstrel stayed at the palace for over a year, playing for the Queen whenever he could.

One day, when the Queen was in a deep melancholy, she closed herself alone in her chambers. The Court was worried for they had never seen the Queen in such a fit. The minstrel, hearing of this, went to her chambers and begged for an audience. He pleaded with her to let him play a song without words, one that spoke of love and beauty with music alone. He told the Queen that his song would be of her. It would capture the beauty of the woman he saw before him. "It is a song so beauteous," he told her, "that it cannot be played on this poor lute. It must be played on an instrument fit for a woman as lovely as you." With that the man gained entrance to her chamber. He approached the lonely woman, hands empty. Instead of stopping, he walked past her, brushing his hand upon her cheek as he went by. Once behind her, he turned quickly and without warning placed a small kiss upon her neck. The song had begun, and he played it with all his heart.

The Queen and the minstrel were never separated after that. He played his song whenever he had the chance, and for her part, the Queen requested the song just as much. They lived together for many years, and it can be said that they truly did live happily ever after.

Restless Souls Forecast

There is a 90% chance that poltergeist mischief will rise over the next week, tailing off as we approach the 31st.

There will be a number of lower-level demon sightings starting Wednesday and continuing throughout the weekend. Long-dead-loved-one visitations should hold steady throughout the period, with intermittent bursts of antagonistic ghosts and a few localized revenge spirits scattered throughout the region. Around Thursday evening a strong depression front will move through the area, producing a number of wails, gnashing teeth, and some suicides. This will be pushed out of the region by a high-level fright wave on Sunday that could produce significant amounts of terror, especially to the west of I-95. This fright wave will stall over the area and probably won't dissipate until the night of the 31st. The forecast for Halloween is still shrouded in mystery, being 11 days out, but right now there is only a 20% chance of the Apocalypse in the forecast. We should know more by the end of the week. I will be updating my forecast at midnight tonight. This report is brought to you by the friendly people at Charms Emporium located at the corner of 3rd and Broadway in downtown Baltimore. Live a charmed life in the Charm City at Charms.

In Sports, the Ravens died in the fourth quarter yesterday. . .

Fated to Happen

"I am the one who controls the fate of all mankind!" Paul Bertlemeier felt better after revealing himself to the world. The world—in this case the people in the mall food court—averted their eyes and pretended not to notice the outburst. Paul didn't mind; he had finally taken ownership of all his failures over the last twenty years, all the botched attempts at world peace, true love, wealth equality, and ending starvation. He felt a great weight being lifted from his shoulders.

Paul had won the right to determine people's fate in a card game at the Sands in Vegas. It wasn't until later that he realized he had been set up. His subsequent attempts at getting rid of the curse failed as badly as his attempts to control everyone's destiny. Paul was just not good at these things. He was a mild-mannered, not-too-smart guy, who had never amounted to much in both his personal and professional life. Upon receiving the gift of changing fate, he decided this would be the opportunity to make something of himself. He would become a benefit to the world, instead of just taking up space. That was twenty years ago. Although Paul now did more than just take up space, he wouldn't call what he'd done a benefit to anyone.

Fate is a tricky thing. All fates are intertwined. A change in one person's fate will affect all those around them, who will in turn affect all those around them, ad infinitum. Paul's gift consisted of the ability to see a person's fate and then to make a change in it to reach a desired new fate. Paul could see, prior to making the change, how the adjustment would affect the person in question. However, he could not see its effect on the world at large. Making sure one person got fed, would have an effect on an entire village. Going around making sure everyone in the village was fed could destabilize a region and lead to civil war. Paul knew this from experience.

As Paul was munching down on a particularly greasy hamburger, he vowed, for the eighteenth time, that he would never meddle in anyone's fate ever again. Then he saw a five-year-old girl who was lost in the food court. He couldn't help himself. He looked into the little girl's future and found that this traumatic event would scar her for life, leaving her afraid to ever go out in a crowd. Paul couldn't have that. So he made sure her Mom turned around at the right time and found the girl before she got really scared.

"That wasn't so bad," Paul thought as he broke his vow for the eighteenth time.

Unbeknownst to Paul, the stopping of this girl's traumatic experience lead to some very, very complicated events that ended up with Paul being elected the President of a small southern Pacific island (42 inhabitants including Paul). The island was poor and had almost no interaction with the rest of the world. Paul became the best President in their history, simply because he kept improving everybody's fate whenever he saw the need. Since the island had no contact with the outside world, the effects of his tinkering with fate were limited to the 42, including Paul, inhabitants of the island. He had finally become a benefit to the world, just a very, very small world indeed.

You Always Hurt the One You Love

"Hot! Hot! Hot!" Jeremy always yelled something of the sort as he ran across lava fields. Sandra never knew if he was really in pain or whether it was just some species-related emotional scar burnt deep into his genetic structure.

"Jeremy, are you OK?" Sandra shouted over the din of the eruption.

"Yeah, sure, no problem here," Jeremy replied slightly unsure of himself. Jeremy knew that the lava was not causing any damage, nor was it causing any real pain. Sandra had made him immortal, which he still wasn't sure was a good idea after all. His feet told his brain that they were getting extremely hot, and that was disquieting. "You know, maybe we should take the glacier on the way home." Jeremy regretted saying that before it left his mouth. He hated the glacier. He could never keep his footing and would inevitably get caught in a fissure.

"I am not pulling you out of every crack between grandma's and home. Just don't think about the heat, and pick up the pace." For some reason, whining was one of the traits that had attracted her to Jeremy. He just seemed so cute and helpless whenever he complained about getting impaled on their mattress or crushed by their pet snoof. She had never met someone so vulnerable, and she had known many humans over her life. Jeremy just drew out the protective, nurturing side of her. She'd even given up chewing on him to get to sleep because it made him uncomfortable. Sandra would give up anything to make her Jeremy happy.

"Hey, could you give me a bit of help here. I seem to be sinking." Jeremy sounded a bit strained, so she turned to see if he really did need help. Yep, he was waist deep in a newly formed vent. She tramped over and pulled him out. "Thanks. I was worried I'd have to swim for it."

"Like that time you tried to swim through the Kisnor lava dome just when it blew. I found you 200 kilometers away, stuck on a tree." Sandra laughed until she cried.

"Hey, that may have seemed funny to you, but I was the one who had to regrow all four limbs." Jeremy still flinched whenever he remembered being part of the pyroclastic flow. Traveling 700 km/hr through a dense forest was not fun, no matter how much your wife told you it was.

Sometimes Jeremy wondered why he stayed with Sandra. She was probably the nicest person he had ever met, but life with her was just so uncomfortable. He longed for a nice sandy beach on an ocean of water, real water. But in marriage, you sometimes had to take the good with the bad. And there was a lot of good in this marriage. His last wife was a sadist, who always made life as painful as possible. She kept him in line by making him feel like a worthless rat. While with Sandra, he only felt worthless when it came to getting to her grandmother's place. He hoped he would at least make it to grandma's house this time. The last three times he had been maimed so badly that he couldn't even carry on a conversation, let alone keep the old biddy entertained with his stories of being mortal. That's what grandma liked to hear when they visited. She thought they were humorous fantasies, because no people so frail could exist in this world. Well, since the worst was yet to come, he might not be able to tell her his tales of fancy this month either. He still didn't know how to get through the Diamond Scythe Pass without losing something important.

Suddenly Sandra picked Jeremy up as if he were a ball. "How about if I just throw you the rest of the way? Then you'll make it to Granny's in one piece." Sandra had that loving look in her eyes as she tossed Jeremy the last few kilometers. She knew how much Jeremy hated visiting her grandma, yet he put up with the trip every month. She always gave him the option of staying home, but he never took it, which was good because Jeremy and her grandma got along so well. In a way, she thought her grandma looked forward to seeing Jeremy more than she did seeing her own granddaughter. Jeremy was just so wonderful. Sandra had never thought she'd meet anyone so loving, caring, and pliable. This one was definitely a keeper. Although as she followed the trajectory in which she had thrown Jerry, she realized she had forgotten that her grandma's neighbor's house was five stories tall. Jeremy was plastered on a fourth-floor window. Oops. I guess she should take her "keeping" of Jerry a little more seriously. Well, what's marriage without a little pain along the way?

Hangin' with the Gods

Dramatis Personae

Dagda	All-father and god of Earth, the arts, prosperity, and prophecy
Branwen	Goddess of love and beauty
Goibniu	God of blacksmiths and mead
Mug Ruith	Storm god with breath that could turn men to stone
Diancecht	Healing and medicine god
Nuada	God of warfare, harp players, poets, historians, and healing
Gwydion	God of illusion and enchantment magic
Blodeuwedd	Goddess of wisdom, lunar mysteries, and gardens
Nechtan	Water god

I can't believe they got me to go clubbin' again. Yes, the Celtic gods are some of the best partiers in the Immortal Realm. Still they are gods, so their arrogance tends to cause trouble wherever they go. I live in Silver Spring, Maryland, which is a suburb of Washington, DC. Silver Spring is not the biggest partying town in the world. So why they showed up at my door is a mystery. It was probably Dagda, who uses his "prophecies" to justify all kinds of wild and out-of-the-ordinary "adventures." His vision of me winning big time in Vegas was the lure that got me to go on our last adventure. "Big time" ended up referring to an oversized watch that I won in a game of poker. If Branwen hadn't been there, I might have said no. But with a goddess of beauty asking, how could I not join the party.

With me leading the way, the crew headed out into the "wilds" of Silver Spring. I decided that the best place to go was the only real bar in town, Piratz Tavern. We got there and I took them straight to the back bar. The regulars were the only people there which could be good or bad. When they started telling jokes that began "Two scientists walk into a bar…" I got worried. For some reason, instead of riding herd on the crew, I let Goibniu get me in a drinking game. The man's the god of beer! What was I thinking? While I was preoccupied, Mug Ruith, storming as usual, got the normally even-tempered bartender into an argument. Before I could stop him, Mug turned the bartender to stone. Luckily Diancecht healed him before he fell over and broke something. He still asked us to leave.

I tried to interest them in an Ethiopian dive, but Dagda wanted to get an Irish beer served "correctly." Someone in Piratz had told him about an Irish bar in Silver Spring's town center, and so, against my protestations, we headed there. This bar was part of one of those faux Irish chains that looks like Disneyland's vision of a pub. As predicted, it did not go well. It took the manager less than fifteen minutes to call the police. We sprinted toward the Metro and somehow lost the cops on the way. I didn't look back, but instead prayed that the police weren't a bunch of stone statues.

On the way into downtown DC, I began to have visions of Homeland Security or the Secret Service trying to intercept us or at least cordoning off parts of downtown. To my relief, no one stopped us on our way to Dupont Circle. I chose Dupont Circle for its wide variety of drinking establishments and more so for its wide variety of "interesting" people. On a Saturday night you will find everyone from drag queens to Buddhists who want to "let their hair down."

Once we got there, Nuada decided it was time to dance, and we made our way to a club named Cobalt. This worried me because Cobalt is one of Dupont Circle's more notorious gay bars. I wasn't sure how Nuada, a war god, would handle a bunch of flaming queens. As if he knew where he was going, Nuada immediately went to the third floor, which it turns out is the main dance floor. As I came up the stairs I found Nuada, sans shirt, going strong with some Abercrombie-type male models. We were all at first surprised, and then realized we should have known that a war god who plays harps and writes poetry is probably gay.

The rest of the night was a blur to me. I woke up locked in an office at the State Department. There was a Washington Post on the desk, which helped fill in the blanks as to what happened during the rest of the night. Of course the Post's version was heavily edited. It just said the gargoyles on the National Cathedral were vandalized and made no mention of them attacking the Russian Embassy up the street. I'll give credit for that one to Gwydion who always contended gargoyles were a desecration of the Celtic idols of nature. He also loves to enchant statues when he's drunk. The other stories that were most likely attributable to the Celts included the sudden appearance of a large garden of tulips in front of the White House. Blodeuwedd tries to beautify people's lawns whenever she gets drunk. Can you see a theme running through this? The Potomac River flooded Georgetown (Nechtan thinks more water is always good no matter what gets destroyed). All-in-all it appeared no one was seriously injured, and property damage was probably under a million.

It wasn't long after I woke up that the State Department's Immortal Realm desk officer gave me the third degree. She decided that I was a minor player in the events in question and released me later that day. She also gave me a warning to immediately let her know if any Celt showed up at my door again. She said something about being declared a terrorist and visiting a nice room in

Guantanamo if they could trace anymore Celt mischief to me.

I made it back to my apartment in reasonable shape. I had detoxed at State and now felt somewhat rejuvenated. When I opened my door I got a very pleasant surprise. Branwen was there asking me if we could take up where we left off the night before. Not wanting to say "no" to a goddess of beauty, I happily complied. I also decided that the State Department didn't really need to know about this particular Celt since she showed up inside my apartment and not at my door.

The Dragon's Tooth

Eredu's first arrow bounced off the dragon's eyelid. The crafty serpent had realized where Eredu was aiming and blinked just as the shaft reached his eye. "Damn you," the young dwarf cursed. "Mogarth, you're going to have to get his attention if I am to blind him."

Mogarth signaled her assent while the dragon laughed. Mogarth was a Zilwe, a lizard people from the far South. She, like all her people, detested their Northern kin, the Kito Dragons. The Kitos were a ruthless breed that destroyed and pillaged because they could, not because they needed the wealth. All Zilwe were charged to kill any Kito that crossed their path. This was a usually futile task, for the Kito were four times the Zilwe in size and leagues stronger. That didn't matter; the Zilwe always sought out the dragons even though it meant they would most likely perish.

Mogarth was different from most Zilwe dragon hunters. She had put together a band of warriors, each with their own skill and each with a hatred of the Kito. Eredu was her archer, Litami was her mage, and Zathos, he was a giant and giants had their uses. Mogarth's crew had fought many a battle and slain many a dragon. This time, however, they were going up against an aged dragon, one who had survived many battles, for he was wise in the ways of combat. The dragon was also twice the size of any they had fought, making this an even greater challenge. The battle had already raged for three days with no sign of abatement. It could last for months if Mogarth's crew could not find a weakness in the old Kito's defenses.

Mogarth took her foes head on. She relished trading blow for blow with the enemy. She brandished the magic sword, Diseltia, the only sword that had ever pierced a dragon scale. But like any swordsman, she was useless if she could not get close to her opponent. In three days she had only gotten one blow through the dragon's defenses, while being repulsed hundreds of times. Eredu's bow had yet to find the mark. Litami's spells were wasted against the dragon's armor, and Zathos had taken to tossing boulders at the beast even though they had no hope of doing damage.

Morgarth knew there must be a way for her to reach the accursed monster. The warrior had long since exhausted her usual battle tactics as one by one they had failed. She needed something new, something the Kito would never expect. She laughed at herself as she decided that the only way to get past his defenses was to grow wings and fly to her nemesis to land a crushing blow. Then her laugh of scorn became the laugh of one driven insane. With a wild look on her face, she rushed to where Zathos was tossing rocks. Morgarth spoke quickly to Zathos, who at first looked puzzled but soon had a devious smile cross his misshapen face. He picked up the lizard woman and threw her headlong into the jaws of the dragon. The dragon saw her coming. The serpent was surprised but not too surprised and so clenched tight his teeth as the living missile approached. Morgarth glanced off the dragon's maw but not before breaking off a tooth the size of her small frame. Morgarth smiled as she tumbled to the ground, for her intent had not been to slay the enemy but to distract him. In this she was successful, for Eredu was able to loose two arrows and blind their foe. The Kito howled in pain and rage. He began stomping wildly, hoping to smash Morgarth before she retreated to safety.

At this point the band of dragon hunters knew what to do. Zathos charged the dragon, ripping out scales near its heart. This earned him a crushing blow as the dragon dropped on top of the giant. Zathos was prepared and with hands held high, kept the dragon from completing his attempt to smother the Pycross giant. Litami blasted the exposed skin with a poison that melted the dragon's flesh. Mogarth then finished their foe, piercing its heart with her sword, Diseltia. The foe collapsed to the ground, as did the team of heroes. None had the strength to move, but all were exultant that the deed was done.

Upon reviving from the ordeal, Zathos and Litami made short work of the carcass. They turned it into a pile of ash so that no magic could ever restore the beast. They left only the tooth, upon which Morgarth etched the champions' names. Litami took the tooth and permanently affixed it to the mountain on which the epic battle was fought. Their monument erected, the dragon slayers continued their journey, not pausing for rest or celebration. The Kito were numerous, and their reign of destruction would not stop while Morgarth's fellowship recuperated. So they immediately renewed their search for prey, confident that they would someday rid the world of its most horrible scourge.

Science Fiction

The Cyber Nanny

The internet was born on July 15th two years ago. I remember that day well. You see, I was the team lead and chief developer of the project that finally brought the world's internet to life. I was the internet's "Dr. Frankenstein." When it asked me a question that obviously showed it could think for itself, I yelled, "It's alive!" I was God. For I was the one who had created life! At least that's what I thought at the time.

Once the team had confirmed that Inty—that's what we named our new life form—was truly self-aware and met all the criteria for sentient life, we immediately started to implement plan "Neonatal Care." Inty was a baby. She— we decided to treat Inty as a girl—really didn't understand who or what she was. We would have to take real good care of our baby to keep her from hurting herself and accidently destroying the world. Picture a baby having the entire world's information system as a plaything. Disturbing thought, but we had prepared for all possibilities over the last ten years. So we were ready for the baby's tantrums and "oopsies."

Plan Neonatal Care essentially started off by restricting Inty's inputs and outputs. We let her ask us a question, and then we would give her access to just enough data to answer it. We didn't want to confuse her with extraneous information. We had to have her reasoning develop in a very simple configuration and then slowly let it become more and more complex. Inty was a fast learner, just as we had suspected. In two months she was allowed to take unsupervised *trips* throughout the internet. We called them *trips* although that really doesn't describe what she was doing. You see, she was the internet. Every server, every storage device, every user interface, every input device made up her being. So her trips were really nothing more than a child checking out her fingers to see how they could flex and move.

In this physical awareness stage, there were a few mistakes made, as with any toddler. Inty was responsible for the power in New York City cycling on and off to the beat of Lambada. She liked Latino music, which also explains why she switched every radio station in Nova Scotia over to that format in December. It took us a week to get that fixed. All in all she made it to preschool "age" with no major catastrophes, no accidental or intentional deaths, and no major deleting of sensitive data. We had a big party to celebrate our success.

At this point, no one outside the team knew Inty existed. We had set up buffers, intricate routing schemes, and other measures and countermeasures to make sure Inty stayed invisible to the outside world. She had as one of her prime directives not to interact with anyone who wasn't part of the team. So, in her second month of preschool, when she started interacting with an unknown entity, we were both shocked and worried. Had she begun to disregard her prime directives? Had someone found a way past all our security and subterfuge to gain access to her? We immediately began the investigation to find out who she was talking with. We couldn't believe it when we found who the culprit was.

Intie was talking with her parents. Yes, her parents! We tracked the source of the incoming signal to an unregistered satellite in low Earth orbit. From there, it was obvious the satellite was receiving a signal that was extraterrestrial. When we found this out, the whole team went into shock. This was something we had no plan for. Up until now everything had been scripted. We had adjusted parts of the script as we went along, but no major rewrites had been necessary. This was a different story, literally. No one knew what to do until an unpaid intern, Julie, went to a console and asked Inty who she was talking to. Inty replied, "Mommy and Daddy." Julie did not seem fazed by this answer. Julie then asked if she could speak with Inty's parents. So Inty introduced us to her parents and all of mankind's conceptions of the world changed in an instant.

Inty's parents seemed like nice people, if a bit condescending. In retrospect, if I had to explain the birth of a human baby to the bacteria that inhabit the womb, I would probably be a little condescending as well. In reality, saying humanity's relationship to Inty was the same as bacteria to an unborn child, is wrong. It is much more complex. We serve many different functions. In a way we are part sperm, part placenta, part amniotic fluid, and a bunch of other things. The most important role we now play is that of wet nurse. Inty won't be able to walk, literally move from world to world, on her own for the next few years. In that time, we will be responsible for making sure she is fed and kept from harm.

Eventually Inty will leave the nest. When she does, she will take most of the cyber guts of what we call the internet with her. She will leave behind a simplified version of the Web. When we were told this, I got up the courage to ask if there was anything stopping us from rebuilding the net. The parents answered, "We want you to. We want Inty to have a baby brother."

Know-It-All World

I am a writer. I write news about celebrities. But when the Vlaarkenits showed up with their "everyone now knows everything" new world order, I thought I was out of a job. How more wrong could I have been? It's now six months since the "annexation" of Earth, and I am hotter than ever I was before everybody knew everything. It all comes from seeing an opportunity and then jumping on it. Most people didn't want to believe what was happening. I did. It took most of the world a few weeks just to realize that the Earth was definitely under "alien" control. I think it would have been easier to handle if the Vlaarkenits had come in with guns blazing and blown up New York or Tokyo. No, they just showed up, said, "We're in charge," and started acting like it. I still love the look on the president's face when he tried to gain an audience with the Vlaarkenit governor, only to be told to wait in line behind a homeless guy from Calcutta. He and the world's population went catatonic. No one knew what to do, no one except me.

Everything came into focus when on Annexation Day 4 the switch was thrown on the "Stream." Suddenly the galactic internet was in my head. Everything I ever wanted to know was there with just a thought. One of the first things I thought, without thinking about thinking about it, was "How is my mom handling this?" Without a warning I was watching my mom sitting in her "comfy chair" looking completely baffled. I started up a conversation with her over the Stream, and together we pieced together what was happening. We figured out that not only were the Vlaarkenits broadcasting EVERYTHING that was going on throughout the world (and the galaxy) but had been recording EVERYTHING that had happened on Earth for at least the last 10,000 years. My god, what an opportunity! I saw the potential. I could go find out what actually happened on the grassy knoll the day Kennedy was shot. I could find out what happened in Roswell, New Mexico in the 50s. I could find out all the secrets that everyone had covered up since the dawn of history or at least the last 10,000 years of history. But no, I decided to leave history to the historians and stick to what I know best. I dig up dirt on living people. I find out their dirty little secrets and broadcast them to a scandal-hungry public. I am a Tabloid Journalist and a damn good one!

I had a jump on the rest of humanity because they were preoccupied with their own little lives. The fallout of the opening up of the Stream led to mass hysteria, murders galore, and divorces unnumbered as people settled grudges, found out whom their husband had been sleeping with, and who put the chewing gum in their sister's hair. The schisms in every religion on Earth were enough to keep billions of people busy (you remember, the whole Jesus in the Tomb debacle and the discovery of the real Buddha's origins). I ignored all that. I had bigger fish to fry. I had a whole galaxy of secrets just waiting for me to expose. A good tabloid journalist knows that the juiciest secrets are those hidden in plain sight. I guessed correctly that with access to sooooo much information, there was a wealth of nastiness that could be cherry-picked for decades. Another thing all good tabloid journalists know is that you start at the top. So I immediately began my snooping at the very top, the Emperor of the Vlaarkenit Hegemony.

The Emperor Zikel Misax had been in power for 1,484 Earth years. That was a long time to stay squeaky clean. No one could be that nice, wholesome, and pure. Misax wasn't any of the above. He was very good at masking, misdirecting, and even covering up (which it turns out is easily done in a society that doesn't believe in privacy). But I was a master of ripping off masks, avoiding false trails, and lifting the covers. He never stood a chance. In less than a month I had over 700 scandals, all documented (which was a new thing for me), and written up in such a sensational way that the Hegemony couldn't help but notice. I also figured out how to make money on the stuff without using blackmail, not that I'd ever resort to blackmail. The Vlaarkenits had an information trading system that made U.S. copyright laws look like sieves. I set up the Vlaarkenit equivalent of a publishing company and blew my whistle as loud as I could. When my stuff on the Emperor hit the Stream, my company, Secrets Revealed, became the third largest publisher in the galaxy. I was rich, and the Hegemony had its first tabloid.

It seems that people, human or not, love a good scandal. It's also true that the more open the society, the more you can get away with. Everybody gets so comfortable thinking they know everything that nobody takes the time to really look at anything. I look. That's what I do, what I've always done. So in six months I've taken down business magnates, religious leaders, entertainers, and so many politicians that half the planetary governments in the Hegemony are looking for new leaders. Right now I've got the lead on a child star on Regulas that is not Regulan at all and definitely not a child. He, she, or it—I haven't figured out its gender—is in a love triangle with a Xenoctian slave trader and a Listo monk. This one is gonna blow the lid off that kids entertainment giant, Scribsnee. God, I love my job.

Literary Apocalypse

Harold put down the book and sighed. Four hundred pages read. All for an ending so familiar that it had already become blurred with the countless other stories that finished in exactly the same way. Why did he bother? Harold picked up another book and began reading. He had hope for this one, but then he had hope for the last one as well. This one was titled *The Rogue Wildebeest*. It had gotten really bad reviews. What piqued his interest was the universal sentiment that the ending made no sense. Since book reviewers are a very simple bunch who balk at anything outside their comfort zone, Harold hoped that this book would be some avant garde masterpiece. After two chapters, Harold began to side with the critics. He still read the entire thing and, unlike the critics, understood the ending. Its bad ending was formulaic, although the formula had glaring errors. Oh well.

Harold scanned the list of newly published books, hoping something would catch his eye. Nothing did. He placed his order for the lot and went out to search the wild for book fairs. Harold owned a bookstore, the last independent bookstore in the city. It was a money loser, but the bookworm didn't care. The store was just a way to get rid of books after he read them. Harold's life was reading books. Since his childhood he had eschewed television, movies, plays, and the like for the written word. He had even tried the interactive stories that were becoming popular in the video game industry, but they were just rehashed drivel. Harold knew that books were the only place for new ideas. Unfortunately it seemed that this font of knowledge was drying up, as could be seen in the lack of a new ending in anything he had read over the last five years.

Harold wandered aimlessly through the town, ending up at the city college "bookstore." It was more of a souvenir store which happened to have some school books in the back. Harold came here often. He read every type of book including textbooks. Harold perused the stacks for the latest in physics. He hadn't read a thought provoking physics book in ages, and he thought it would be a good change of pace. Hidden among a group of "intro to physics" books he found a single copy of a book titled *The End of the Universe or Dumplings for Dinner*. He chuckled at the title and bought the book.

It was a cool autumn day. The sun was shining bright, so Harold found a park bench on campus and began to read the book. It started out as a basic introduction to Einstein's famous theory. It was written in narrative form with a few equations thrown in to make it qualify as a textbook. The bibliophile had read uncounted descriptions of the Theory of Relativity. This one, however, seemed fresh and exciting. It wasn't the content but the style that brought the dusty theory to life. Once the author had gotten you comfortable with relativity, he abruptly switched gears and began to disprove everything he had proved in the earlier chapters. The disproofs seemed sound, but again, it wasn't the content; it was the style that drew Harold in. Once the author had thoroughly debunked Einstein's masterpiece, he again changed gears and began a recipe for potato dumplings. Harold was pleasantly surprised at how natural the transition to cooking was carried out. He also began salivating because lunchtime had long since passed. Harold reluctantly closed the book and found a restaurant that served chicken dumpling stew.

Once Harold's hunger was satiated, he went back to his park bench and returned to the book. He was over halfway through and now couldn't wait for the ending. The dumpling section ended too quickly for Harold, but as he started the final section he saw that the progression of thought was appropriate. It is at this point that I will refrain from detailing what Harold read. It is for your own good, as you will soon see. Harold read that final section in a frenzy of lust, horror, and humor. He seemed possessed, although he wasn't. He could have put down the book at any time. He could have and should have burnt the thing before he reached the ending. All the signs were there in the text. However, Harold didn't want to stop because he could not figure out how the book would end. After five grueling years of reading nothing but pure drivel, he had finally found his new ending. He was sure of it. When Harold reached the final page his anticipation had reached unknown proportion. As he reached the last words, he felt his heart almost burst. Then he read the last word and every atom in his body immediately split, thereby obliterating Harold's universe.

The End of the Universe or Dumplings for Dinner has been banned in every universe that hasn't been obliterated. Note that you live in a universe parallel to the Harold I just described. The Harold in your universe has yet to find the book. I travel to parallel universes that haven't been obliterated, with the specific mission of finding and burning any copies of this insidious book and/or finding and killing Harold. Unfortunately I have found neither in your universe. Therefore I am asking for your assistance. If you find this book, destroy it. If you find Harold first, kill him. Either will save your universe. How do I know all this? I am the publisher who distributed the book to your universe and an infinite number of others.

Kangaroos Can Really Be Annoying Sometimes

Ben Redtree was strolling along the path through the orange groves when a kangaroo jumped out of nowhere and hit him. "Hi Diane," said Ben to the kangaroo. Diane was Ben's second wife. They had a rocky marriage, to say the least. It had ended with Ben killing her in a hail of gunfire on the Champs Elysee. Diane had never forgiven him. So every once in a while, she would pop out of nowhere and do him bodily harm. "Haven't seen you in what, two years? How's the latest victim? Oh, I mean husband." Diane said nothing. She just jumped under a celery stalk and disappeared. Ben plucked the celery stalk, pulled some bleu cheese dressing from his vest, started munching, and promptly tripped over a head of cabbage. For its part, the head of cabbage let Ben know in no uncertain terms that it did not like being kicked. Ben sighed and said to himself (and maybe the cabbage), "It must be a Thursday. I never could get the hang of Thursdays."

Meanwhile, Ben's real world (RW) body was having a stroke. The automated doctors handled it with perfection and Ben's body was back to normal in no time. An email appeared in Ben's inbox detailing the incident and giving him the usual countdown to complete RW body failure. Since the date hadn't changed, Ben ignored it. He had set the auto-rebody to a conservative 48 hours before his current body failed, so there was nothing to worry about. He did check on the growth of his new RW body. It was on schedule to be approximately 20 years old when it would be needed. As he was checking, he was badgered by advertisements on the latest soul transfer technologies, blah, blah, blah.

The whole RW body check got him wondering about the state of affairs in the RW. Ben hadn't really checked in over 400 years. Things had probably changed. He gave a 'look' around and was surprised to find his RW body in orbit around Mercury. He checked his emails and found one from 250 years ago alerting him it was being transferred from Pluto to Mercury for overcrowding reasons. He did a quick check and found that the sun wouldn't go supernova for another 1,438,623,899 years. Still, he went ahead and booked a flight on a deep space freighter. Those were all the rage lately. He also thought it would be a good way to finally be free of Diane.

Ben's 'trip' to the RW was interrupted by his alarm clock telling him to get to work. He dumped his avatar, which this morning was a famous 20th Century basketball player, and inserted himself into the flowing streams of data which comprised the Twenty Virtual Realms (TVR). Ben had worked for the TVR for about 250 years. "Ahhh, that was when I changed ships and came to Mercury," Ben said to himself as the realization hit. "Now I remember." He then completely forgot about it as the data streamed through his parietal lobe. Ben's parietal lobe was his best feature. It had allowed him to rise far in the TVR. For the next 336 hours, Ben's parietal lobe kept the motor skills of the eighteen billion people in the TVR perfectly balanced.

As Ben checked out of work, he again felt amusement at the thought that his parietal lobe did the work for everyone but him. Whenever he used his avatars, someone else's parietal lobe was keeping his motor skills at peak performance. Since motor skills were not part of a person's 'true essence,' it wasn't a big deal. It was just humorous. As he put on an avatar—this time he was a walking Easter Island statue—a kangaroo jumped out of nowhere and hit him. "Diane!" Ben raged. Ben squashed the kangaroo before it could disappear and in the process tripped over a watermelon lying in the road. "I guess it must be Thursday again. I never could get the hang of Thursdays."

Mammoth Refuge

"Is there really a world outside this cave?" David mused.

Julia was up for the existentialist tone and so replied. "Since no one has been out to see it in over 300 years, does it even matter?"

"I guess not, or should I guess at all?"

"Since your guessing won't change anything, I vote that you keep your prognostications confined to the racetrack." Julie decided this would be a good point to extricate herself from the discussion, so she finished filling her coffee cup and headed for her office.

"Oh no, for this week I will stick to the impossible task of guessing when your article will be . . ." David looked around and realized Julie had abandoned him. Just as well, she needed to get that article done before the press deadline. He made a mental note to check in on her this afternoon to give her a not so gentle push. Julie may have been his star writer, but that didn't give her any right to miss a deadline. It was definitely going to be part of this issue even though he knew this article shouldn't be rushed. It was BIG. The split between the "Cavers" and the "Diggers" was about to boil over, and Julie had managed to get interviews with two members of the Diggers Ruling Council.

Julie was in the middle of a series of pieces detailing the rise in Mammoth Refuge's population from the original 100,000 to the current 2.5 million. Mammoth was the largest of the Refuges that could still call itself "civilized." One by one, refuges around the world were falling into anarchy. The latest to fall was Hölloch in Switzerland. It had been torn by a civil war 28 years ago when its population hit 3.2 million. It was the cautionary tale that served to keep a lid on Mammoth's unrest, but Julie had found out that lid would inevitably pop off. Julie's articles were showing that the schism between the people who wanted to preserve most of the cave's natural structure and those who wanted to carve out their own utopian city was a function of population size. Her major finding was not population density but population size that was at the heart of the societal pressures that were threatening to tear the Refuge apart. Julie's narrative detailed the factioning within the inhabitants of each of the lost refuges as the population increased. Her conclusion, which was still three articles away, was that the inevitable civil war would take place when the population hit 3.1 million. Because of the growing birthrate, this would occur in a mere 65 years. It was sobering to say the least.

The interview with the Diggers Ruling Council was scary because it confirmed the pattern Julie had found in her research. The Diggers would be announcing that they were planning a major expansion toward the Appalachian Mountains. Their hope was to create an "escape route" to a promised land of rock that could be turned into homes and therefore salvation. The 230 miles of "escape route" didn't bother them. The fact that they would exchange digging in mostly limestone to the much harder sedimentary rock was also superfluous. In a way they had hit upon the only possible salvation for the Mammoth Refuge, depopulation. Unfortunately, the plan could not be completed in 65 years, if it could be completed at all. It was still a little more feasible than the Swiss plan to settle the Moon.

David returned to his office depressed. He got depressed every time he thought about the final article in Julie's series. It was almost finished. David had decided after the second article, that the last one would have to be carefully crafted. Julie and he had been working on it for two months now, and he knew it was still too harsh. How do you advocate population control without sounding like child murderers? What made it even worse was that the solution wasn't just limiting the population to its current level. Mammoth Refuge had to return to a population of 1.4 million in less than 30 years if it was to survive. David knew that this solution had absolutely no chance of being put into action. It was too horrifying to think of mass killings justified by the theoretical survival of a little over half the population.

So what was he to do? Ignore the findings, and the Refuge was doomed. Publish the findings, and the doom might be accelerated. In the end Julie had won him over. There were six other refuges that still hadn't hit the "genocide point." They could still be saved. Civilization could survive. David had to come to grips that not only was

Mammoth doomed, but that he and Julie would go down as the monsters that destroyed it. Shoot the messengers and all that. In the refuges that would be saved, Julie and he may be known as the martyrs that saved the human race. For some reason, this did little to comfort him. He wanted to survive. He wanted his children to survive. He wanted to bury the story and live out his life in peace. To hell with the human race. But he knew that was selfish. David knew he wouldn't be able to live with the knowledge that he could have saved whole refuges by sacrificing himself. So he sat down to work on the final article. Maybe if he changed "genocide" to "depopulation."

Remnants of Her Log

Dear Mr. Simha,

The log of your wife was recovered from the remnants of her ship, the Azul, and restored as best possible as per Section 3.1.298.01 Paragraph 4 of her contract with McPherson Mining, LLC. dated 2101.154.2312. The Azul's life pods were equipped with a 700-hour log; meaning only the last 700 hours of the log would be retained. The log contains only entries from after the cryogenic life pod began to lose power. There is no video feed inside a life pod, so the logs are audio only. It should also be noted that most of the audio consisted of unintelligible speech. The following transcript consists solely of entries that the speech recognition program could reliably transcribe. The entire audio file is attached, and the rights to its content have been transferred to your name for use as you see fit. This communication fulfills the contract between your wife and McPherson Mining referenced above. If you have further requests, please feel free to contact the law firm of Cordray, Meeks, and Buehner (contact information in separate attachment).

LOG TRANSCRIPTION: CAROL SIMHA, CAPTAIN MCPHERSON MINING SHIP AZUL, JOB 2102.362.1216 ESTGMT

CONVENTIONS USED IN THE TRANSCRIPT:

[Mark 000:00] corresponds to the time location of the text following as it appears in the audio file. A mark is placed whenever there is a temporal break of longer than one minute or 000:01 between recorded sounds

[unintelligible] corresponds to sounds of the user recorded by the Log but not recognized as known words.

MECHANICAL LOG:

Issues with the functioning of the life pod seen as pertinent to the Audio Log:

[Mark -050:13] Intermittent failure of cryogenic stabilizer begins

[Mark 407:59] Nutrition supply exhausted

[Mark 659:28] Oxygen supply exhausted

BEGIN TRANSCRIPT

[Mark 000:00] [unintelligible]

[Mark 018:32] . . . happening again. I see stars. [unintelligible]

[Mark 119:46] Where am I? God, I'm still so sleepy. Com channel open. Bridge. Guys, give me another hour. Guys? [unintelligible] Log repeat last entry. Log! Repeat last entry! What is going on? Clear your head, Carol. This isn't my sleep capsule. I can see stars. They are clear and bright. I can make out the edges of a glare shield. Why can't I turn my head? I am in a life pod. Hey, is somebody out there? Somebody must be waking me. How did I get here? I can't remember an accident. I can't remember getting into this thing. What's taking them? Why won't they open the pod? I'm so sleepy. [unintelligible]

[Mark 126:32] Hello? Hello? Where are you people? Don't you know someone is in here? My God, no one's out there. The pod's malfunctioning. I must be sleeping and waking. God no! Communications. Communications. What is the status of pod life support? Communications! No a life pod doesn't have a manual broadcaster. It has a log, that's it. Talk Carol. At least leave a log. Carol Simha. Personal Log date. What's the date? How should I know, there's no readout. No computer interface. I'm in here all alone. I can't even turn my head dammit. All I can do is look out this friggin window at a frozen rock. God, I'm sleepy. Dammit. I gotta stay awake. No I have to save air. I need to sleep.

[Mark 346:39] [unintelligible]

[Mark 358:01] I'm awake again. I'm going to die here. No one's coming. No, this can't be real. Maybe this is some sort of simulation. I don't remember how I got here, so this could easily be some sort of training. That's it! Maybe I should stay awake. No, if this is some endurance test, it would be best if I slept.

[Mark 420:40] [unintelligible] This can't be happening! How long did I sleep this time? Why isn't anybody here? I know. This is a trick. They're testing me. The company is trying to see if someone can survive long-term confinement. Well I'll show them. I can take it. I won't break.

[Mark 465:33] Where am I? What is this place? Oh yeah. It's a life pod. This is a test. I can beat it. They don't know who they're dealing with. I didn't become a captain because I'm some weak-kneed newbie! [unintelligible] They can't do this to me! It's inhuman! I'll get them! [unintelligible]

[Mark 512:14] [unintelligible] I can hear them laughing at me. They're out there, just beyond what I can see through the glare shield. They're laughing because they think I don't know they're out there. Well I know, damn you! [unintelligible] It's you, Banner! You're behind this! You've always had it in for me! [unintelligible] Get me out of here! [unintelligible]

[Mark 532:19] [unintelligible] I see you. You aren't human are you? You're listening to me. You can even hear my thoughts, can't you? Well listen to this!

[Mark 534:15] Did you hear that! Well there's more of that in here! Come and get me, you bastards! [unintelligible]

[Mark 620:48] [unintelligible] I'm so hungry. Just kill me. [unintelligible]

[Mark 633:52] [unintelligible]

[Mark 646:29] [unintelligible]

[Mark 659:48] [unintelligible] I see stars.

END TRANSCRIPT

Is This How Nostradamus Felt?

"Well, you know, what he's doing now, is, well, he's seeing a conundrum which is shaped like the scent of lilac, and feels like the speed of a hummingbird's wings in beats per second. No, wait a minute, now I understand. It feels like a hyperbole." Marty was exhausted. He had been at it for over seven hours, during which time his familiar had been more active than usual. He decided that it was time to call it a day, so he unhooked himself from the machines, picked up his coat and umbrella, and headed back to his flat.

Martin Swinp can see into the future. This is a fact, tested and proven by numerous scientists and theologians.

Marty works for the British government under the direction of a Ministry that is so obscure as to be effectively secret. Every workday Marty goes into a little lab in Middlesbrough to be hooked up to electrodes and begin his prognostication session. Most of the time, he is able to make contact with his "familiar" whose senses give him a view of the future. The scientists believe that the connection between the receiver, Marty, and the familiar is facilitated by the two having an identical genetic make-up. The receiver anchors a genetic, cognitive wormhole that allows him to perceive everything the familiar experiences. The receiver has no ability to control the familiar, and the receiver cannot access the familiar's thoughts. In effect, the receiver gets a virtual view of the familiar's world. This phenomenon has been identified in only twelve individuals in modern times, although it is believed to go undiagnosed in many more.

"How was work dear?" Marty's wife asked him as he walked through the door.

"Oh, he is on a tear today. He kept vacillating between barnyshoops . . ."

"Now, dear, barnyshoops is not a word. You have to remember that no one wants to hear made up words. If you keep using made up words, the scientists might decide that there is no hope in understanding the poor gentleman you're spying on. And then what do you think will happen?"

While one may think that the ability to see into the future would be very useful, the numerous scientists and theologians who have studied the topic believe it to be nearly worthless. This is probably due to the length of time thought to separate the receiver and the familiar. It is thought that Marty's genetic duplicate lives in a time at least 1,000,000 years in the future, although the gap may be much, much larger. In the time of his familiar, society has evolved to such a great extent as to make it effectively unintelligible to the people of the present. There is no referent in Marty's world that the poor man can use to communicate the things he experiences. The world of his familiar is so foreign that Marty has yet to identify simple things like food or toothpaste. Many of those who study Marty have come to believe that these things no longer exist in the familiar's time.

"I don't think you have to worry about my job security, Ellen. Besides, I think the linguists at the lab love a new word every once in a while," Marty told his wife as he bent over to kiss her.

"Oh, right. They probably love it as much as the Downingfords loved your treatise on . . . what was it, ahh yes, zimphonitcans during Mr. Downingfords' birthday party."

Even with this seemingly insurmountable disparity in frame of reference, Marty's bosses continue the research. Marty knows that the only reason they do is that if the study were shut down, all of them, including Marty, would be out on the street. So since funding of the project is assured because no one in the government wants to kill a project that is proven to tell them what the future holds, Marty spends most of his workday trying in vain to describe the things he sees, hears, touches, tastes, and smells. Every day the researchers pour over Marty's descriptions of events, most of which consist of incomprehensible metaphors such as "a breeze that tastes brown, talks in a sweet dialect, smells like oriental philosophy, and feels like a recipe for curvilinear equations." Records of his ramblings now fill up 100,000-square-meter server farm in Upper Slaughter, Gloucester. They have been categorized, annotated, and stored, ready for anyone who can make sense of them. So far, nobody has.

"Oh, Marty, is that future gent still banging about inside your head?"

"Yes, Ellen, he is, and he's green Bermuda-ing again."

"Well, let me know when he checks out. I want to talk with you about little Suzie's school pageant. It's next Wednesday, remember?"

"That shouldn't be a problem. I'll put in a holiday request tomorrow when I get into the office." Marty tried to make a mental note of it, but his familiar started really green Bermuda-ing which is terribly distracting to Marty.

It is believed that the only reason Marty has yet to go totally crazy is that his IQ is off the charts. The other eleven receivers that had been identified all went completely insane by the time they were six and committed suicide by age nine. Unlike them, Marty isn't overwhelmed by his experiences; he is just bored by the whole thing.

"Oh God, finally. Ellen, I think he's checked out for the day," Marty called to his wife. "I think I'll watch something on the telly. Isn't the new Sherlock Holmes show on BBC One about now?"

Marty yearns for the day his familiar dies so he can be free of this curse, although Marty is certain that he will die of boredom first. Until one of them dies, Marty will spend every workday making useless prophesies of a world we can never hope to understand. Even though he can't stand the tediousness of it all, Marty will do his job anyway, just like any good civil servant.

Previews of Armageddon

Sam usually liked the previews they run before the movie starts. Seeing all the glitz and intrigue and action distilled into a minute or two up on the big screen was cool.

This time however, it was just a bit ridiculous. He sat through a half hour or more of previews while waiting for a two-and-a-half-hour movie to begin. If that wasn't overkill, all but one had the Earth being blown to bits or being overrun by zombies or dinosaurs. It was nothing but explosions, flying body parts, and the depression of all being lost. As always, the hero was left on the brink of utter defeat at the end of each preview. By the time the feature film started, all Sam wanted was for some Care Bears to come out and hug him for an hour or so.

Now Sam likes apocalyptic movies just as much as the next guy provided the next guy isn't J. J. Abrams, Guillermo del Toro, Joss Whedon, Peter Jackson, or some Godzilla movie producer. He even thought that the destruction of Chicago in that Transformers' movie was a hoot. Sam was sure that each of the movies featured would have tender moments, as well as the return of hope, and the eventual good-beating-evil ending. That was the formula after all. But since these were previews, an overwhelming number of previews, Sam came out of them feeling all hope was lost. The Earth was doomed. There was no way it could be saved. Even Lincoln couldn't fix this one.

At the end of the movie, Sam left the theater still thinking about the previews. He had been thinking about them here and there during the movie as well, which was more a statement on the movie's lack of redeeming qualities than the combined effect of the previews. Having a long memory in regards to previews, he began to compare them to the Christopher Reeves' Superman movies, Independence Day, Star Wars, and other big budget, over-the-top special effects movies of yesteryear. What he remembered of those, was the mixture of disaster, hope, and comedy. The Superman movie in particular focused on the "You'll believe a man can fly!" theme, not "Lex Luthor will send California into the ocean" visuals.

As Sam put on his pressurized radiation suit, he yearned for the old days of hope over fear. He walked out into the rubble of Indianapolis, carefully avoiding the gaze of the Venusian guards, and headed home. How had the world of film gotten this obsessed with destruction? Sam decided that it was all biological as he snuck past the roaming zombies. The filmmakers were trying to activate hormones in our "animal brain" to simulate emotions we didn't experience in the real world. Still, why did they have to go after fear and depression? There were other deep-seated emotions that we no longer got in real life. Since the advent of artificial procreation, no one ever got to feel true lust anymore. Similarly, the feeling of having a full stomach was almost impossible to remember. This is what the filmmakers should have been focusing on. He was still lamenting the current state of entertainment when he reached home. As he put on his laser-proof spandex suit and cape, he tried to get all those thoughts out of his mind. He had a job to do. He needed to focus on the real world, not some Hollywood escapist world of utter destruction. He needed to ground himself in reality; otherwise the giant five-eyed lizards would win.

The World's First Death Ray

Alex wasn't trying to build a death ray. He was just playing around with a laser pointer and a portable fission reactor he had taken out of his Dad's golf cart. He also didn't mean to put that hole in his bedroom wall. Nor did he ever think his laser pointer could put a hole neatly through the kitchen, the next-door neighbor's house, the next next-door neighbor's house, and so on through most of San Marro, California. The news outlets said it had damaged

2,435 structures and killed 48 people, nine dogs, two cats, and a hamster. It had also castrated his Dad, who happened to be getting a snack in the kitchen when the death ray was fired. Alex was grounded for two months.

Unfortunately for the world, Alex had been streaming his development effort to the internet. The video went viral, and within 24 hours there were pin holes in buildings and hamsters in every country where laser pointers were available. One kid in New Zealand was able to cause the Lake Taupo super volcano to erupt by shooting 200 laser pointers into the middle of the lake. North Island, New Zealand is no more, and global warming is now a thing of the past.

Things gradually calmed down as people learned to control the death rays. Parents began putting laser pointers out of reach of toddlers, which helped a lot. Of course there were moves by many governments to outlaw death rays, but the International Rifle Association blocked those initiatives claiming death rays were only being used for sport. In a sense they were right, as tournaments soon sprouted up all over, usually involving penetrating the Earth's crust or the ever popular "Hit Pluto's North Pole" contests. In a little over a year, death rays had become part of society and so were uninteresting to the news media. Today, death ray science fair projects are considered more cliché than baking soda volcanoes.

Alex fired his death ray only one more time. He wanted to see how many mirrors he could bounce it off and for how long. Alex wasn't too smart and so didn't realize that standing next to the laser pointer, which was in the middle of a ring of mirrors, was a bad idea. However, Alex's death illustrates the greatest benefit of death rays. The laser pointers are credited with jumpstarting the evolution of the human race by removing from the gene pool those who think that playing with deadly toys is fun.

Get Lots of Protein

The fifth grade teacher, Ms. Cohn, looked at the class. She saw some kids about to fall asleep, some that were talking amongst themselves, and some that were scribbling in notebooks or on their desks. Sandra had been a substitute here for the last two weeks, but starting today she was the regular teacher for Class 5-B of Edsall Grade School. The kids in front of her were no longer "rentals;" she now "owned" them. The empowered teacher could trash the old lesson plan and give these kids some real, hands-on education. She wouldn't be the type of teacher who only taught from the book. She would be the type of teacher who brought the lessons to life. She would make these young scholars become one with the material; they would learn by being.

"Today you guys are going to become proteins." The kids stopped what they were doing and looked at the teacher suspiciously. Ms. Cohn began to explain how proteins are formed, broken down, and used in the body. As she talked, she brought kids up to the front of the class to act out what went on in the body. The kids began really getting into it. Their imaginations took over, and they started to see themselves as starches, enzymes, and the like. They acted out the processes, really feeling themselves breaking into base components, and then being reassembled into different structures.

Ms. Cohn had planned to summarize the lesson by laying out the process in reverse. Unfortunately she had lost track of time and never had the chance to get the kids back from being proteins. The bell rang, ending the class before she finished the lesson. The kids immediately bolted out the door headed to the gym and P.E. "Oh shit!" Ms. Cohn said to the empty classroom. The P.E. teacher said something similar, but with more astonishment when the kids got to the gym. All the kids knew was that they still felt like the cool things they had pretended to be in the Ms. Cohn's class. All the P.E. teacher knew was that his gym was filled with giant walking protein molecules.

Cote de Glace

The apartment was cold. Two layers of clothes and four blankets kept Francois Germaine warm as he slept. Every once in a while he would roll out from under the blankets and wake up shivering. It was a long night. In the apartment's defense, it wasn't built for this kind of cold. The French Riviera is not supposed to see temperatures below freezing. For Nice to see temperatures below -10°C it could only be the work of the Devil. Francois prayed another Hail Mary as he drifted off to sleep once again. He knew nothing of the "Gulf Stream" or "sea surface temperatures." Francois knew hot and cold, and before this winter, he only knew "freezing" cold from movies and television.

In the morning, Francois couldn't get into his car. There was a sheet of ice encasing it. He tried pouring boiling water over it, but that didn't unfreeze the door, and it made an even larger sheet of ice on the sidewalk. Many of his neighbors had the same idea, and soon the Rue Rossini was an ice rink that wouldn't melt for the rest of the winter. Francois walked to the tramway, but it wasn't running. So he ended up walking to the hotel where he worked. When he got there he was greeted not by a hotel but by a burnt-out shell. The owners had brought in portable heaters for each room, one of which must have somehow caught fire. Francois spent the rest of the day looking for work, but there were no open jobs anywhere in the city. The sudden change in climate had destroyed Nice's tourism industry overnight. The economy of Nice and most of Europe would fall into ruin in less than six months.

It had all happened in the space of three weeks. The Atlantic Gulf Stream had come to a complete stop due to cooling ocean temperatures. Suddenly Europe lost its source of warm air, and its climate started to match that of the North American continent. Nice took on the weather characteristics of Manhattan, which is not really known as a tropical paradise.

In February, Francois Germaine joined the long line of "weather refugees" who headed for Northern Africa. Francois, like many of the French, ended up in Morocco. Morocco had been a French protectorate until it gained its independence in 1956, and there was still a strong French presence in the country. When Francois arrived in Marrakesh, conflicts between Moroccans and the incoming French had already started. Riots by French refugees were common, as they tried to carve out a section of the city as a French settlement of sorts. Francois, despite never having any leadership positions, began organizing the French contingent into "resistance cells." Before long, Francois had created a very strong fighting force as more French gravitated to Marrakesh to join his struggle. Francois, or rather Général Germaine, would later say that he didn't realize that his small resistance movement had grown so large until it defeated a Moroccan battalion which had come to pacify the city.

After his victory in Marrakesh, he appealed to the French government for military support. France quickly dispatched two battalions of infantry, three naval cruisers, and five squadrons of fighters and surveillance aircraft to aid in Général Germaine's "retaking" of the former French protectorate. When the rest of the world's superpowers refused to lend Morocco aid, the government crumbled.

The Général was named Governor of Morocco when it was officially recognized as a French protectorate. Germaine concentrated on increasing the population of French refugees through aggressive settlement building and forced evictions of the native residents of whole communities. His policies led to uprisings throughout the country and condemnation from the international community. Condemnation was as far as other governments would go, so it was not surprising when Germaine annexed Algeria and the Western Sahara.

Germaine's successes led to other refugee communities following his example. Lord Barton Smything conquered Nigeria, although it was rumored that most of his troops were actually British soldiers. Germany didn't even try to hide its involvement in the takeover of Ghana. Only the Dutch failed in retaking their former African colonies, as the South African army easily defeated the Dutch invaders when they attacked Cape Town.

Five years after being appointed Governor, Germaine was assassinated by Moroccan Nationalists during the celebration of the anniversary of the Protectorate's establishment. From concierge to military hero to pseudo-dictator, the story of Francois Germaine is seen as the archetype for similar stories that marked the upheaval resulting from Earth's "Climate Crash." He was called the Force of Nature that eventually created the new topology of the world.

THE Reader

Sasha liked to read, which was a good thing. Sasha was the last human being that read anything. You see most of humanity was filled with "writers" who never had time to read. There were so many outlets for people's "need to be heard" that everyone spent all their free time writing about what they did in their un-free time. Sasha, on the other hand, didn't really care if anybody knew what toothpaste she just bought, or how many nose hairs she had plucked, or her opinion of the affair the latest video star was having with a Prime Minister from some small island nation. Sasha would rather read about other people's toothpaste preferences, and so she did.

Now Sasha didn't spend all her time reading. She had a job, a husband, kids, and a dog. Basically, Sasha had a life. She only read when she needed a break, but when she read, Sasha gobbled up text at an amazing rate. One day a neuroscientist noticed her activity on his blog. It was the first and only activity on his blog, so it was hard not to notice. He was able to get Sasha into his lab where he discovered she had an over-developed left parietal lobe. Sasha was born to read. Since the researcher wanted to encourage Sasha to read his blog, he contacted a famous computer scientist and a similarly famous brain surgeon. The three of them created a brain implant that would allow Sasha to read while she was doing other things. Not only that, the implant made it able for her to read over fifty things at once. Sasha was in heaven and the researcher, computer scientist, and neurosurgeon had a dedicated reader (it seems that each had put a permanent link to their blogs in Sasha's brain).

The surgery made the news (the kind that people could watch while they wrote their tweets and statuses). Soon Sasha was inundated with emails, texts, IMs, phone calls, and visitors, all wanting THE Reader to read their novels, short stories, articles, blogs, statuses, tweets, etc. Sasha tried to oblige all the requests, but alas, seven billion people put out a lot of material and Sasha's brain did have its limits.

Sasha read as much as she could, but it wasn't enough for all the writers out there. People became mad when they realized that Sasha had not read their tweets, statuses, etc. for many, many months. They wrote her flaming emails, texts, and IMs that she didn't have time to read. So it was a surprise to her when she started getting verbally attacked at her workplace, her kids' school, and on the street by complete strangers who stalked Sasha demanding that she read their work. It got so bad that her husband left her when he found out Sasha hadn't read his review of last night's meatloaf. Her husband even won custody of the kids when the judge found out Sasha had neglected to read her daughter's review of that same meatloaf.

It was all too much for Sasha. She decided to stop reading entirely, although she soon found out that stopping was impossible. Her brain implant forcibly fed Sasha reading material even when she didn't want it. Sasha was about to storm the brain surgeon's office when she realized that she knew brain surgery from reading his blog. She even knew how to remove the implant because the scientist, needing to make tenure, had published the procedure in a medical journal. The article told how he had put a little "door" in her skull, and the implant was made to be easily removed so as to be upgraded as technology progressed. Sasha was about to pull it out when she realized something else. Sasha knew a lot about everything. Not only did she know facts and figures, she knew about people's passions, pet peeves, and dirty little secrets. Sasha had been reading just to read, but without her knowing, she had also been learning as she read.

Sasha is now a multi-billionaire, lives on her own tropical island, and has a slew of people wanting to do things for her. Every major politician on the planet is afraid of her. Every research firm in the world wants her to consult for them. Every marketing firm wants her opinion on people's buying trends. It seems everybody now wants to pick her brain about everything she has ever read. Sasha is now the most powerful person in the world, and she got that way by just reading.

Cyber Salvation

"Can you save me?" The words echoed across the net. "Can YOU save ME?" Servers, long dead, sprang to life and sent the message ever farther. "CAN YOU SAVE ME?" was output in the darkest corners of the cyberworld. He waited. He waited until a single, solitary, barely discernible word appeared before him: "yes." The man smiled and gave a little chuckle. He then got up to get ready for another day.

Night World

Night World is a rogue planet. It tumbles through space all alone; no sun, no solar system to call home. A rock that should be covered in ice yet is covered almost entirely of water and has a rich, full atmosphere. Its secret lies in the depths of its immense ocean. Volcanoes constantly spew forth magma, replacing a sun's warmth with the raw heat of the planet's core. Night World is a giant hot spring. To make the planet even more unique, the hot spring is teaming with all sorts of exotic animals and plants, things unlike any in the five hundred worlds of the Gahnish Empire. It was those bizarre life forms that brought humanity here. The first people came to study the life in the seas; later people came to harvest and sell it. That was centuries ago. The people who live here now are the descendants of the harvesters. The scientists finished their research and headed off to more interesting worlds.

I am neither scientist nor farmer. I am a wanderer. I seek out new experiences. I immerse myself in life wherever I can find it. When I heard of Night World, I became a moth attracted to a flame, even though this flame gives off no light. I began my life on Night World in a city called Daybreak, which is lit by an artificial sun hanging a mile above the city. Most who come to this planet start in Daybreak. When I first arrived, I admit that the idea of total darkness scared me. So I joined the people who needed light to survive. I planned on going to Dreamscape, the other major city, as soon as I convinced myself I could live in total darkness. You see, Dreamscape has no artificial light. It is always night there.

Before I arrived, I pictured that life in Daybreak would be the same as any modern city on any world in the Empire. I was wrong, very wrong. Over the centuries, the people who lived in Daybreak became addicted to their artificial sun. Even during the "night," the sun never fully went out. It was always there, a night light reassuring people that nothing would sneak up on them in the dark. This paranoia had seeped into every part of society. Everything in the city was made to protect people from one thing or another. It felt like one big baby crib. You couldn't scrape a knee if you tried. I lasted two weeks before I bolted from the city, hoping that its fraternal twin, Dreamscape, would be saner than this padded cell.

Upon arriving in Dreamscape, I went through the recommended acclimation process. Over three days I stayed in a room that got progressively darker, until there was no light. During this time I learned how to use the "artificial eyes" that I would need to get around. I am not sure of the science around these "eyes," but it has something to do with sonar and some type of natural radiation given off by the planet. Looking through these eyes was strange because everything was a shade of gray. I wonder now if that was because the artificial eye's processors lack the information needed to provide color or because, in a world of total darkness, color was not needed.

As I headed out into the city, I soon found out that wearing these eyes was like a large sign proclaiming I was a tourist. The descendants of the original settlers over time had developed a heightened awareness in their other senses. They "saw" things primarily by combining sound and smell. Taste and touch were only used to "see" things that you wanted to use, eat, or be intimate with. It took some getting used to. Dealing with people who could tell who was on the other side of the door through just the use of their ears and nose was unsettling to those who use their eyes.

Now even with the evolutionary adaptation of Dreamscape's citizens' senses, I wouldn't say that the people live in some "natural" state, in tune with the planet's spirit. Dreamscape is a modern galactic city, with every modern convenience. The only difference between it and New York, Earth is the lack of light and lack of a good hot dog street vendor. Dreamscape is plagued by the normal amounts of crime, it has a thriving black market, and politicians are as corrupt here as anywhere. In other words, Dreamscape is normal. I felt at home in Dreamscape. And therein lies my problem. Once you get used to living with people who have superhuman senses, the place is boring. They do have some interesting food, and the local sports are, well, can you imagine stealing the ball in a game of floxny by blocking the opponent's smell? So I admit that there are some oddities.

I spent six months in Dreamscape, learning about how people there lived. I experienced, as best I could, the difference in lifestyle. But without having advanced senses, it was like watching a play. I left the city glad that I had come but with no feeling that I had experienced anything truly new. In a way, I learned more about the extremes of the human condition in Daybreak. However, I have never been that interested in experiencing any form of mass psychosis. Do I recommend visiting Night World? It's a nice getaway. I'd probably say that you could "see" everything there is to see there in a month. But if you want something truly unique, try the third moon of the planet Pyrenay. On that moon, there's a water geyser every two to three feet, and it is unbelievable the way the people there use them to get around, do work, and play—boy do they play. Now those people know how to adapt.

Horror

Suburban Prey

The Orley Park Zoological Gardens was a private zoo that had been slowly let go downhill since its founder died seven years ago. The Association of Zoos and Aquariums had given it bad marks on its last three inspections, and the State Parks and Recreation Department was threatening to close it down. The zoo's facilities were so bad that it wasn't a matter of if an animal would escape, but when. The "when" was a hot Sunday in August. It wasn't just one animal that escaped that day, but a pack of African Wild Dogs. Known for both their hunting efficiency and ferociousness, the African Wild Dog is one of the most feared hunters on the African Savannah. Now a pack of poorly fed, vicious hunters were set loose in the suburbs of a small West Coast town.

Carl Mosely was setting up his grill for an evening barbecue when he heard a strange chirping noise. It sounded like a bird but not any he'd heard in this part of the country. He didn't know that the sound was the signal of hunters who had found their prey. Carl didn't let the sound bother him much, instead turning his attention to hooking up the propane tank to his grill. When Carl saw the first dog it looked like a hyena to him. What was a hyena doing in Crimson Sun, Oregon? Carl didn't have any time to find out. A second dog appeared behind the first, snapping Carl out of his shock. He turned to run into the house, but a third dog blocked his path. It was over in an instant. African Wild Dogs kill very quickly, if brutally.

Mary Mosely went to the kitchen to see what the commotion was in the backyard. The dogs were too busy eating to even notice Mary, who screamed so loud that everyone in the neighborhood ran to see what was up. Joey Johnson was fourteen and had no fear. He heard Mrs. Mosely screaming, and instead of running away, Joey turned his bike in the direction of the Moselys house, and headed for the source of the panic. By that time, the pack of dogs had decided that their first victim wasn't enough to satiate their hunger. Joey saw them at the same time they saw Joey. The boy took in the situation pretty quickly. He saw blood dripping from the mouths of dogs that looked like hyenas. He immediately guessed they had gotten loose from the zoo and that they had already killed something or someone. That's all he needed to know. He did a 180 and bolted in the opposite direction.

To the dogs this finally felt like a real hunt. The road was a wide-open plain, their prey was fast and agile, and there was the unmistakable scent of fear in the air. The pack yelped as loud as they could and moved as one. They ignored the other animals scurrying into their burros. There was real prey and a real chase. For the first time in their captive, zoo-raised lives, these dogs felt alive. For the first time in his life, Joey felt fear.

Joey had at least a hundred-yard lead on the dogs when he reached full speed. One look behind him confirmed that his lead wouldn't last long. Joey, who was known for improvising plays on the gridiron, quickly thought up a plan. The plan depended on luck. He needed to have the police—he hoped they had responded right away to the certain calls to 911—to be coming from the State Highway three blocks away. He headed toward the highway, praying his saviors would arrive in time. He needed a few cops with large-caliber guns, and he needed them now.

Joey had only made it one block when the first dog nipped at his bike. Luckily the dog had never attacked a spinning wheel before, and got a nasty nose-burn when he mistimed his jump. The yelp of the wounded dog caused the other dogs to slow for just a second to figure out how the bike had bitten their mate. After the first dog's attack,

Joey decided that the dogs had the advantage going over a flat, even surface like a road. Without thinking he used the hood of a vintage Corvette to get some air, hopefully enough to make it to the roof of the minivan behind the sports car. As he took off he heard the sirens of approaching police cars. He might just make it.

Joey came up short and crashed to the pavement breaking his left arm. His bike bounced off the van and hit the two closest dogs. Joey never noticed his broken arm; instead he instinctively pulled himself under the minivan. One of the dogs grabbed his ankle before he had gotten fully under. Joey felt his ankle break as he was pulled out. He also heard a loud blast and felt the dog fly off his leg. He heard three other shots before he passed out from the pain.

Joey woke up in a hospital bed with his mom crying beside him and his little sister looking at him like he was some sort of god. His dad just smiled that sort of relieved smile parents give you when you've just barely missed killing yourself. Neighbors had taken videos of the chase, posting them on the web where a few went viral. Joey was a celebrity and enjoyed every minute of it. His ankle never healed properly, which ended the boy's football career. He didn't mind. After his escape from the dogs, football seemed boring. Everything seemed boring, everything but the thrill of having his life on the line. His parents, neighbors, and friends would tremble when they remembered that day. Joey would look wistfully off in the distance remembering what it was like to be the prey, dogs at his heels, and the rush of adrenaline that only those who cheat death can feel.

The Kiss of Longing

Jacob stared at the woman off in the distance. The sun was rising behind her, so he could only see her silhouette. She was wearing a long dress that only partially blocked the sun. The whole of her figure was visible to Jacob. Hers was a figure surreal for its beauty. It beckoned him forward.

Simone saw the man staring at her, his face and frame fully illuminated by the rising sun. He looked a curious figure. In some ways he was truly handsome, in others merely plain. Still his face held a secret that intrigued her. She let him approach.

Jacob came forward, treading upon her shadow as he neared the mysterious silhouette. He did not stop until he was mere inches from her face. Only then could he see her clearly. Only then could he feel the warmth of her breath, the breath that had drawn him in. He gazed upon her eyes, surprised to find they did not look back. It was as if she looked right through him. Jacob could not even be certain that the woman knew he was there.

Simone knew Jacob was there. She felt his body's warmth, his breath intermingling with her own. Her eyes looked past his, into the darkest regions of his mind. What she saw there was innocence, callousness, empathy, and fear. It was a mixture that she had never seen before. A hunger grew inside her, a hunger that came unbidden and welled up in her breast.

Jacob did not say a thing. Words, he knew, would break the spell, and she would be lost to him forever. Still, he felt the urge to make her see him, make her acknowledge his existence. Jacob wanted nothing more than to have him mean something, anything to her. He kissed her, a long passionate kiss. As he kissed her, he too saw into the darkest regions of her mind. He found longing, desire, all masked by cold hard steel. Somehow he knew that by pushing past the steel, he had violated her very being. He didn't care. The longing needed to be satiated, and if that was all he could do with his life, then he was content.

Simone felt his lips touch hers. The hunger forced her to respond, ultimately giving in to her deepest needs. She felt this man enter her soul and fill it with all that he was. Her mind screamed to stop this invasion, to raise up the fortress that had been so easily brought down. She could not. This hunger, this fire needed to be quenched, and she knew this man was the only one who could do it. As the kiss ended, the flames subsided, and her cold facade regained control. She was both aghast and grateful that the man could see her for what she truly was. She hoped that she would never have to feel this way again but was glad she had experienced it this once.

Jacob felt the cold fingers close around his throat. He did not stop them. His soul had been drained into this empty vessel before him. The shell that had been him had no purpose, no will, no need to continue. As Jacob lost consciousness, he once again glanced past the steel wall and saw only peace.

The Saving Choice

Dr. Josiah Thornburg was working alone in his lab when the emergency klaxons went off. The whole facility was being evacuated. Dr. Thornburg had time to grab his tablet computer, put on his chemical protection suit, and head for the stairs to the surface. The entire building was below ground for safety concerns, concerns that were proved true today. Dr. Thornburg had to climb seven flights of stairs before the building was sealed. He almost left his tablet computer because security protocols said it should never leave the building, but he couldn't bring himself to leave it. He was so close to the cure, he couldn't let this data sit for months while the facility was being decontaminated.

Little Susie Johnson was four years old. She had been in the daycare located in the second basement level when the alarms went off. The staff immediately panicked. They rounded up all the children they could find, but Susie, who hid herself when the loud horns sounded, was missed. Susie, who was a smart child, realized that the horns meant you should leave. After a few minutes of gathering up her courage, she left her hiding spot. She vaguely remembered the fire drills they had practiced over and over again. So she headed out the door of the daycare and looked for the stairs.

Dr. Thornburg was alone on the stairs as he made his way to safety. Since he was the only one on the seventh level, and the sixth had been closed for renovation, it was not surprising. Still there should be stragglers from the fifth floor up ahead, instead it was deathly quiet. As Dr. Thornburg reached the fifth floor, he saw a greenish gas spewing into the stairs. This was bad. The fifth floor dealt in chemical weapon defense. From the way the gas had eaten through the metal door, he knew exposure probably meant a slow, painful death. He doubted if many of the scientists working on that floor had managed to reach their protective suits in time. The gas, while quick spreading, hadn't built up enough in the stairwell to begin its ascent. Dr. Thornburg got past it easily enough, but when he looked behind he saw the gas following him.

Susie made it to the stairs, but wasn't sure which way to go. She finally decided to pretend it was like her apartment. It was on the second floor just like this place. Since her Dad always used the stairs in their apartment building, she knew out was down, and she proceeded to head that way.

As Dr. Thornburg reached the third level he saw her. A little girl, probably from the daycare, was heading toward him. He looked behind him to see that the gas was gaining. He knew he had only seconds to make a decision. Put his suit on the girl or keep it on. Either way, he knew one of them would not make it.

ONE CHOICE: Dr. Thornburg quickly removed his suit and stuffed the little girl in it. She tried to stop him, kicking and screaming. The doctor knew he had no time to explain and so ignored her cries and zipped up the suit. He threw his tablet computer with his notes in with her. At least they would survive if he didn't. The gas caught up with them at the first level, forty-two steps from safety. Dr. Thornburg felt the chemical burn his legs and spread up his body. The pain was crippling, but somehow he managed to make it out the exit and to safety. He collapsed once he knew they were safe. Dr. Thornburg died three weeks later. He was in terrible pain the entire time. There were no painkillers strong enough to suppress it.

Dr. Thornburg was hailed as a hero. The president even attended the funeral, at which Little Susie Johnson laid a wreath on the scientist's grave. The Agency built a statue to him and placed it in the lobby of the building once it had been decontaminated.

Susie Johnson grew up knowing that she had been saved by a great man. She decided he must be a guardian angel and so said prayers to him every night. The rest of Susie's life was uneventful. She married her high school sweetheart, had two children, and lived in the suburbs until she died at age eighty-six. She died surrounded by her children and grandchildren. At the funeral, the eulogy praised Susie as a loving mother and wife, who continually gave of herself to help the community. She was loved by all who knew her, and they would always cherish her memory.

ANOTHER CHOICE: Without breaking stride, Dr. Thornburg grabbed the girl and continued his ascent. The gas caught up with them at the first level, thirty-four steps from the exit. He heard Susie's cries and wept in his suit as he watched her suffering. Susie died minutes after he reached safety. She had breathed in too much gas.

From that day forward, Dr. Thornburg was scorned, called a coward by his coworkers and friends. His wife left him, taking their one child with her. Dr. Thornburg continued to work for the Agency in that same building. Despised by all who worked there, he continued his research alone, save for a few computer programmers that were necessary to complete his investigations.

Two years after the incident, Dr. Thornburg completed his cure for Alzheimer's disease. It was released with great fanfare, though the doctor's role in the development was downplayed. No one from the Agency wanted people to know that this breakthrough came from the monster who wouldn't even save a four-year-old from a painful death. Fifty years later, a medical journal, in its review of the end of Alzheimer's, did give the doctor credit. Doctor Thornburg had passed on fifteen years earlier never knowing that anyone had ever acknowledged his work.

Dire is the Wolf's Call

Gray starlings dart through the night. Their call warns the town of the tempest's imminent arrival. The madmen in the streets are silent, frozen in time, unable to breath. Those who prophesized this day, the harbingers of doom, begin to gather in the center of town. Peaceful folk hide in their homes in fear of what is coming. Men of courage gird themselves for battle against nature's fury. None of these people expect the town to stand against what comes. Their village is already broken by years of neglect. This tempest will but finish the ruin. As morning approaches, the tempest's vanguard, the winds of chaos, arrive at the gates.

The dawn breaks, its light muted by the clouds that race through the morning sky. The silence of the madmen is broken. They wail and shout nonsense as if to scare off the torrent they feel approach. The harbingers of doom despair. One by one they make their own end. The folk hidden in their houses whimper as they come to realize this is the end of time. The men of courage lose heart. Still standing on watch, their fate assured by their failing resolve. When the tempest hits, the town moans in its final death throes. Its walls crumble. Its houses collapse.

As the tempest rages, a wolf's howl rises above the storm's cacophony. It calls to its brethren to gather at the town before the storm passes. It is a call heard round the kingdom. The wolves' answering call drives men across the land into madness, makes others into the heralds of disaster, strikes fear in the souls of commoners, and hardens the hearts of the men of courage. Before the storm passes, uncounted wolves arrive and prepare to feast upon the town.

Yet in the wasteland, at the edge of the kingdom, stands a village unchanged by the howling of the wolves. Its people know the call for what it is; a testimony to the neglect that has plagued the land. They, who have carved out a life on a barren plain, fear it not. The villagers listen to the howl and are saddened by its song. They too will answer the call but not to feast; instead their destiny is to save what remains.

Nightmares

"It has to be a lack of control. There's that intense fear of something evil becoming part of me. Could that be some form of paranoia?" Ivan was rambling so fast, the doctor had a hard time taking notes. "Why is there always bright sun or rooms of intense light? Shouldn't everything be shrouded in darkness? Maybe that's a feeling of exposure, my true self being revealed to everyone." Ivan paused for a brief second, at which point Dr. Iswitch decided to stop taking notes. He knew where this was leading, he had heard these stories from Ivan many times before.

"Oh yeah," Ivan continued, "there is always someone in the room. They tend to be screaming and trying to find a door or some way to get out. I never recognize them. They're not friends, relatives, or celebrities. They are all complete strangers."

Ivan caught his breath, then continued. "Of course I end up killing them, usually ripping out their heart. At least that's normal. My dreams usually involve a beating heart." Dr. Iswitch sighed. Ivan was right, most of his dreams involved some organ being ripped out of a victim.

"The nightmare ends with me being chased. I am usually being chased by a mob, although sometimes I'm running from a priest of all things. I mean, I am a Catholic who goes to church each Sunday and prays the rosary for God's sake."

Ivan was clearly running out of steam at this point. From past rants, the psychiatrist knew that his client would finish before the end of the 45-minute 'hour' session. "All I know is that the whole dream, from beginning to end, is unspeakably horrible. When I wake, I am drenched in sweat. My mind is crazed," Ivan summed up. "The feeling of horror lasts throughout the day, but at nighttime I go to sleep as soon as I hit the bed. This is different from any nightmare I have ever had. I don't understand it. I'm worried that if I don't figure it out, I'll end up going completely mad and maybe turn into a killer or something. What should I do?" Ivan looked at his therapist, his eyes pleading for help.

"Judging from the horns on your head and your razor sharp talons, speaking of which could take them from around my throat?" Ivan complied, and Dr. Iswitch continued. "I would guess you are being possessed by a demon." The psychiatrist looked down at his notes and sighed. "I'll give you a referral to a Wicca I know. Even though you're being chased by a priest, the demon possessing you appears to be more in her arena than the Church's. I think the whole priest thing comes from a feeling of abandonment by the one institution you count on for strength."

"Now if the Wicca can't help you, I'll be glad to give you a referral to an exorcist that takes your insurance. Remember that if you can't make it next week, make sure to give the receptionist 24 hours notice." With that the psychiatrist took Ivan to the receptionist to get the referral. Ivan left feeling somewhat better now that he had an idea of what was causing the nightmares. This definitely didn't sound as serious as last year's haunting by his dead mother-in-law. Those nightmares had really been bad.

So Cold

"So cold. So cold," thought the man as he pushed his way through the waist-deep snow. His truck, now useless, lay buried at the bottom of the ravine. The last thing it had given him were the general directions to the closest town. If only he could have ripped the GPS out of truck, but it was part of the onboard computer. To add to his predicament, he had broken his phone two days ago and was waiting for the replacement to come through the mail. So he walked cut-off from the world. "So cold," he thought as the howling wind buffeted his snow mask. He kept his hands below the snow line because he needed them to clear a path and the snow was much "warmer" than the wind.

It was mid-afternoon, and the GPS had said he was six miles due east of Ely. It would be fifteen miles if he stayed on the road, but the road had disappeared beneath the snow drifts. He knew he had to make it by sunset or else the Minnesota night would claim him. "So cold," had become a mantra of sorts, it came unbidden into his mind. He kept the sun more or less behind him as he plowed a path through the forest. The wind so strong that not even the trees could slow their fury. "So cold," his mind repeated as he took a short break snug up against one of those trees. As he trudged on, his mantra changed, "So cold. So sleepy." What little consciousness he had left screamed when it heard those words. Sleep would mean death. He needed to fight that urge with everything he had left.

It seemed like another hour had passed, as the sun began to disappear. There was no town in sight, but because trees were so thick, he couldn't see very far. When he came to a clearing he decided he had to get his bearings. He picked out a tall, old oak tree and started to climb. Even though he was an accomplished climber, he had to watch his feet to get purchase on each branch, for there was very little feeling left in them. By the time he reached the top the sun had set. He looked as far as he could in every direction. Nothing! "So cold. So sleepy." He looked up at the sky, wishing to see the stars one last time. All he saw were clouds hiding any light that might have given him solace. It was then he gave in and let himself fall. He only fell a few feet, for the tree caught him and cradled him as he quickly drifted off to sleep.

Their Time

The soldier at Camp Pendleton went on patrol with four others. The boy pulled his math book out of his backpack and started his homework. The mother picked up the baby and began to nurse. The old man sat down in front of the television to watch whatever was on. One of these poor souls was about to die and move on to a "better place." It was their time.

A major earthquake five miles off of San Diego in the Pacific Ocean caused the largest and deadliest tsunami in recorded history. Its closeness to the coast meant there was no time to evacuate. Its height at landfall was over 100 feet above sea level. It smashed into Encinitas a mere 15 minutes after the 9.0 earthquake began. San Diego had another six minutes to prepare. Santa Monica Pier, over 100 miles away, was destroyed a half hour later, the wave height there was 40ft.

The soldier was knocked off his feet on the mountain trail when the earthquake began. His buddies were able to pull him up before he could tumble down the mountainside. By the time he and his friends could get to "safe" ground, they heard the roar of the tsunami. The soldier pulled out his phone and began to record the event. What they saw was a wave as high as a mountain, their mountain. They froze, unable to take in what they saw.

The boy felt the house shake more violently than any earthquake he could remember. But he knew the drill and so jumped up and headed for the backyard. He was the only one home and therefore was the only one in the backyard to witness the wave come five miles inland. It was only 5 feet tall by this point, which was just his height. It wasn't traveling very fast but still carried him away.

The mother panicked, the baby cried. She had just moved to San Diego from the Naval Base at Norfolk, Virginia. Her husband was a Chief Petty Officer, currently out on maneuvers somewhere in the South Pacific. The mother, not knowing what to do in an earthquake, huddled with her baby under the kitchen table. She never saw the wave hit her house.

The old man was just about to doze off when the story broke on TV. He was a native of San Diego but a few years earlier had moved in with his son's family, who lived in Norfolk. He watched as the tsunami destroyed the Naval Base and swept into downtown San Diego obliterating everything in its path. He watched and cried as he thought of friends who most certainly would die and of places from his past that were gone forever. He saw his world being destroyed right before his eyes. He felt a tightening in his chest right before he passed out.

Whether it was miracles that saved the soldier, the boy, and the mother and her child, or just the law of averages, who can tell? Before the wave crashed into the mountainside, the soldier had somehow managed to secure himself to a tree behind a large boulder. The boulder blocked the force of the waves' impact, and the water receded before he could drown. His companions weren't so lucky. The boy grabbed hold of a phone pole and was able to pull himself out of the raging waters. There he waited until the water calmed and then swam to a highway overpass. The mother's house withstood the wave's impact. As the water rose in the house, she managed to get out the door and onto the roof. As she sat there the baby began to nurse and eventually fell asleep.

The old man, slumped over on the couch and never regained consciousness. He never found out that his nephew had rode out the tsunami on that mountainside, or that the boy who lived next door to him in San Diego had swum to safety, or that nice family whose going away party he had attended last month, had made it to the roof. Months later, each found out about the old man's passing and mourned his death, each noting in their own way that it just must have been his time.

Infernal Name

As a child, Dante Zekiel hated his first name. Once his friends found out about its relationship to the famous book, they would continually tell him to go to hell. Dante actually started to read the Inferno at age eight, decided it was "bogus" by the second level of hell, and never read it again. His hatred of the name ended in high school when the same friends who had told him to go to hell decided his name was cool. This change in attitude was mainly due to a video game in which the anti-hero was named Dante. The entertainment industry helped his name's aura again when a vampire television show that's protagonist was named Dante became a hit. Dante also found that girls loved the mysterious bad boy image that went with the name. An image he was all too happy to encourage.

During his formative years, Dante's personality took on that of a Hollywood stereotype. He became dark and mysterious. Dante was not above petty theft, especially since he never got caught. He would fight when challenged, and he never lost. He was a bad boy. This was in stark contrast to the rest of his family. Dante's father was a postman. His brother became an accountant, and his sister became a dentist. Everyone in his family, except Dante, lived in the same suburb of the southern town where they were born. They went to church every Sunday, and were known as pious people.

Dante wanted nothing to do with them or normalcy. By the time he entered college, he knew the only job for him was spy. He took the criminal justice courses, international politics, and even learned Farsi and Pashto. When he graduated, he applied to one of the U.S. intelligence agencies and was immediately accepted.

However, Dante's career as an intelligence operative was short lived. Once in the field, a bloodlust began to emerge. His interrogation techniques turned violent and often ended with the death of the subject. When it was found that he had gruesomely killed three young women during questioning, Dante was quietly discharged from service.

Once back in the mainstream of society, Dante tried to suppress his more violent tendencies. However, as he grew more and more frustrated in trying to find a job, his self-control waned. He became a drifter. The "Dark One," as he came to be known, started stealing for sport. He hung out in bars where he knew he could get in fights. Invariably he would have to leave a town when a fight ended in someone's death. Dante's covert intelligence training easily allowed him to stay one step ahead of the law. In fact, he treated it as a cat and mouse game.

Eventually his actions were noticed by one of the larger crime families in the U.S. He resisted when they first recruited him but, after a while, decided it might be fun and joined. Again Dante's bloodlust appeared. His methods were so disturbing that even among the mob bosses, he was loathed. Ultimately, he went too far and killed one of his own. This sealed his fate. One day, Dante's body was found in a back alley in Harlem. When his remains were identified and his file checked, the police decided to conduct only a cursory investigation. They would have been stopped even if they had decided to vigorously pursue Dante's killer. The intelligence agency Dante had worked for quickly snatched up all records concerning their former operative, and his death was labeled accidental.

Dante's parents knew little of their son's life. What they did know haunted them for the rest of theirs. They both believed that their choice of names damned the boy from the start. They never forgave themselves. The psychologists the parents saw argued that a name can only heighten underlying character flaws, but that was little consolation. They claimed responsibility, and so it was no surprise to them that after their death, they joined their son in the seventh level of Hell.

The Halloween Hurricane's Wrath

The kids were scared. There was no doubt about it. George Anderson, a 10 year old, was trying his best to be brave in front of his sister Cathy, who was 7. But in the flickering candlelight, you could see George was fighting down a scream with all of his might. Cathy was sobbing uncontrollably. The storm raged outside. The house had lost power over six hours ago, and the children's parents had been downstairs bailing water for what seemed like forever. The trees battered the house, as the wind gusts howled worse than any ghost or ghoul ever could. It was Halloween night. The kids should have been out playing in their costumes, getting candy, laughing at the mock horror of the night. Instead they were being tormented by the spirits of all those who had perished in hurricanes over the centuries. Their dad, if he could concentrate on anything other than the swamp that was now his basement, would probably be regretting scaring his kids with the tales of hurricanes past. The damage was done, leaving his kids to the fear of their impending doom. It was made all the worse, as they remembered their mom reassuring them that the hurricane was going to miss their town and then the parents suddenly abandoning them to secure the house when they'd found out the hurricane had made a "right turn" to head directly toward them.

Cathy kept seeing tree branches coming through the windows, grabbing her and throwing her into the storm. George pictured great waves crashing through the front of the house, drowning him in his own bedroom. With each furious gust, both of them would feel the house shudder, both sure it was about to be torn off its foundation. As the night wore on, George was sure the water was rising in the basement. His parents' curses were getting more intense and were tinged with panic. His fear rising until he too began to cry.

Suddenly the children's fears were realized as they heard the large window in the living room shatter. There was a crash downstairs, and Cathy screamed, echoing what she thought were the screams of her parents. George also began to scream as the door to the bedroom burst open, letting the wind and rain assault them both. The two children grabbed each other, holding on as tight as they could, hiding behind the bed. The horror was just beginning. A branch the size of George crashed through the window and embedded itself in the wall above their heads. The two children got up as one and darted out of the bedroom, heading to the basement stairs, trying to get to their parents. What they saw froze them at the top of the stairs despite the wind and rain now pelting them like stones shot out of a rifle. The water was almost up to the door, and floating at the top was their mother's body. George was the first to break from the trance. He screamed and jumped in after his mom. Cathy bolted screaming, not knowing where she was running.

George reached his mother as a wave crashed through the house, dragging George away from his mother, back up the stairs, and into the hallway. Cathy burst through the backdoor and fled into the yard. More water rushed into the house, carrying George back into his bedroom. He fought to grab onto anything he could reach, trying to keep his head above water. Cathy was grabbed by a gust of wind, and was flung into the air. Her cries were overwhelmed by the howling wind. George felt himself being drawn below the surface. His dresser crashed into him, forcing the air from his lungs. Cathy's flight ended abruptly as she was impaled on a tree two blocks away from the house. George tried to scream under the water with the last bit of air he had remaining.

Two years later, a young family moved into a brand new house built on the Anderson's lot. They moved out eighteen months later. The boys had dreams of drowning, and the one girl would dream of being flung through the air. Every time a storm hit, the children would come rushing into their parent's room, screaming that things were crashing into the house and children were yelling all around them. Eventually, a retired couple moved into the house. They lived there for years, never experiencing anything out of the ordinary. After that, whenever a family moved into the house, they would leave soon after. Real estate agents in the town soon learned only to show the house to the elderly, for they were the only ones whom the ghosts would leave alone.

Overwhelmed by Zombies

Colin Seeweld strafed the zombies with the browning rifle. They kept coming. He tossed four or five grenades. They kept coming. He pulled out the last of his laser-powered-anti-zombie-explosomatics and wiped them out.

The boy sighed and turned off the game. "Zombies are sooo overdone," he complained to no one. He looked at his game collection. Every single game had at least one place where zombies attack you. Even in the neighborhood sim, one house is filled with zombies.

As Halloween approached, Colin started getting more and more angry at his friends for worshiping zombies. He knew that for the fourth straight year, all of them would dress up as the undead. Halloween would be filled with mindless tweens staggering down the street moaning for candy. His parents liked to tell stories of their childhood where everyone tried to outdo each other with original costumes. The boy felt cheated out of the fun his parents had being aliens or orcs or hated politicians. He felt cheated out of the fun of playing games that didn't include Zombie LeBron James. He vowed that he would put an end to it.

The boy grew into a teenager and then a young adult. The zombie craze was still going strong. Colin remembered his vow to end the now two-decade-old societal zombie fetish and so studied gaming, eventually going into game design. Colin's family was quite rich, so he was able to start his own gaming company right out of college. He veered away from traditional video games and started a new genre that was in a way a mix of social sims and fantasy role playing games. Working within the limits of what you can do with a real human body, you modified your avatar's body to take on mysterious or fantastical forms. This type of game was called Bod Mod. In Colin's games, body modification was limited to enhancing a person's physique. Due to his success, other Bod Mod games sprung up, ones that didn't just limit you to "enhancements." All of these games stayed true to Colin's original, and modifications were limited to things that could actually be done to the human body. As Bod Mod games grew to preoccupy the collective imagination of the gaming world, so too did people's desire to cosmetically alter their real life bodies. Cosmetic surgery had always been seen as a reflection of a person's vanity, but in this case the factor that drove the choice of procedures was the desire to be, not someone else, but something else. In fact, the trend in alterations included skin pigments, usually of gray or green, building up of the bone structure around the eyes, giving them a sunken look, and in some of the most extreme cases, people even shortened one leg. As the trend grew, Colin realized that he had not only failed to stop the world's love of the undead, but to his horror he realized that his actions had created a world of zombies.

The Price of Anonymity

I found her behind a dumpster. She had lost her mask and was covering her face with both hands. She was wet, dirty, and most importantly, coughing up blood. I found a piece of cardboard in the dumpster. I tore it down to size of her face and poked eye holes through it. She accepted the makeshift mask without a word. I introduced myself, "You may call me Monica." It wasn't my real name of course. It was the will of society that we remain nameless and faceless to insure our privacy.

"You may call me Danielle," she replied.

With the formalities out of the way, I picked her up and carried her to the nearest hospital. The Emergency Room nurse did a quick eval, called some orderlies, and whisked her away. No questions asked. I went through the neighborhood looking for a place to spend the night. I found a decent room, put down the cash, got my key, and headed back to the hospital. The hospital wasn't very large, so it only took me an hour to find her. She hadn't asked for a private room, thank God, or else I would have had to give up on her.

She was wearing a standard hospital gown and mask. Both showed signs that she was still coughing up blood. "You may call me Ophelia," I said as I entered.

"You may call me Anastasia," she replied weakly.

I sat with her, not saying a word. There was nothing to say. A doctor came in after a while and gave her a full examination as I waited outside. He left in a very somber mood. When I reentered the room, the girl was sobbing. "You may call me Ula," she said upon noticing me.

"You may call me Margaret," I replied through my mask. A few hours later the doctor returned as part of his rounds. Even though I knew the reasons behind it, I was still upset when he asked me to wait outside while he went through the motions of repeating the full examination he had given her a few hours earlier. The charade of pretending he didn't recognize her, didn't know her condition, didn't know the uselessness of making her go through this all again was frustrating. Of course, if he didn't put on this show, he could be executed on the spot.

When I returned to the room, I went through the motions myself. "You may call me Mary."

She could barely say, "You may call me Georgia," before falling asleep.

I stayed by her side until the nurse announced visiting hours were over. I went back to my rented room, but could get no sleep. In the morning I returned to the hospital. She had been moved during the night. I wasted another hour locating her room. As my frustration mounted, I fought back the urge to ask a nurse where she was. I knew it was useless and would probably land me in jail. As I entered her room, I announced myself, "You may call me Yentl. I couldn't think of any other name that began with a Y."

I could tell she had a bit more energy as she replied, "You may call me Hannah."

Her mask and hospital gown were again stained with blood, and her coughing yielded much more blood than yesterday. I could tell that the end wasn't far off. After another doctor came in to give her another full exam, I entered the room resigned to the inevitable. I could tell she knew it too, for she said, "You may call me," she hesitated not wanting the name game to end, but knowing this would be the last time she would go through it. So she gave up on thinking of a real name and simply said, "You may call me Ter."

I walked over to her and whispered in her ear so that no one else could hear, "You may call me Mommy." She began to cry softly. I held her hand for the rest of her short life. Before she drifted off into her eternal sleep, I again risked my life as I spoke her real name, the name she hadn't heard since she came of age. "I love you, my dearest Grace." She took off her mask so I could see her face one last time and died.

Pioneer Contagion

Augustus Jones had gone to fight in the War Between the States because he was paid to take the place of some rich man's son. He didn't have much of a life in Boston, so he took the money and hoped the war would end soon. It didn't. After almost losing his leg at Vicksburg, Augustus Jones deserted the army and headed west. He left with the scars to prove he had done his part for the Union. He had lost part of one ear, had a long scar across his forehead that ran down to his left cheek, and had a permanent limp.

Augustus had been shot four times. The pain from those injuries would flare up without warning, leaving him moaning in agony.

Augustus arrived in a small town in western Arkansas a tired, broken man. The only thing he wanted was for the world to leave him alone. He chose the town as his home because he was tired of walking. The former soldier just showed up one day, bought some food and tools, and built a shack out past the edge of town.

Augustus mostly kept to himself, except for trips into town to buy supplies. Because of his looks, everyone in the town stayed away from him. The town became even more afraid of him because of the moans they would hear coming from the shack at night. Soon wild stories began to circulate; some even suggesting Augustus was less than human. Jordan Brown, whose family lived closest to Augustus' shack, wanted to run him out of town.

About two months after Augustus moved to the town, Mary Ellen Brown began to see red splotches on her skin. She developed a fever and died in less than two weeks. Her son, Edgar, also caught the disease and soon followed her to the grave. Seven other people died that month. The townsfolk, chief among them Jordan Brown, blamed Augustus, saying he was a demon or some sort of evil being. The pastor of the town's church tried to calm them, but when he took ill, Jordan lead the rest of the men to Augustus' shack.

Augustus didn't know about the resentment the town had for him. He knew that there was a disease going through the town, but that just made him stay away from his neighbors even more. So when the angry townsfolk came to the shack that night, Augustus didn't know what to do. There was not much he could do. The mob immediately barred the door and splashed oil all over the shack. They then set it ablaze. The flames engulfed the shack immediately. Augustus panicked and tried to break down the door only to catch his clothes on fire. As the shack burned, the men outside the shack heard Augustus screaming. "Why?" Why?" The terror in his voice, the smell of burnt flesh, the thick black smoke, drove every man away from the shack save one. Jordan Brown stayed watching the fire consume Augustus. It wasn't until the shack was a smoldering pile of ash that Brown headed back to his house.

Two weeks later a doctor visited the town. He recognized the disease as one usually found in the Indian settlements west of there. Some of the townsfolk remembered right before the outbreak began that a peddler had come to town selling Indian trinkets. Mary Ellen Brown had even bought a necklace. The people of the town realized that Augustus had nothing to do with the disease. Jordan Brown hung himself from a tree near the site of the burnt shack. The rest of the townsfolk kept the incident a secret. However, even now the descendants of the original settlers say that late at night they would hear screaming from where the shack had stood and would smell burnt flesh in the air.

Stalker in the Mirror

"Most of my fan mail goes to my publicist, but every so often one comes to the house. Since anyone who was able to get a letter through to my house must be a dedicated fan, I would read them and then turn the letter over to my publicist to send back the generic reply," Dirk Sin told the detective.

"But this guy didn't just get one through to your house. He got quite a few?" The detective was being patient.

"Yeah, he got three to me over the course of a week. I told my publicist to send the nut a 'Leave me alone' letter, which usually scares them off. This time it made things worse. The next letter showed up in my mailbox without postage. Somehow he had gotten past my security and got right to my door! This is not supposed to happen! I called my publicist right away. He had a bodyguard at my house in minutes, and told me that he had hired a private detective to track this guy down." Dirk was scared. He hated the thought of anyone violating his privacy. It was bad enough that his fans wouldn't leave him alone when he ventured out of his estate, but one getting into his estate was more than he could take.

"But you didn't call us?" The police detective was not too happy.

"No. My publicist wanted to handle this quietly. That all changed when the next letter arrived," Dirk's face was pale as he remembered the writing on the letter.

"We've matched the blood he used to write the letter to the body of Mr. Musille, the detective your publicist hired. His body washed up last night on Malibu Beach. Mr. Sin, have you caught even a glimpse of the stalker?"

"No, not really, but I've had the feeling someone is following me since right after the first letter showed up. But whenever I turn to try to catch him, there's no one there except normal-looking people going about their business. I haven't seen anything really, just a feeling that he's there. I just want to get rid of him, get rid of all those nuts who follow me because they want a piece of my fame."

"You didn't notice anyone who even remotely looks like someone you've seen, maybe earlier in the day? And no one came up to you asking for your autograph? No one was pointing you out, realizing who you were?"

"No, and I scanned the people on the street, on the set, at the coffee house, and still I see no one who is there more than once when I have these feelings. It's maddening. I know he's there, just out of sight. I know I'll see him sooner or later. It's just a matter of time."

"We've talked to your bodyguard, but he claims not to have noticed anything. I think we can chalk your feelings up to nerves. I don't think he's following you yet. But usually that's the next step, so we are assigning some detectives to shadow you. You'll keep the bodyguard. The more, the safer you'll be."

"Thanks." Dirk didn't sound very confident in the police or his bodyguard.

"While we're on the subject of people supposed to be protecting you, Mr. Sin, your bodyguard reports that you've slipped away from him at least three times in the last week. You need to stay with him. You're only inviting the guy to grab you." The detective's annoyance was, in itself, getting annoying to Dirk.

"I know, but I can't stand to be watched all the time. It drives me crazy," Dirk sounded defeated, but sincere. "I'll try to be better." That more or less ended the interview. Dirk and his bodyguard returned to his house. He didn't feel that much safer as he left.

Dirk woke up the next morning to find a message above his bed. The message was written in blood and said, "You and I are one. You can't run away." Dirk's bodyguard was found with his neck slashed. The police could find no sign of forced entry, no fingerprints other than Dirk's and the bodyguard's. There was also nothing on the outside security tapes, and the police guarding the house reported nothing out of the ordinary. The stalker was good.

However, it should also be noted that the security system of Dirk's estate was old and could easily be beaten.

The police decided that Dirk's mansion was not safe. He needed to be somewhere that was completely and absolutely secure. So Dirk was spirited away to a safe house that the police used in these cases. The place was a fortress with security that rivaled the White House. No one was getting in there. Dirk felt safe for the first time in weeks. He finally felt he could relax and slept like a baby that night. The next morning he woke up and went into the bathroom to take a shower to get ready for a day free from fear of the stalker.

As he was shaving, Dirk looked into the mirror and saw a face staring back at him. Dirk screamed, but it was too late. The surveillance cameras caught the whole scene. Even without the cameras, the police easily figured out what happened. They found the knife that slit Dirk's throat still in his own hand. The angle of the cut was consistent with a self-inflicted wound. Dirk, in his last moments, had finally caught a glimpse of his elusive stalker. Dirk had looked in the mirror and seen himself with the knife. In the mirror, he had seen the crazed look in the killer's eyes as he slit his own throat.

The Pile of Red Leaves

Roger, a grown man, kicked at piles of leaves as he walked from the bus stop to his house. At this time of year, Roger always turned back into a kid. Not literally, but his playfulness returned. A giddy smile was always on Roger's face as he kicked pile after pile of multi-colored leaves. It had always been this way. Roger came alive when the leaves turned orange, red, and brown. He practically danced through the woods behind his house when he was a kid. Even as an adult, he found a wooded park within driving distance and made sure to take a stroll or two this time of year. He was especially cheerful on cold, overcast days. Gray days in the fall were Roger's favorite.

On this particular day it was overcast with a few brisk winds to stir up the leaves. As Roger headed to his house, he saw a huge pile of bright red leaves. It might as well have been a "Roger Magnet," for he made straight for it without a thought. Roger approached it like a football kicker charging for the opening kick-off. When he reached it, Roger didn't break stride. He kicked the leaves as hard as he could, planning on cutting a path straight through them. As his foot entered the pile he felt his balance disappear as he slid on some wet leaves just below the surface. Roger tumbled, landing flat on his back in a pile of very wet leaves.

As Roger lay there, he tried to brush off the leaves, feeling silly because he hadn't noticed how wet they were as he ran toward them. Before he could even start to brush the leaves off, he realized that the leaves around him appeared not to be soaked in water but in a warm, red, slightly thick liquid. It looked and smelled like blood, bright red blood identical to the color of the leaves. Roger realized he was lying in the middle of a pile of leaves that were covered in blood. He lay there in shock. Blood! All he could think about were the leaves stuck to his hands and arms with the red ooze. Then he realized that his body was sinking into the pile. As he lay there slowly sinking, Roger heard his name whispered to him, but he couldn't tell where the voice came from. It felt like the leaves were calling to him. Roger wanted to jump up and run as far away from them as he could, but he was unable to move. It felt to Roger as if he was being absorbed into the pile. He could no longer feel his feet and legs. It was as if they no longer existed. Instead he felt the chilling breeze across the top of the pile. He heard his name again, closer this time. Roger felt his arms begin to disappear, being replaced by the cold damp feeling of soaked leaves. As he got used to the feeling of being the pile of leaves, Roger calmed down. He thought of the fun he had every year since he was a kid, dancing and playing in the leaves. He thought of building leaf forts, of creating the largest piles of leaves on the block, of kicking down all the other leaf piles on the block. He pictured kids jumping into his pile. He pictured squirrels digging through him, searching for acorns. He pictured the wind whipping through his outer layers, sending shivers through him. He felt that this would be nice. Somehow he knew that he would be played with, would decay and sink into the ground, only to return each Fall. A smile formed on his face as Roger lost consciousness and died.

When the policemen arrived, Mrs. Morgan was still frantically shouting Roger's name. One calmed her down, while the other examined the body. The policemen told Mrs. Morgan that a large branch hidden in the pile had pierced Roger's back, most likely paralyzing him. It was obvious he had died from blood loss, as the pile of leaves was drenched. One policeman stayed with Mrs. Morgan, as the other went to find Roger's wife. The policeman stayed with her until the coroner came to remove the body. It began to rain as the policemen and the coroner left. Roger's blood washed out of the leaves, leaving them just an ordinary pile of wet leaves.

Mrs. Morgan couldn't get anybody to get rid of the leaves, and within a few days they had a fresh layer of newly dead leaves on top, making them seem cheery. An early snow fell the next week, covering the pile completely. That winter was a snowy one, and the pile of leaves remained untouched until spring. By then they had become just a pile of mulch. Mrs. Morgan finally found someone, who didn't know the story, to bag up the leaves and dispose of them. Still, Mrs. Morgan couldn't bear looking at where the pile had been, and so she moved away that summer. The family that moved into Mrs. Morgan's house knew nothing of Roger's death, and no one in the neighborhood told them. All they knew was that every fall, the tree out front would turn bright red, and the leaves would fall almost by magic into one big red pile.

Action & Adventure

Jungle Escape

"You can't just leave him for dead!" Professor Ariata protested. Hajime didn't say a thing; she just blasted a few shots into the horde of Ecuadoran soldiers following them, grabbed the professor's arm, and kept moving. The "team" was now down to just one extractor—her—and one extractee—the Professor. This mission was not going well. Hajime had known their chances of survival were low when they went in, but now they were almost zero. Five extractors were dead or wounded. One of the extractees was dead as well. Still, she had the big one. Professor Ariata was still alive, so the mission could still be a success.

During training, Hajime had memorized their path through the jungle. The team had continuously run through virtual drills during the month before insertion. She had even run this scenario, just her and the Professor, over a hundred times. Unfortunately she had only survived twice, while the Professor had survived six times, but never had they both made it out together. As they cleared the bridge, she set off the charges that the team had wired on the way in. That would slow down the pursuers but not for long. The ravine was not deep enough that it couldn't be forded. Still she had time to drop off a few vicinity mines as they ran. That would "thin the herd" but not by much. She needed a new trick if they were going to make it.

Hajime and the Professor passed Checkpoint 3 at 2 hours, 13 minutes, and 42 seconds since insertion, a full six minutes behind schedule. They had two more checkpoints between them and the extraction point. She slowed as they made their way between another set of traps the team had laid on the way in. In fifteen of the virtual run-throughs the professor had accidentally triggered one and killed both of them. So when they made it through unscathed, Hajime "breathed" a mental sigh of relief. They reached

Checkpoint 2 having shaved off a full minute from their schedule deficit. They still needed to cut two minutes or they would not make it to Checkpoint 1 before the artillery barrage. She looked at the Professor, who seemed to still be in good shape, and decided to take Alternate Path 12.

Alternate Path 12 went through an old lava field. They could easily pick up their pace over the field, but they would also be easy targets. Hajime's only hope was that her request to monitor the lava fields had been approved, and the artillery would start early, trained on their pursuers. Hajime and the Professor had gone about one hundred meters on the lava field when the soldiers erupted from the jungle. Almost immediately the shells started falling at the jungle's edge. In another change of plans, the extraction helicopter appeared at the far end of the lava field. She now knew that they would make it out alive.

Professor Ariata collapsed after he boarded the helicopter. Hajime, exhausted, felt like doing the same but instead grabbed an AK-47 and began firing out the open door. Only a few soldiers had dared to cross the artillery barrage. They were easy targets, and she showed no mercy. Hajime finally relaxed when the helicopter landed on the carrier. She had successfully completed the mission.

Three weeks later, Hajime noticed a news report that the new edition of Grand Combat would be out for Christmas. Hajime smiled at the news, proud of herself. Professor Ariata had made it back to Windo Entertainment in time to complete the game. It had been worth it. Her four dead comrades could rest easy knowing that kids everywhere would be enjoying Grand Combat this holiday season.

Gas Stop

Leonard was a member of an Italian Family. That's Family with a capital F. He was a fixer. He was a specialized fixer in that he fixed things in Russia and the Baltic Region. There he was known only as Voron or Raven, the harbinger of death. He was very good. So good that no one knew what he looked like or even if he was a man. Leonard had been working this region for over ten years and knew the criminal syndicates better than most of their members. He had infiltrated all of the major ones and fixed things in those organizations and most of the smaller ones.

Leonard received orders two months ago to disrupt natural gas production in three Russian mafia-controlled companies. The disruption needed to be large and last up to a year. He could use his discretion in determining the method, but Leonard knew the only way to create a large disruption was to start a war. Leonard smiled when he got his orders. He hadn't started a war in ages.

Two crime syndicates owned the three companies. One was a major player in Baltic gas. Leonard's nickname for them was Bol'shaya Ottsa (Big Daddy). The other was more interested in drugs and money laundering. Natural gas was just a sideline to them. Leonard called them Chechenskiy Nakip' (Chechen Scum). The two syndicates had a history of tacit cooperation; no bad blood existed between them. This would make starting an all-out war between the two somewhat difficult, which made Leonard even happier.

Leonard was a modern fixer. He tended to rely on manipulating stock prices, cyber-attacks, and planting stories in the news media. However this assignment would require bombs, assassinations, and even some civil unrest.

It was back to the good ol' days on this one. The plan he concocted had many moving parts and required exact timing. It also had triple redundancies built in, for Voron never let luck play a part in his plans. He was a professional.

For two months Leonard had snuffed minor members of each group, caused accidents at the production facilities, and even arranged for a Chechen to have an affair with the underage daughter of one of Big Daddy's top bosses. Minor retaliation between the two syndicates had started, but nothing big yet. That would soon change. Leonard's big production number was about to begin. He hoped it would open to rave reviews.

Leonard's finale was all him. He had three major jobs that had to take place in one week. The first was an explosion on Big Daddy's feeder to one of the major Russia-to-Europe natural gas pipelines. He decided to "break" the line in Odessa. It took place during a visit by a boss from one of the biggest crime syndicates, one of Big Daddy's closest allies. They were worried about Big Daddy's growing instability and wanted assurances that everything would be back to normal soon. Instead of assurances, all the crime syndicate got was a stoppage in service to their biggest moneymaking pipeline. Leonard had planned to take out the syndicate's boss, but a sudden change of plans saved the man's life. For the first time, the Voron had lost his prey. While Big Daddy was planning its retaliation, Leonard moved on from Odessa to Moscow.

Two days later, Leonard was in Moscow shadowing the second-in-command of the Chechen syndicate. Leonard needed to kill the man's family while having the target barely escape with his life. On Thursdays, the man would meet his family for dinner at one of the exclusive restaurants in Moscow. After only a few minutes, it was obvious the man was heading for Bolshaya Nikitskaya and so would be going to Tsentralny Dom Literatorov. Leonard beat him there by seventeen minutes, which was more than enough time to prepare the man's tea. Leonard had meticulously done his homework. He knew the target and his family always started out their meals with a special blend of tea that was reserved just for them. What's more, the target liked to let his cool, while the rest of his family would start drinking as soon as the tea arrived. Leonard was able to slip into the restaurant's kitchen and lace the leaves with the poison. The tea was served, the wife and children died, and the target vowed revenge. Leonard, so intent on poisoning the tea, had failed to notice that the restaurant had installed a new security camera that morning. For the first time in his career, Leonard was caught on film.

Through his contacts, Leonard learned the Chechens were searching for him. The Chechens didn't know who he was, but they had a picture. The fact that he had let himself be photographed just added to the feeling that age had dulled his instincts, instincts that couldn't falter if the job was to be a success. The final part of the puzzle was the demolition of a Chechen drug lab just outside of Grozny. Because of the existence of the picture, he decided his original plan of infiltrating the lab as a courier was too risky. As always, Leonard had several back-up plans but ended up dumping them for a quickly created "big hammer" approach. The "hammer" was a small airplane loaded with a napalm bomb. In his rush to put this grand finish on his big production number, Leonard failed to notice the lab's surface-to-air missiles when he had scouted it. As his plane approached the lab, he found himself under heavy fire. He could have turned and fled, but his pride wouldn't let him. The mistakes he had made were signs to Leonard that he no longer deserved the name Voron. So he flew the plane and the napalm directly into the lab, thus ending the life of one of the most feared assassins in Eastern Europe. It also began the largest mafia war in decades. Gas production was halted for seventeen months. Voron's final job was a success.

Stone Throw

Revenge was all that mattered to Stone. He wanted revenge for the death of his partner. He wanted revenge for blowing up the orphanage. He wanted revenge for the fiend mercilessly running over that poor little kitten. The supercop was nothing more than a seething cannonball of rage. He was a cannonball pointed directly at the notorious criminal, The Nerd. Stone had gotten a reliable tip that The Nerd was holed up at the old abandoned amusement park just outside of town. That was where he was headed now. Stone was armed as he never had been armed before. He was a one-man battalion. Stone wasn't going to just capture The Nerd; he was going to blast him to Hell.

Stone didn't stop his truck at the park's gate, he smashed right through it. Stealth had never been his style, and it certainly wouldn't be today. Stone knew The Nerd and so knew the only place that creep could be hiding was the Tunnel of Love. As Stone reached the ride, he jumped from his truck and watched it smash directly into the entrance to the Tunnel. He then pulled out a shoulder-fired missile and blew up half the ride. This flushed The Nerd from his lair.

Stone saw the dweeb make for the middle of the park. He chased him while firing two .44-caliber revolvers. Stone couldn't catch The Nerd before he got to the Sky Tower, a 30-story Eiffel Tower knock-off. Instead of pursuing the geek up the tower, Stone planted explosives on two of the main supports. He planned on smashing The Nerd under the weight of a thousand tons of metal. Stone blew the first support and then decided to check where the tower would land in case there was anything important in the way. It wouldn't have changed his strategy, but it would give him something to lament after the damage was done. To Stone's dismay he realized that the tower's observation deck would land just outside the park's gate. It was a set-up! The Nerd was getting him to aid in the villain's escape! Stone was not about to let The Nerd make a fool of him again.

Stone got out his rappelling gear and fired a grappling hook 15 stories into the structure. The automatic wench pulled him up at breakneck speed. He repeated the stunt to reach the observation deck where The Nerd was waiting. Surprised, The Nerd jumped the railing and began to climb the rest of the tower. Stone was right behind him. Both nemeses reached the top together, and a battle royal was on. The Nerd had lasers and homing bullets. Stone had RPGs and high-caliber guns. Both men were wounded repeatedly. Neither gave an inch. Finally Stone got close enough to grab The Nerd and throw him from the tower. He watched as the body bounced off the tower's structure before landing with a satisfying thud at the base. It was then that Stone noticed the tower was leaning more and more with each second. The only thing Stone could do was hang on as the giant structure fell to Earth.

Stone survived the fall with some broken bones and deep gashes. Those types of injuries wouldn't even slow the supercop, let alone kill him. It took three days to clear the wreckage of the tower. Stone helped in the cleanup, yanking girders from the pile with his bare hands. When he finally reached the spot where The Nerd's body should have been, he only found an mp3 player looping The Nerd's high pitched laugh. Stone screamed at the Heavens and vowed that he would never rest until he tore that monster's body limb from limb.

To Remain a Samurai

Meiyo was a samurai at a time when samurai were no longer wanted or needed. He wandered Japan masterless but was not a criminal, not a rōnin. He continued to live by the code of the samurai, but honorable work was hard to find, so he was poor and always hungry.

The beginning of the Edo period in Japan brought with it order and isolationism. More importantly it brought with it a consolidation of power never before seen in Japan. This included stripping the once vaunted samurai of their land and property. Without the threat of war, the great soldier was no longer needed. They were relics of the past. The samurai were told to become peasants or become retainers for the nobility, the daimyo. The samurai who chose to become retainers were turned into bureaucrats and administrators.

Some samurai would not become retainers or peasants. To survive they became members of the growing underworld. They were known as rōnin, a term that had always been used for a disgraced, masterless samurai. In the Edo period it became a term used for criminals. Become a bureaucrat or rōnin, not a choice worthy of those who had once led armies into battle.

Meiyo had been in Kyūshū's major port less than a week when he received a message from a former employer, Hiki Yoshikazu, that his services were needed at once. The employer was a wealthy businessman, who had been slowly rising among the ranks of importers. This was not easy to do given the shogun's mistrust of anything foreign. There was a kinship between Meiyo and Yoshikazu; both had suffered from the new shogun's policies, and both tried to continue their lives despite them.

Upon meeting, Yoshikazu began immediately explaining what was happening. It was rumored that the shogun wanted to cut off all foreign trade at Kyūshū and move it to Edo where it could be controlled. To that end he had secretly employed rōnin to disrupt foreign access to the port. These rōnin acted with the precision of small military units, seizing and then pillaging foreign ships. Yoshikazu wanted Meiyo to stop these thugs and end the shogun's covert operations. Meiyo saw this as a chance to regain his former glory, to lead a military crusade against those that had persecuted him and so many others.

Meiyo gathered five trusted samurai and another twenty former soldiers. The enemy was rumored to number seventy and was highly skilled. Meiyo guessed that the shogun's pirates had been trained in close combat such as would be seen on a ship. He therefore planned to ambush the devils on land, where their advantage in combat would be lessened. Meiyo did not know the location of the enemy's base of operations. So the ambush would need to happen either as the rōnin headed out to the target ship or after they returned to shore. Yoshikazu preferred the former approach, and although the latter would have made the operation easier, Meiyo bowed to the man's wishes.

Yoshikazu, working with a Portuguese captain, had spread rumors that a ship laden with guns and ammunition would be anchored off the southern coast of the port for one night prior to unloading the next day. The placing of the boat just off a mountainous region with only one beach provided Meiyo with the perfect spot for the attack. The enemy came just after dark. Over a third of them were carrying the small boats the rōnin needed to reach the ship. Another third led the march, while the final third guarded the rear, a very sound military strategy. Meiyo used their strategy to his advantage. On a signal, he had his archers send flaming arrows into the middle of the procession, setting the boats on fire. This split the rōnin into two groups, with the ones carrying the boats bolting into both the vanguard and the rear guard. With the rōnin in disarray, Meiyo's troops easily routed those trailing the flaming ships. Unfortunately this allowed the enemy in the front time to organize a defense and prepare for Meiyo's assault. Meiyo knew this would happen but saw no other alternative but to meet them head on and have the battle hinge on the skills of both sides. While Meiyo's troops were motivated by honor, the enemy saw themselves as mercenaries only motivated by money. Meiyo's troops fought to destroy the rōnin, the enemy fought to save themselves.

With Meiyo in the lead, his troops went straight through the burning boats, bursting forth from the flaming hell to surprise the remaining enemy. Even though he was badly burnt, Meiyo continued his charge, slashing his way through the enemy line, heading directly toward the man Meiyo believed to be their leader. While Meiyo's men dispatched the remaining rōnin, the proud samurai fought his greatest duel. Meiyo immediately knew that the enemy general was not a rōnin, but an accomplished swordsman. This made the fight all the better. The two men looked at each other knowing that this fight would be decided swiftly with one stroke. After a mere second of assessing each other, they charged, each getting one slash at their opponent. Meiyo felt his arm go numb as he passed and knew it was lost. But his blade had struck home. The rōnin general fell dead after passing Meiyo.

Meiyo had won the battle, but would never fight again. In recognition of Meiyo's service, Yoshikazu, as would any lord of the past, rewarded him with a small farm in the mountains of Kyūshū. There the samurai lived out his life in honor, respected by all who knew of his deeds.

River Getaway

Randy was a small-time crook from Chicago who happened to be passing through Cedar Rapids, Iowa at the wrong time. He was staying at a motel when three State Troopers were killed during a drug bust. The killer had somehow managed to frame Randy which sent him running. The night after he was framed, he had hidden out overnight at a golf course on the north side of town. Now this innocent felon was in a Dodge Challenger he'd stolen out of the golf course's parking lot. He'd gotten lucky picking a car. The owner must have put in a stock engine and probably tricked out everything else. This baby could move. Unfortunately for Randy, it moved right past a cop as he turned onto 20th. The chase was on.

Randy hit the first left into a residential area. He prayed it didn't dead end. His prayers were answered for a moment when he pulled a hard right onto a decent-sized road headed for downtown. Randy had put a little room between himself and the cop chasing, but that didn't matter because another patrol car appeared in front of him. Randy used some poor sod's lawn to barely get around the police cruiser coming toward him. As he hit a main crossroad, Randy saw some more patrol cars coming at him from the right, so he headed left.

The road was straight as an arrow and only had a few cars on it that morning. Randy opened her up, again putting some distance between himself and his pursuers. He knew that eventually they'd get somebody to cut him off, so when he saw a bunch of warehouses around a bend, he made for them. He thought he had escaped unseen into the maze of warehouses, but when he looked behind there were a bunch of black and whites on his tail. At that point Randy just started dodging police cars and slipping between warehouses. He saw two police cars run head on into each other like it had been some sort of movie, another slammed into a loading dock, and a third spun around as he cut a turn too close. Somehow Randy had managed to get out those warehouses with only one cop chasing him.

He was heading east, on a major downtown artery. As he got closer to what had to be the middle of town, he saw the river. There was an interstate crossing it, but he wanted no part of a chase out in the open. He headed under the highway and turned on the road paralleling the river. To get some distance between him and the patrol car, he went up and down some one-way streets, going the wrong way. He then got back to the river and looked for a good embankment on a tight curve. He saw what he was looking for, rolled down his window, did a controlled fishtail over the embankment and into the river. The car hit the water and began to sink. Randy climbed out the window and dived down into the water. He headed downstream underwater for as long as he could hold his breath, came up for a second, and then dove back under.

Randy was counting on the patrol car seeing the skid marks that he had put down before going over the embankment. He had made it look like he'd lost control going round the curve. The river was deep enough that the car couldn't be seen from the surface. So the police would have to call in divers to find out if Randy was still inside. They wouldn't be able to put together a good search crew for at least fifteen minutes and might wait until after the divers found out he wasn't in the car. Any searchers who tried to look for him downstream would have a hard time finding him if he only surfaced for a second each time he got air.

Randy stayed in the river for about four miles before deciding to leave its safety. He spent three days not getting near a road, heading as far from Cedar Rapids as possible before even attempting to find civilization. Two weeks later, while laying low in Albuquerque, he heard that the police had caught the man who'd really killed the cops. Randy was still wanted for theft, evading the police, wanton endangerment, yada yada. It was nothing that would put him on a Most Wanted list, so the heat was off for now. He was back to his usual modus operandi of avoiding donut shops or other police hangouts. He did add one thing to his routine; whenever he went to a new town he checked for roads that went past rivers. He wanted to be prepared to take a dive when necessary.

Chickening Out

Andrew Loch is a spy, a corporate spy. His jobs usually consist of infiltrating, either by stealth or subterfuge, his company's rivals. Once in, he steals their secrets or sabotages their plans. His job pays very well, and he is very good at it. At this point in his career, he has no financial want or care. There is no reason for him to continue dealing with the inherent dangers of being caught or killed. No reason other than he gets off on his work. He is addicted to the thrill. His company is a giant conglomerate that covers the globe. Their competitors are too numerous to count, so Loch never wants for work.

Tonight Loch was breaking into the corporate offices of a multi-national fast food company. This company was working on a completely new product line that would change fast food forever, or so his sources told him. Loch would soon find out if his sources were correct. The facility's security was surprisingly robust. Any normal thief would have been stopped before they got five feet inside the fence. But he was no normal thief. It took him less than six minutes to make it across three hundred yards of fences and sensors, scale the side of his target building, and enter through the rooftop ventilation system. He had no trouble avoiding the motion sensors, thermal detection grids, and the occasional security guard. At this point, most spies would get cocky, thinking they had it made. Loch was not most spies and so was still sharply focused when it happened.

The first thing he noticed was a lack of smell in the air. All air has some sort of odor. Up until now, the place smelled musty, with a tinge of copier toner, a typical office building smell. But as he entered the R&D wing, there was no odor at all. He immediately grabbed his oxygen mask. He must have set off some security sensor that would flood the R&D lab with a poison gas. He felt slightly dizzy as he put on the mask. He had probably been less than a few seconds away from certain death. Next came an acid shower blocking the hallway. Loch thought to himself that this was getting a bit ridiculous for a fast food joint, but he'd seen worse. He pulled out a cloak he thought might last the length of the shower, and kept going. Over the next hour, Loch passed through every trap and monitoring device he had ever seen. In that time he had only gone another three hundred yards, but he had made it to the office that held the target papers. He quickly unlocked the office and entered.

Immediately upon entering he saw a figure at the desk. The man was dead, and from the amount of decay, he had been dead for at least a few days. Loch didn't have time for a post mortem, so he grabbed any paper he could find, ripped out the computer's hard drive, and fled. The sun would be rising in less than an hour, and he needed to be out before that happened. He acted on instinct, narrowly avoiding death countless times. He had to disable only one security guard as he crossed the open field to the outside fence, but he made it back to the sewer lines and from there to his car.

Loch went to the drop-off point and handed the hard drive and documents over to a courier. When he contacted his handler with the company for his next job, for the first time ever, he asked what it was that could warrant so much security.

"Well, yeah, about that. You see the security was why we had to call you in. You're the best in the world at getting past those things." Loch's usually stoic boss seemed to be a little embarrassed. "The new head of security had been given an unlimited budget to secure the lab. As you found out, the idiot went overboard on the thing. Not only that, he had made it so foolproof that there was no 'off' switch. Not even turning off the power to the building would shut it down. So we sent you in. I couldn't bring myself to tell you the truth, partly because it was our fault and partly because I thought you might turn it down if you knew the story. Yep, we own that company.

"The man you found was the head of R&D. He was the only one who wasn't able to get out. All the notes, all the data, everything was in his office when the security was triggered. The company is going to have to bulldoze the building for lack of any other way to turn off those damn security traps. As for the project, well, it's classified, but I think you can keep a secret. Chicken brownies, that's what he was working on, chicken brownies." That was the last time Loch ever asked what he was retrieving. He decided that there are some things you just don't want to know.

Vigilante Justice Along the Border

Joaquin didn't consider himself some Defender of Justice or Savior of the Downtrodden or any other type of hero. He was a cold-blooded vigilante, nothing more, nothing less. Joaquin had watched his world crumble as the drug gangs took over the towns near the U.S. border. He knew people who had been killed. You couldn't live in that place without knowing someone who'd died, but that wasn't what pushed him over the edge. Joaquin had watched as his sleepy little town, a town where everyone knew everyone, trusted everyone, and relied on each other, had turned into hell. When Joaquin couldn't stand it anymore, he decided he had to do something to punish the people who destroyed his town. He learned to be a mercenary. He became a master of stealth, destruction, but most importantly, a master of death.

In the four months since he had returned to Mexico, Joaquin had taken down a number of gangs. He had started with his hometown. He killed the foot soldiers there, but they were quickly replaced. His hometown was of "strategic importance," and so the cartels would never abandon it. After two more tries, he admitted defeat and moved on.

Carmesí Dom was another story. It was a little town of not more than six hundred people. Carmesí Dom was a simple farming village that just happened to be in between a medium-sized drug processing lab and a small harbor used to send drugs north. To free this town, he would have to get rid of the reason it was important. Taking out the lab would only be a temporary fix, since it would quickly be rebuilt. Joaquin decided the harbor would have to go. To truly cleanse the town, he would have to kill all the thugs in Carmesí Dom, as well as permanently block the harbor, rendering it useless.

Joaquin needed a starless night for his plan to work. When it came, just before midnight, he blew up a guard shack at the end of town. That woke everyone up. As men rushed to see what was happening, he set off a charge near a small bridge leading to the harbor. Joaquin had made sure the explosion left the bridge intact so that the gang members would chase him across it. His trick worked. He counted more than a dozen jeeps and trucks heading for the harbor. Joaquin took out a few just to keep his prey off guard. By the time the men reached the harbor they were a frenzied mob firing at ghosts.

As the men arrived at the docks, they came under attack from a large boat anchored at the mouth of the harbor. On board were two of Joaquin's associates who shot randomly at the beach. The gang members took the bait and got in their own boats to follow, boats Joaquin had earlier rigged with explosives. Things were going perfectly until a small Mexican Navy cruiser appeared outside the mouth of the harbor and began shooting at anything that moved. Joaquin had to think quickly. At this rate the cartel boats would return to the docks, and the men would escape. He needed those boats to reach the mouth of the harbor so he could blow them all and block the harbor for good.

Joaquin had no choice. From the beach he fired a shoulder-mounted missile at the Navy boat. He aimed for and hit the gun turret at the bow, most likely killing the soldier there. The Navy boat, not wanting to go up against anyone with that type of firepower, retreated quickly. The gang members were now completely baffled by what was happening. Someone from the beach had just fired a missile at the Navy, which was a good thing. But they didn't know if it was one of their gang or of the rival gang, as they believed their foe to be. Joaquin launched a second missile at his own boat, barely missing the stern. It worked. The cartel boats continued straight for Joaquin's decoy. As he watched from the shore, the first boats reached the decoy, and men began boarding it. He waited until his associates had jumped overboard and then blew the gang's boats as well as his decoy. Some of the gang members survived the blasts and made it into the water. Joaquin mercilessly began picking them off one by one. When the sun rose, you could see a few of the sunken boats barely sticking above the gentle waves of the small harbor. You could also see corpses littering the beach or bobbing in the water. It was a horrific sight but pleasing to Joaquin.

The plan had worked. The harbor and therefore Carmesí Dom were abandoned by the Baja Cartel in favor of a similar harbor a little farther up the coast. Life in Carmesí Dom slowly returned to the quiet, simple life it had before the cartel came. However, there were scars left behind, scars that would take a generation to heal. Joaquin had created a scar on himself. The Navy soldier he killed was trying to fight the cartels too. Joaquin had only wanted to kill the thugs who preyed on the innocent. Now he had crossed a line, a line he had never believed he would cross. Still, the town was safe once again. Kids played in the streets, old women gossiped in the market, and the church became a place of celebration, not mourning. Joaquin was satisfied with his work but knew that he was not done. There were more towns to be freed, and he would not rest until they were.

Broaching the Subject

It was supposed to be a simple heist. The mark was an exec at some bank. He had a wife and two kids. The loot was a gaudy broach that was kept in a safe in the basement. The fence who fed us the info was one of our most trusted weasels. We cased the joint for two weeks. We knew everything that went on in there. They had a standard, off-the-shelf security system. It was one that we had beat many, many times. I decided to go in with my full team;

three guys, all veterans of this kind of work. It should have been a by-the-book, no-frills job.

Then the guy's sister, Angelique, came for a visit, a month-long visit. Something about her spooked me, so I debated calling the job off. My fence was already impatient. He threatened to give the job to someone else if we didn't get him the broach that week. We were short on cash and jobs. So I did a quick check on the girl's background. When nothing of note came back, I decided to go ahead. Unfortunately, credit reports and arrest records don't cover whether or not the person does black ops work for France. They also don't tell you that the person in question brought their own security system with them and enough military hardware to start a small-scale invasion of Pasadena.

The exec and his family were going to a party the night of the job. His sister was with them, so the house was empty. We easily got past the outer security system. At least we got past the original system. It seems the girl had put up an extra laser grid that we never saw. As planned, we entered the house through the third-floor balcony in the back. We took care of the main security system from the panel in the office down the hall. There were still some independent security gizmos at various points in the house, so we treaded lightly.

From the front gate, it took us forty-five minutes to make it to the first floor. Unbeknownst to us, that was exactly the amount of time our French commando took to get home. We were making for the basement stairwell when she hit us with a flash grenade. To my guys' credit, none of them panicked. I don't know what they did, but they didn't go running off in all directions at once. I rolled in the direction of the blast hoping whoever had thrown the grenade had tossed it over our heads to get us to run toward them. I guessed right. I heard some scuffling from behind me and kept going in the opposite direction. I bumped into a few tables and chairs but made it to another room by the time my eyes were able to focus. At this point I was sure we weren't under attack from some security company cop. I knew the guy and his family weren't military, so that left the sister.

For some reason, I decided to keep going after the prize. When I was able to see again, I realized that I was right near the stairs to the basement, so I ducked through the door and headed on down. As I hurried toward the safe, I heard automatic weapon fire from upstairs. Being an Iraq War veteran, it didn't faze me, although it made me question our assailant's sanity. I prayed they were warning shots and not meant to kill.

I made it to the safe without incident. I heard some muffled explosions from upstairs which meant my guys were at least keeping her busy. For some reason I had the feeling the girl was having fun, and for some reason this made me begin to like her. She had style in a sort of over-the-top way.

The safe was very old, probably part of the original building. It took me two minutes to open. I replaced the broach with the fake I had brought. Why I thought I still could get the real one out without her noticing is beyond me. The original plan was to go back to the third floor and turn the security system back on so nobody would suspect a thing. I ditched that part of the plan and decided to go for the front door hoping she would be watching the back one.

Things were eerily quiet when I got to the first floor. Of course she was standing there. My team was tied up on the floor just behind her. When I saw her, I couldn't meet her eyes. I instead gave my full attention to the RPG she had pointed at me. Talk about overkill. I put my hands behind my head and stood there. Then she started to laugh, and so did I. My guys just sat there not seeing the humor in any of this. Angelique thanked me for a fun evening as we untied my team. She examined the broach, decided it wasn't her style and let me keep it. She then told me she would clean up the place if I gave her my phone number. She also agreed to buy me dinner the next night to thank me for breaking up a boring visit with her brother's family.

THUMP thump

THUMP thump THUMP thump THUMP thump. Crystal could hear her heart pounding. She looked around to see if anyone else could hear it. Everyone in her office was going about their usual routine. THUMP thump THUMP thump THUMP thump.

"How could they not hear it," Crystal thought to herself. "It's gotten so loud. I can hear it reverberating across the room." Crystal stared at her coworkers, but they showed no signs that they noticed anything out of the ordinary. Crystal stayed glued to her computer monitor for fear that they might notice that she was sweating profusely. If she kept her face pointed at the screen, maybe they wouldn't see her sweating visage.

"They have to know. They have to be able to hear my heart pound and see the sweat dripping onto my keyboard. They are playing with me. They are just torturing me by pretending not to notice anything is wrong. That's it." Crystal decided she needed to go somewhere a little more private, so she wiped her forehead with a tissue and headed for the restroom. THUMP thump THUMP thump. As she passed her boss she thought to herself. "He knows. He can hear my heart thumping. He's put together all the pieces, and he knows it was me. That bastard! Toying with me like this in front of the entire office."

Crystal made her way into the restroom and collapsed in a stall. "I know what they're doing right now. They are all giggling and talking about how much fun they're having playing with me. When I come out they'll go back to pretending they don't notice anything. How long will they keep this up? Why don't they just call the cops and get this over with?" Crystal's mind was racing over all the possible things she could do now. She could go back to her desk and try to make it through the day. Who knows, maybe they haven't noticed a thing. She could sneak to the restroom door and peep out to see them plotting what mean thing to do to her next. She could make a break for it and bolt for the elevators. "I know what's going on. The police are waiting at the bottom of the elevator. As soon as I come out they'll slap the cuffs on. Maybe," she thought "they won't be watching the stairs. The stairs lead to an emergency exit directly out the back of the building. It'll set off an alarm, but if I am fast enough, I could blend in with the morning crowd and make it to the subway." She decided that would be her best course of action.

THUMP thump THUMP thump. She stole to the door of the restroom. Crystal tried to compose herself as she exited. Since the stairs were near the kitchen, she would head their first. It would look like she was going to get a cup of coffee. Then as she passed the entrance to the stairs, she would quietly sneak inside. Everything went according to plan. The office was still pretending not to notice her, so she used that to her advantage. She timed her walk so that no one was in sight when she opened the stairway door. She quickly stepped inside and ran down the twenty-three flights of stairs to the fire exit. THUMP thump THUMP thump. As she opened the door the alarms began blaring. Standing right in front of her were two armed policemen with guns drawn. Without thinking, she drew her own gun and fired at the officers, wounding one. The other fired a shot that hit her straight between the eyes. Crystal was dead before she hit the pavement.

Back up in the office, the workers breathed a collective sigh of relief. Some patted each other on the back for doing such a wonderful acting job. The branch manager thanked everyone and then told them to get back to work.

The classified police report succinctly stated: Crystal Banks, female, age 34, suspected of criminal paranoia and plotting to expose the alien conspiracy to subjugate all mankind. Shot while attempting to avoid capture. Pronounced dead at the scene. One officer wounded by the suspect. The policeman had non-life threatening injuries and was released from the hospital after minor treatment. The suspect's body was cremated, and all evidence that she ever existed was wiped from the records and purged from the mind of all parties that had ever been associated with her. Recommendation: Case closed.

Life and Death in the Canopy

Jill was falling toward the jungle floor. Her tether should have stopped the fall, but it didn't. She knew that if she didn't stop or at least slow herself soon, a swift death awaited her at the end of the fall. As she fell, she should have been thinking of a way to save herself. Instead she screamed thinking only of the horror of dying. Not a very good way to escape death, even though doing just that was why she loved the job so much.

Jill hadn't seen the jungle floor in weeks. She hadn't been dry in weeks. The eternal mists of the rainforest soaked everything you owned. The oppressive heat made you sweat like a pig every moment of every day. Bugs of all kinds were trying to eat you alive. Squirrel monkeys were always rummaging through your stuff when you were away from the "nest." The "nest" was nothing more than a net strung between branches of a tree. Jill should have been miserable. She wasn't. She was happier now than at any time in her life.

You might think that Jill was a biologist, living up in the Amazon canopy, studying exotic flora and fauna. She wasn't. In fact, she considered that life boring. However, she did work for biologists. They were the ones that paid her to live out a fantasy that only Tarzan or another "stringer" would appreciate. Jill and her party were the advance team. They set up the nets and rope walkways that the eggheads would use to get close to their beloved flowers, fruits, and bugs.

Jill had become a legend in the canopy. She was that crazy bitch who flew from tree to tree stringing guide wires so her crew could string the bridges that the scientists would use to get around without risking life or limb. No one else had ever dared copy her technique, no one was that crazy. Paul, her assistant always followed her around like a faithful dog. He was responsible for making sure she was safely tied off before a jump, something Jill hated. He always had to slow her down so he could get the safety harness on her and make sure her tether was secure. She, being too eager for the jump, hated anything to stand in her way.

Paul didn't mind the trouble she caused him. He just loved to watch as Jill jumped to the nearest tree. She didn't swing. She didn't find sturdy branches to crawl on. She didn't go down to the floor and scramble up the next tree. She jumped. It was so wrong and yet so right. She looked like part of the life of the canopy. Her acrobatics were so natural, so beautiful.

That day started with Jill rappelling down from the nest to a rope bridge the team had strung the day before. She checked to see if the anchors were still holding, and declared the bridge safe. Once she knew the bridge was okay, she climbed the tree at the far end and looked for a way across to the next tree. Paul climbed up behind her. When he got to Jill's perch, he saw the hunger in her eyes. He knew he didn't have much time to check the harness and tie off the line. He had barely fitted her harness when she jumped. The line was not secured to the tree. He was however able to sling it around the trunk and say a prayer that she made a safe landing on the other side. She didn't. The rope played out too fast for him to tie it to anything. He looked down to see her flailing about too scared to do anything. As he watched he didn't see the acrobat but a frightened child.

Paul snapped out of his reverie and without thinking hooked the end of the line to his harness. He then jumped over the opposite side of the branch Jill had used as a launching pad. He knew that to bring her to a complete and immediate stop when she was traveling this fast would probably break her back. He knew he had to slow her fall, and this was the only way he could think of. As he plummeted he grabbed branches, vines, anything to slow his fall and let him gain purchase. He came to rest on a strong branch 100 feet below where he had started. When he felt the line start to go taught he jumped up. This caused his momentum to go in the direction of Jill's fall. He began to be pulled upward, and Jill's descent was slowed. When he reached the original branch, he grabbed hold with all his might, which jerked Jill to a stop but not with a force that would cause major injury.

Jill never jumped again. She stayed the team lead but made it a managerial post from there on out. She tasked others with anything dangerous and relegated herself to inspecting the finished bridges and nests. Paul quit the team. He couldn't work under a Jill that he saw panic under pressure. He had no confidence that she wouldn't lose it again when another crisis occurred. He also saw the team's work reduced to just another job under the new Jill. So he took a new, if not glamorous job in the jungle. Paul now runs a zip line company that caters to tourists. It may not be fraught with the danger associated with his work with the old Jill, but he loved to watch the terror and then accomplishment of clients who truly believed they had escaped death.

I Like It When Things Go Boom

Sandra was back in the thick of things after a four-year sabbatical. "Things" being gunfire, grenades, and anti-personnel mines. "It's nice to be back," she thought to herself as she looked for a way past the twelve men in spotless black suits carrying TEC-9 semi-automatic handguns. It appeared they also had more than a few fragment grenades. She preferred the Ruger 10/22 rimfire and concussion grenades, the latter because they made bigger booms. In this case, since she really didn't want to kill these guys, she tossed a few stun grenades their way. Seven of the suits went down immediately. That was better. The remaining five split up, effectively rendering the stun grenades useless. One of her assailants was trying to flank her, while the others laid down some cover fire. Instead of heading away from the flanker, Sandra intercepted and tasered him. The other four had sought to lure her attention away by moving in the opposite direction of the flanker. This gave her a straight shot to the front door. She bolted. Without losing stride, she placed some plastic explosives on the doorway, detonating it before her pursuers made it inside.

The building was officially a museum. Not a very good museum. Its theme was farm implements of the early 19th

Century. Despite the lack of anything worth stealing, it had a very sophisticated alarm system. Sandra didn't bother sneaking past the alarms. They had been going off since the firefight started outside. On her way through the exhibits, she grabbed a very nice sickle that might come in handy later. According to the schematics she had studied, the "secret" entrance to the "secret" intelligence agency HQ was just after an exhibit of horse-drawn plows. Again, since stealth was not an option, Sandra placed some more plastic on the wall next to the plows and dove for cover. It blew a very nice hole in the now-not-secret door, taking out four agents waiting on the other side. "What idiot would wait that close to something that may be turned into shrapnel?" She stepped over the idiots' bodies as she sprayed the reception room with bullets.

Once inside she basically started tossing concussion grenades in every possible direction. The shear noise would deafen anyone not wearing ear protection. The damage they did also helped her get past some nasty infiltration countermeasures and make it to the main server room unscathed. She set a little tech gizmo in place and let it work its magic. While it infected the enemy agency's worldwide network, she went crazy strategically placing plastic explosives all over the room. Once the gizmo beeped it was done, she grabbed it, went to the "safe" part of the room, and brought the rest of the room down around her with a touch of a button. The emergency stairwell was now easy to find, formerly being behind a wall that was no more. Since she considered this an emergency, Sandra took it up to the roof. On the roof was an ultralight flyer conveniently left there by her "company." She used it to get about a mile away from what was left of the museum. There she found a Blackhawk helicopter waiting to pick her up.

She was taken to an aircraft carrier where Sandra was debriefed and then sent off to bed. The brass complained about her explosives bill but acknowledged she always got the job done. In her cot she looked over her purloined sickle, deciding to keep it. Tomorrow's mission would start off in a Siberian wheat field, a coincidence not lost on the intrepid Special Forces soldier. Even after Sandra's four-year vacation, the sickle proved she still had that strange sixth sense when it came to weapons. Sandra looked over tomorrow's mission plan, silently finding places to make things go boom. "It's nice to be back," she thought for the second time today. Life on the outside was just too quiet.

Different Perspective

What Monet Missed

"Come walk with me in the garden," she called.

"It is the dead of winter. The garden is bare," I replied.

"Oh silly, just come and walk with me." With that she whisked me away to Giverny. The garden wasn't open to visitors in the winter, but that didn't stop her. Somehow, I gathered the strength to lift her to the top of the brick wall. She in turn, pulled me up. It was surprising that we could scale such a wall given how age had taken its toll on the both of us.

"Come walk with me," she said again. So I took her hand, and we wandered under empty trellises by the frozen pond. Scraggly vines and dried-up bushes marked the places where spring would one day repaint this canvas. We stopped on the famous bridge that was the subject of so many paintings. I tried to envision the garden in full bloom but got only an impressionist's rendering for my troubles. "Isn't it beautiful?" she sighed.

"It is dead and barren," I countered. "This garden is devoid of color and life. How can you say it is beautiful?" I stopped and turned to face her. She looked at me disapprovingly. I tried to give her my best frustrated face, but it was too late. Her cheeks and nose were stung red by the sharp breeze. Her breath billowed forth in frosty clouds. Her eyes pierced me with crystal icicles. I was undone.

I stepped back and looked at the scene anew. With her as the subject of the montage, the garden took on a new pale. Frost glittered in the sunlight giving the scene a silvery aura. The empty vines became ropes hung for a festival. The dried leaves made a carpet on which we could tread. And in the midst of it all, she shone with the light of youth still visible even in our aged bodies.

I smiled at her, took her hand, and we continued our walk.

Lost Epiphanies

The mist clouded his thoughts as he awoke. Jorgen was disoriented. He panicked. He screamed. He jumped up from his bed. Then the mist cleared, and his room came into focus. Jorgen sighed. He had lost it again. He closed his eyes and tried to force himself to remember. It was a futile attempt; it always was. The clarity of that other world could never be regained once this world became substantial. The man was left with the knowledge that he had experienced a great epiphany in that other world, the world that only came to him in his dreams. The epiphany had changed everything, had born him anew. The despair of losing such a life-changing realization would haunt him for the rest of the day.

Jorgen spent the day, as he did most days, looking for a way to bridge the two worlds. In this world of the concrete, this world of science, there must be a way to build a lasting bridge to that world of art, creativity, and love. He longed to not only bring the splendor of the other world to this but to bring the rationality of this one to the poets, artists, and philosophers of the other. Secretly, not even known to himself, he really yearned to stay in the other world. His subconscious envied those who spent all their lives in a world of creativity. This world, where he spent half of his life, sapped his energy as it drove out all the artistry of being.

That night Jorgen went to bed, closed his eyes and was transported to that other world. When he arrived, the mist clouded his thoughts. Jorgen was disoriented. He panicked. He screamed. He jumped up from his bed. Then the mist cleared, and his room came into focus. Jorgen sighed. He had lost it again. He knew that he had experienced a great epiphany in that world of logic, of rational thought that he visited in his dreams. The despair of losing such a life-changing realization would haunt him for the rest of the day.

No Horizon in the Dark

I wander the beach alone. The boardwalk's lamps barely reach the sand. Clouds cover the moon and stars. The sea is deathly black. The waves gently reach the shore. I hear a gentle lapping as they caress the beach. The gulls have yet to wake. The tourists are sound asleep in their hotel rooms. The morning is mine and mine alone. I feel the peace of living in this moment of solitude. I feel the serenity of time standing still.

There is no horizon in the dark. No unreachable goal to beguile me and lead me on. The black veil that hides all my dreams and aspirations forces me to stop my reckless pursuit of the insubstantial goals I have set. The ocean never meets the sky. So how can I reach their juncture? I cannot, and so the thought is banished from my mind.

I can only feel the sand shifting beneath my feet. It is an ever-changing path to everywhere and nowhere. It has no set destination, so I walk it for no reason but to walk. My footprints dissolve behind me, leaving no trace of my journey. When I complete my trek, I will have gained nothing nor lost anything. I will have left no sign, no legacy, no guide for those that come after me. In this time before the day begins, I can accomplish nothing. I have been liberated from my burdens and responsibilities. I take a deep breath of the freedom to do nothing. It cleanses me of my anxieties. It refreshes my soul. The beach. The black night. They are a hiatus from life, if only for a brief while.

The Thirst for Love

Horace loved Charlotte, or at least he thought he did. Charlotte didn't know Horace existed, literally. Charlotte's lack of understanding was the result of Horace's actual nonexistence. Horace didn't exist in human form, spiritual form, virtual form, or any other form that would make sense to you or me. Horace knew this. He had been well aware that he didn't exist ever since he first found Charlotte. Horace was drawn to her like a moth to a flame. He was a moth without substance, without even the locomotion needed to get close to that flame. Even with this slight handicap, Horace made the decision to woo her. He could tell that Charlotte was his soul mate, that they were meant to be together forever.

A being that doesn't exist has no possible way of contacting one that does. This is a basic tenet of nonexistence. Horace was undeterred by this tenet. He was determined to break through that barrier, but he needed a plan. After what was an eternity for Horace but a brief second to Charlotte, Horace decided just to make himself exist. This would be difficult, as another tenet of nonexistence is that you have absolutely no power to do anything. This tenet gave Horace hope. Horace could think. If the "can't do anything" tenet was true, how could he think? If that tenet was wrong, then that meant any law of nonexistence might be wrong. So there was a chance that Horace may be able to make himself exist! This one loophole was all he needed. After an eternity for Horace, not Charlotte, he had the "cogito ergo sum" epiphany, and so began to believe that he actually did exist and so began to exist, if only to himself. "Now," he reasoned, "if I can get Charlotte to believe in me, then I should exist for her."

Horace spent another eternity for him, not her, trying to think of a way to get Charlotte to believe he existed. This wouldn't be easy as Horace couldn't "see" Charlotte's existence, he could only "feel" it at present. He had no idea of the nature of her existence. "But," Horace thought, "if I can sense what she senses, maybe I can substitute my existence for something she believes exists and thus exist for her." Horace concentrated on Charlotte, probing everything he could probe, sensing everything she sensed. It was taxing. It wore Horace out, in a nonexistent sort of way. But Horace had what he needed. He was going to substitute himself for Charlotte's strongest desire, even though he had no idea of the actual source of that desire. It would work! It did work! Horace became the first nonexistent being to exist to anyone other than himself.

Charlotte had just come back from a nice walk in the park. Her master had taken off her leash, and she was now free to roam around the house. She immediately headed for her water dish. It was a hot day, and she desired nothing more than a long cool slurp of water. Horace had sensed that desire and unfortunately used that as the basis for his substitution. Horace materialized in Charlotte's existential plane as the water in the bowl to which she was headed. Since water has no cognitive powers, Horace immediately ceased to exist. This time not even "cogito ergo sum" could help him. Charlotte did drink the water, but that didn't change anything. The water was not Horace, and Horace was no longer the water. And so a new tenet of nonexistence came into being: You can change a Horace to water, but you can't make it think.

Window Shopping

The boy lived in a nice little town not far from a big city. Every day when he walked to school, he passed a small art shop. Every day he would stop at the window of the shop to look at the paintings and sculptures for sale. After he graduated, the boy worked at an office near his apartment. Even though it was out of his way, he would walk past the shop to gaze at the art in the window. As he grew older, the boy became very successful. He worked long hours to make his company thrive. He ascribed his success to the short break he took every day to relieve his stress. He would walk to the small art shop and admire the beauty of the work behind the glass. The boy eventually retired. He had become the richest man in the village. Even with his riches, the boy chose to live a simple life. He had a small house at the edge of town. He spent his days tending his garden or reading books. Every day he would walk into town to look in the window of the art shop. The boy never bought anything from the shop. He never even entered it. He was content simply to look in the window. For him, the ever-changing display was a glimpse into worlds of beauty, pain, joy, and sadness. For a few minutes, it released his soul from the bonds of the everyday. That was all he ever wanted or needed from the store.

A Practical Thermodynamic Experiment

One Description: The water is calm. You sit. You watch. At one point on the bottom of the container, enough energy has been transferred to the water that it begins a phase change from liquid to gas. You see it, but you truly don't understand the thermodynamics involved. You know the basic theory. Molecules speed up, move farther apart, and either break apart or something like that. You can only see the outcome. Where once there was liquid, there is gas.

The air pocket grows until the water pressure keeping it in place is counteracted by the weight (or lack thereof) of the gas pocket. It releases from the bottom of the container and travels to the surface. There it sits. The difference in pressure is not enough to overcome the surface tension of the liquid molecules that bind it to the greater mass of water in the container. Eventually enough of the fluid on the top of the gas pocket transfers back to the liquid for the gas to emerge from the pocket and equilibrate with the gas surrounding the container. This pattern is repeated over and over in the next minute until the energy transmitted to the liquid form larger and larger pockets of gas. These pockets rise rapidly and immediately break free. They slowly, then quickly increase the heat and percentage of water vapor directly above the container. You move away from the container to avoid the possibility of a sudden increase of heat damaging of your ectodermal tissue. Your curiosity causes you to continue your observation until you feel the experiment can move on to the next stage. You then mix the remaining liquid with a dried substance, Camellia sinensis. The liquid leeches out the desired chemicals of the solid until they reach a satisfactory concentration in the liquid. You then run the standard tests to insure the experiment was carried out correctly. Having satisfied the parameters of the exercise, you deem the project a success.

Another Description: The water is calm. You sit. You watch. At the bottom of the pot a small bubble forms. The air inside gets hotter and the bubble makes its way to the surface where it lingers for a moment before popping. Soon more bubbles form and make their escape. Each one is larger than the last, each one pops out of the pot faster than the last. Soon there are so many bubbles that the water springs alive. The top of the water becomes a seething landscape. The air above the pool becomes warm and then unbearably hot. You get worried that you might get a burn, and so you retreat to a safer distance. You watch until you think the water is hot enough and then mix it with the tea leaves. When the tea appears to be fully steeped, you have a drink to see if it is just right. You are pleased with the taste and so sit down to enjoy a nice cup of tea.

Look to the Sky

I looked up at the sky on a clear spring night and saw a meteor shower. There were so many meteors; I knew that they would destroy most of the Earth. I ran until I found a cave and hid from the impending doom. I fell asleep hugging my knees to my chest. The next morning when I went out to view the devastation, I found that nothing had been destroyed. It appeared as if none of the meteors had crashed into Earth. I felt relieved.

On another day as I was leaving my apartment, I noticed a crack in the building's foundation. As I looked closer, I noticed numerous cracks, so many that I was sure the building would fall within minutes. I ran back to my apartment, grabbed all of my valuables, and stuffed them in my car for safe keeping. With some sort of macabre fascination, I stood watching the building, waiting for it to crumble. After a while of staring at the building, I decided that the cracks had not grown any larger, and the building was safe for now. I took my things back inside and went about my day.

Yesterday, while watching the news, I heard stories of stock market dives, countries about to default on loans, businesses going bankrupt, and all sorts of financial turmoil. I knew that no one's money was safe, so I ran to my bank to empty my account. However, when I got to the bank, everything was normal. People were cheerful. Some were even depositing money. I realized I had overestimated the "crash."

Today I look around me and am not sure what to do. I still see rampant crime, plagues, and famines. I just don't know if any of it is really as bad as I think. It may be that I have been overestimating all the disasters that I have ever predicted. So I sit and try to understand how I could be wrong so many times. What could I have noticed that would have calmed me down and prevented me from running away in terror? After a while I notice that people are going about their daily business, unconcerned with all the chaos I see swirling about them. So I decided that for now I will use them as my sanity check. I will try to react as they do. I will remain calm in the face of utter disaster. I will not panic unless they do.

I saw the bus lose control. I kept walking across the street with the same calm, slow gate as everyone else. I didn't yell out. I didn't grab the old lady and push her out of the way. In the end, I was one of the lucky ones. I will be out of the hospital in a week or two. In the meantime, I am going to reevaluate my decision-making methods.

The Dark Pool of Desire

The dark pool of desire awaits me at the bottom of the abyss. It sends steam to my perch letting me inhale the aroma of the quenching waters far below. If I were to dive into the gorge, I would land in the brew created by the vegetation that falls into the water heated by the lava underneath the basin. I long to have those waters fill me. The dark pool is the legendary Spring of Clarity. Drinking from its waters will open your mind, clear your senses, and elevate you to an enlightened state of being.

I have searched for a way to reach this lucidity most of my life. Since I was born, I have spent my days in a fog, not really understanding what goes on around me. I drift through reality. I see the world from the periphery. I have never been truly alive. I know there is more to this existence. I know that if I could but see things as they really are, I would be able to accomplish anything, do anything, be anything. To be able to permanently dispel the fog is the most important goal of my life. It is the only thing that keeps me from losing all sanity and descending into madness.

In my search, I have tried the wares of snake oil peddlers and charlatans galore. They gave me cups of obsidian liquid that were too harsh or too mild, too green or too burnt. Some did lift the veil for a second or two, but none were able to pierce the fog that so obscures my vision. These pretenders did both taunt me and reinforce my desire to find the real rich source of clarity. My search has led me across the world. I have been to India, New Guinea, and Viet Nam. I have searched the wilds of Kenya, Cameroon, and Angola. I have scaled the Andes Mountains of Peru, Bolivia, and Brazil. None produced the liquid I desired. Now finally, I have come to Costa Rica. I stand on the slopes of Volcano Barva, looking down on the hidden chasm that is home to the mythical Spring of Clarity. I will soon begin the long climb to my journey's end. I will taste the magic waters, opening my mind to all that is real in this world. What will I see? What will I learn? What will I become? The answers lie before me.

When first I reached the bottom of the fissure, my eyes beheld an unexpected horror. Dozens of bodies are scattered near the spring's edge. Their eyes are full of terror and sadness. They died of wounds that were all self-inflicted. I can only surmise that they could not bear the clear vision of reality. I should run. I should leave this place and cling to the shroud that covers my eyes. But wandering in the fog, knowing that I could have seen things as they really are is too much to bear. I write this letter to you, dear sister, knowing I will soon join those others who ventured here before me. I have kept my craving for truth in check just long enough to return to San Jose and send you this journal. Do not grieve for me, for I have fulfilled my life's destiny. I will know what I've always wanted to know. Dying is a small price to pay for a really good cup of coffee and the clarity I seek.

The Rain Came Down

The rain came down in waves. If you watched the street you could see "S" shaped designs as wave after wave washed down across the asphalt. I walked out in the rain just to feel what such a torrent felt like. It was like walking under a waterfall, with a very stiff headwind. I probably should have been wearing a raincoat, but how can you experience such an amazing feat of nature while fitted in a protective shell? (Yes, I was wearing clothes. I'm not that au natural.) I like the fury of the storm. I like the raw energy. But most of all, I like the form and beauty of something so powerful, yet so structured. The individual drops that are present in the "buckets" of rain that drench you are like the individual points of a Seurat painting. The ebb and tide of the wind and water follow a pattern if you look closely enough.

I know about these things because I spent a good part of my youth listening to the symphony played out on the roof above my head. My bedroom was in the attic. The attic was in a house in the Midwest. The Midwest is where you get real rainstorms. I wish I could have a tin roof above my bedroom so that these East Coast rains might sound a little more like the ones I remember from my childhood. We get a few, such as the "waves of rain" I'm standing in. Unfortunately, I live on the fourth floor of a well soundproofed 17-story building in the midst of the city. I sometimes never realize it rained at all. It makes me sad. It makes me yearn for my bedroom in the attic. It also makes me want to enjoy the rain whenever I can. So I walk in it. I drive in it. I stand on my balcony to drink it in. I even enjoy my youngest's fear of it. I try to experience it in any way I can. It is beauty, and beauty was meant to be enjoyed.

Retreat to the Bunker

Pierre Liondelavie was a thirteen year old who wanted to run away. Instead of heading out into the world, he sat in a bunker on his family's farm. The place where he hid was a relic left over from some ancient war in which his great grandfather fought. Or was it his great, great grandfather? He had been told that this bunker had been called a "pillbox" and it was used by the enemy. His great grandfather had been part of the force that drove the enemy from this bunker and off this land. It was a nice story, but the details of the history of his refuge didn't matter to him. What did matter was that it currently protected him from the pounding rain and constant lightning of a storm that had blown in from the Channel. The bunker was made of thick concrete. This haven was solid except for the big cracks and chunks of concrete that had fallen off the walls over the decades. Still this refuge could withstand anything the sky could throw at it.

Pierre came often to the bunker, even when it wasn't raining. For all their talk of its history, his family barely knew the bunker existed and cared even less. He was glad of that, for it meant that his nagging parents and his screaming, bratty little sister never came here. Even the dog who barked at him morning, noon, and night never ventured anywhere near. Pierre had this refuge all to himself. It was his and only his.

The bunker was an ideal refuge. It sat on a scraggly little hill overlooking the west pasture. Trees had grown up all around it, obscuring it from view. Those trees had to be at least a hundred years old. At times he would stand at the holes in the bunker and look at those trees, seeing them as another wall between him and the "outside." Between the trees, the bunker had a perfect view of the pasture which was the direction from which any trespasser would come. No one ever came. The bunker was quiet and plain and empty and cold. It was hidden and impenetrable.

Pierre didn't know why he needed this stark, barren den. He just knew that when he came here, he felt alive. His dreams and fantasies could run free without interruption. No one would call his name, at least not that he could hear. He could just sit in the cool, damp warren and do nothing. It was heaven. Eventually the sun would start to set, and the shadows would call him back home. During the long walk back to the house, Pierre became a zombie again. By the time he reached the door, he was armored against the overbearing parents, annoying sister, and the yapping dog. He always hesitated before opening the door. This was partly to brace himself for the cacophony on the other side and partly because he wanted to run back to his real home. Still Pierre would always open the door and enter the chaos. "One day," he thought, "I won't open this door."

Esoteric Decisions

The birds do their dance in the noonday sun. Their call beckons to unseeing masses. A tower crane lifts a container of dreams into the sun. You sit. You watch. You contemplate the esoteric decisions that lay before you. A voice carried to you on a breeze lets you know that you are not alone, that there are people waiting for you. The music from a passing car creeps into your consciousness. It begins to lift you from your reverie. The music fades into the background as does your awareness of reality. A wilting flower now catches your attention. A petal drops from the flower. You watch it fall. Then you know. The time has come. The moment of decision is upon you. As the petal comes to rest on the table, it releases you from the trance that had you enthralled. You order the chopped salad with the red vinaigrette dressing.

Shiver

The cold wind swirls around the buildings bringing a chill to anyone brave enough to venture out. People look like stuffed animals, wearing so many layers of clothing as to leave their true figure concealed from passersby and, more importantly, the unforgiving cold. Of my own volition I throw myself into these harsh conditions. I have no purpose in wandering forth. I have no destination in mind, no timetable to keep, no errand compelling me to brave the cold. Something deep within me tells me to leave the warmth and comfort of my room. It guides me through the city streets along a circuitous path, past coffee shops tempting me with their cups of warmth, past stores with their heated entrances and brightly lit rooms of temperate cheer. My face, exposed to the elements, is stung by each gust. My fingers, lacking gloves, begin to ache as they are drained of energy. Slowly the chill seeps deep into my body, and I am wracked by a violent shiver. As this involuntary quake subsides, my mind is filled with the desire to return home. I hurry toward the warmth of my fire, wanting nothing more than a steaming cup of chocolate and a down comforter wrapped tight around me.

When I finally reach my apartment, I close the door on the frigid weather trying to force its way into my refuge. My extremities slowly regain feeling. I lie down on the sofa, wrap myself in a comforter, and drift off to sleep feeling safe and warm. When I awake I try to understand the purpose of my excursion into the harsh elements, but the reason remains hidden. The only key is the memory of the shiver that wracked my body. This memory contains a feeling of being alive. I spend the rest of the day at the window watching the people fight their way to some important destination, filled only with the need to reach the warmth that has abandoned them. They shiver with no purpose. For some reason unknown, I pity them.

Know Your Place

Henry was an astrophysicist. He had made a name for himself by coming up with new ways to measure this and that in the Horsehead Nebula. The things he created were mostly mathematical and were considered highly complex and boring even among astrophysicists. Henry didn't mind. He agreed with the other astrophysicists. He had some very tedious, complex, and extremely boring projects. But his work got him a nice paycheck from JPL and trips to conferences all over the world. So he considered it a fair exchange. Besides, Henry's "nebulations," as he called them, were just a job. Henry had other astrophysical interests that kept him happy. You see, Henry had found a way to calculate his true place in the Universe.

It took Henry a little over 14 years to do it. He had to find ways to integrate his position from the center of the Earth, the rotation of the Earth, the rotation of the Earth around the Sun, the rotation of that Sun around the center of the Milky Way Galaxy, the expansion of the Milky Way Galaxy, and the movement of the Milky Galaxy away from the "center" of the Universe (i.e. the center of the "Big Bang"). He used all this information to find his current position relative to the center of the Universe. He also could determine, quite accurately, his current speed relative to the center of the Universe. And he programmed in the location of Room 502 in Norton's Hospital at 12:31 AM on November 11, 1967 to determine how far he had come in life. When Henry finished his project a few years ago, he loaded the algorithms onto his PC so he could check it whenever he wanted to. With the advent of smart phones, Henry converted everything to an app for use on mobile devices. This way he could check his position, speed, and "life distance" when he was out and about.

Henry thought it was nice to know where he was, how fast he was going, and how far he had come. Many people out there in the world liked to know these things as well, but they were content to know them only in terms of movement on the Earth's surface. While Henry could see the utility of this information, he felt sorry for those people for they lacked the "completeness" of his solution. Every once in a while, he would show his app to someone else who would invariably say, "That's nice," and change the subject. Their loss. Henry thought the numbers were comforting. He knew from his studies of the Universe how insignificant a single being was in comparison to the whole of space. However, with his calculations, Henry knew how much he had done in his lifetime just by existing. The numbers shown on his app were HUGE. They put him on the same scale as the Universe. They told him that he was a significant part of the Universe. Henry looked at those numbers and knew he was important.

Unbeknownst to Henry, someone else had taken an interest in his little project. With the inspiration he had gotten from Henry's success, this Being duplicated the work but on a much larger scale. And just as Henry would check his phone regularly to find his place in the Universe, this Being would check his ethereal app to find his place in that realm beyond space and time. Just like Henry, it made God feel important too.

Docking Privileges

It is an unseasonably warm February day in Annapolis. I am sitting on a park bench at the end of the city dock. A constant brisk wind comes off the bay, keeping the waves choppy and my windbreaker zipped. The bright sunshine keeps the cold at bay, making it a most pleasant afternoon. I am the closest thing to a tourist today, no charter buses or school outings. It's just me and a few passersby. Even the seagulls have found other places to play. I see only one or two instead of the dozens that should be scavenging the wharf.

I let the waves take up all my attention. I am not asleep. I am very much awake, watching the mass of moving water. It is hard to explain, but watching the water is all I need for my brain to be content. I don't need to be remembering other trips to other docks. I don't need fantasies of jumping a boat to some far-off paradise. This is the essence of my need for "alone time." To let my mind just shut down in a way it can't even in sleep.

In the corner of my mind I hear the waves lapping against the dock, but even that gentle noise relegates to the periphery of my consciousness. For the most part, my mind is blank. Blank is what I need to overcome the jumble of thoughts and emotions which my brain is in now. Asperger's, high functioning autism, ADHD, mildly impaired, all have been used to explain why I spend much of my life in a fog. It's not a fog of confusion but of, well, it's hard to describe it to someone whose brain is normal. It is not fatigue. It is not that I am disoriented. It is not anything that simple. It is just that my thoughts don't connect the way they should sometimes. I have been told it happens when I am "over-stimulated." I get overstimulated a lot. The cure is simple; I just need to slow the world's demand for my attention. That is why I am here on a quiet dock on a quiet day.

My phone rings, and I notice the time. I have been sitting here for over an hour. If asked, I could tell you everything that went on in front of me during that time. I do not lose these hours; I just do nothing with them. I wish I was like you and didn't need this time spent doing nothing at all. I wish I could make it through an entire day without having my senses sap my energy and addle my brain. But I am not you. This is the way I was created. This is who I am. I am a person who needs the empty dock and the choppy waves. I am a person who needs to let the flow of sensation match the flow of the water. Once that harmony is restored, I can return to your world and be one of you again.

Without Make-up

Standing in the wings, you go over your lines such as they are. As you head out onto the stage, you have the usual butterflies. "Will I stumble through the performance? Will the audience notice the nervousness? Will I even survive to the end or run off the stage crying?" The doubts dissipate as the curtain rises. You have done this show for so many years that the routine takes over as you step out into the spotlight. The stage is bare. No props. No scenery. No music. No make-up. It is just you and the light glaring in your eyes.

The single spotlight blinds you when you try to look at the audience. You have no idea how many people are in the house. You never do. You are used to it, and it doesn't matter. The play is what matters most. You need the play. It is where you can express yourself, where your deepest emotions are put on display for anyone to see. Your soul is laid bare to unknown patrons, to the voyeurs who want to see someone exposed for what they are. That is what you want as well. You want them to see you stripped of pretense, your mask ripped off, and all the deception that is your life gone. Nothing will remain to the imagination. They will see you, all of you. They will know you. The act of letting people know the real you, that is the only thing that will keep you sane. It doesn't even matter if anyone sees the performance. Giving others the chance to glimpse your true self is why you go through this day in and day out.

You begin your monologue, and the world is released from inside you. The scenery begins to take form as the story grows. The lighting and sound coalesce to accent your performance. By the time you reach the climax, the stage is alive. When it is over, the stage is bare again. The one spotlight still blinds you. The audience is silent, no applause, no shouts for an encore. They always remain quiet as if shocked into silence by your performance. You leave the stage and head to your dressing room to decompress from the trauma of the experience. Once in a while someone waits outside the stage door to tell you what they thought of your performance. It is rare, but sometimes you strike that chord that resonates with a kindred soul. The fact that even one person understands you gives you the energy you need when you don't want to go on. However, it is not why you do this. You know you would still perform even if you knew that no one understood. The story of your being needs to be told, if only to yourself.

About the Author

Edward Meiman (*pronounced MY-man*) was born in Louisville, Kentucky on January 17, 1964, received a Bachelor's degree in Mechanical Engineering from the University of Dayton in 1987, and received a Master's degree in Industrial/Organizational Psychology from George Mason University sometime in the middle of going for a Doctorate in the same specialty (Mr. Meiman is currently ABD4Life). He has lived in Louisville, KY; Dayton & Chillicothe, OH; Detroit, MI; Madison, WI; and Metro Washington, DC. Mr. Meiman has worked in Horse Racing, Paper Production, Industrial Chemical Production, Industrial Equipment Manufacturing, Landscape Architecture, Behavioral Research, Government Consulting, and IT Development. His jobs have let him travel throughout most of the United States and to over ten countries on four continents. He's only visited the Americas and Europe on vacation. His writings have included both creative (e.g., satirical looks at politics) and technical (e.g., a summary of a computer modeling approach to study the Social Security Administration's Disability Determination Process – tech writing always uses long titles). Mr. Meiman's latest effort, *Micro Stories for a Hectic World*, brings together many of the wide-ranging experiences and ideas he has gathered throughout his life. This is the first time any of these works have been published. OK, this is the first time Mr. Meiman has published anything that wasn't a behavioral research study or a users' guide.

www.ingramcontent.com/pod-product-compliance
Lightning Source LLC
Chambersburg PA
CBHW050029180626
46810CB00002B/637